WEDDING BELLS AT THE LAKESIDE HOTEL

MELINDA HUBER

Wedding Bells at the Lakeside Hotel

All rights reserved.

Copyright © 2024 Linda Huber

The right of Linda Huber to be identified as the Author of this Work has been asserted by her in accordance with the Copyright Designs and Patents Act 1988.

Apart from any use permitted under UK copyright law, this publication may only be reproduced, stored or transmitted, in any form, or by any means, with the prior permission in writing of the author. All characters appearing in this work are fictitious. Any resemblance to real persons, living or dead, is purely coincidental.

1

SATURDAY, 1ST JUNE

It was the best feeling ever. Stacy Townsend plumped down on a chair at the kitchen table, excitement pulling at her middle. She reached for a croissant to slather with butter and raspberry jam, then gaped at it. In seven days' time, she and Rico would be getting ready to say 'I do'... While her wedding was absolutely the most amazing thing that had ever happened to her, every time she thought about it, butterflies the size of seagulls started flapping about in her tummy – not particularly conducive to breakfast. Did every bride-to-be feel this way? Come to that, did her prospective bridegroom? Rico, the love of her life and her fellow hotel manager was downstairs already, as if this was any old Saturday morning at the Lakeside Spa Hotel in their corner of N.E. Switzerland, but oh, wow – in just *seven days' time...*

Grimsbach church clock in the distance broke into her daydream as she was chewing her way through the croissant. *Bim bam bim bam bim bam* – quarter to eight, almost time to start her shift helping Alex on reception. Saturday was the main changeover day in the hotel, and the desk was much too much work for one person. Flavia, Alex's second-in-command, wasn't due in until the afternoon, when reception would be even busier as new guests checked in with all their questions and concerns.

Stacy swallowed the last calorific mouthful and reached for her coffee. Beneath her, people would be packing and having their last breakfast, then the housekeeping staff would move in to prepare the rooms for this week's arrivals. Weekends were always busy, but hey... Stacy waggled the finger with the diamond and emerald engagement ring. Next Saturday, she'd be slipping into the floaty white dress which, while not a traditional wedding dress, was as romantic a garment as she'd ever worn. It was going to be incredible. And oh, heck, here were the giant butterflies again. Breathe, Stacy.

The flat door banged open as Rico burst in and thudded a pile of letters on the table. 'Post. This lot came yesterday, but they got mixed up with a load of stuff for the spa and Margrit only found them this morning. More cards, by the look of them. Ready for a hard morning's work on reception?'

Stacy got up to wash her hands. Wedding cards tended to be white, and raspberry jam finger marks wouldn't be the best look. Her mother – still in sunny England – would have a fit. 'Yup. We're pretty full until Friday, which is good. It'll make up for being closed for two days for the wedding.'

Rico was pushing buttons on the coffee machine. He turned and leaned back against the worktop while his coffee burbled through. 'As manager, my love, I'm telling you we're allowed to close for two days for our own wedding. It's not like we'll be getting married every other week.'

Stacy raised her eyebrows. 'Oh, so you're the manager? I thought we were equal partners in this business? But you're right.' She opened the first card, then passed it over to Rico. 'From Sarah and Paul. Sarah and I did our nursing training together.'

She went on to the second card, from a distant cousin in Ireland. Next on the pile was a postcard of Zurich. Stacy flipped it over to read the message. *Looking forward to seeing you soon! MJ xx*

She waved it at Rico. 'Who's MJ?'

He came to peer over her shoulder. 'No idea.'

'Hm. Maybe it's a hotel guest due to arrive this week. We don't have any MJs coming to the wedding, do we?'

'Not as far as I know, but why on earth would a guest send us a card from Zurich? And it's addressed to us personally, not the hotel.'

Stacy was going through the list of expected wedding guests in her head. The arrangements were a little complicated. The civil ceremony (and a big party in the hotel) was here in Switzerland, and all the Swiss family and friends were coming, plus family and a couple of close friends from her old home in England. Afterwards, she and Rico were having their wedding trip to the Bernese Oberland in the diagonally opposite corner of Switzerland, and was she looking forward to it! She'd done lots of travelling closer to home here by Lake Constance, not to mention in the Italian-speaking part south of the alps, but she couldn't wait to see the Jungfrau and the Eiger, and the twin lakes at Interlaken. The Swiss part of the honeymoon would end with a couple of days in Basle, then they'd take the train up to Paris for two days in the city of lovers before hopping over the Channel. The trip would finish with a visit to London and another train up to Elton Abbey near Manchester, where Stacy's mum was planning the fanciest church blessing plus poshest dinner party ever, and as far as Stacy could see, she'd invited all their friends and relatives as well as half the village to come to that. Mum was splendid at OTT.

She handed MJ's postcard to Rico. 'It could be someone going to the do at Elton Abbey, I suppose. But if they're in Zurich already, you'd think they'd come by, wouldn't you? I'm calling Mum this weekend, so I'll ask her then – if I manage to get a word in. She has something to show me, apparently.'

Rico stuck the postcard on the fridge with a daisy magnet, and Stacy put the rest of the cards to one side to open later. Time for her stint on reception.

***

At ten past ten the final pair of departing guests left the hotel, and Stacy high-fived Alex, beside her at the desk. 'Teamwork, huh? That's another set of happy customers en route for home, and with any luck, some of them will book the next trip here as soon as they get through their front door.'

Alex grinned, shoving a hand through his fine sandy hair and making it stick up in all directions. 'Four from last week have booked in for the Advent Special in December, did I tell you? Lakeside really is going from strength to strength, isn't it?'

'We are, and I meant what I said about teamwork. You're the best receptionist we could wish for, and with your mum in charge of organising the spa shop – well, it all adds to the family-run hotel atmosphere that keeps the guests coming back.'

Alex blushed. 'One big happy family, huh? And Flavia's out helping Mum with her shopping as we speak.'

Ah. Stacy turned away to tidy her side of the desk. Flavia was a bit of a worry. She was a lovely girl and was shaping up well as a receptionist, but she'd fallen hard for Alex, who was lovely too, and while there was nothing to stop the pair of them getting together, even nearly six months after splitting up with his previous girlfriend, Alex didn't seem in any hurry to get back into the dating game. To add to the complications, his mum suffered from agoraphobia, though she was in a much better place these days, coping with her work for the hotel and managing to get out and about with minimal support. This was often provided by Flavia, whose own mum lived on the other side of Switzerland, so theoretically it was win-win all round, but still... The girl must be aware of Alex's indifference, and that would hurt. Stacy sighed. She and Rico were so happy – it was hard not to want the same rose-tinted feeling for everyone around her. Problem was, life wasn't like that.

A bang came from outside, and she pulled a face at Alex. 'Keep up the good work, anyway. We'll need all the guests we can get for the next year or two to pay for these renovations at the boathouse. I'd better see what Rico's up to out there.'

Leaving Alex at the desk, she grabbed her phone and set off. Rico should have been back by this time; he'd only gone for a quick look at what the builders had done yesterday. The boathouse was a long, grey stone building bordering on the lake bank, and they were turning it into a sauna and fitness room to replace the facilities currently in the cellar of the main building. Humming, Stacy hurried out through the terrace bar, where day tourists as well as remaining hotel guests were sitting outside in the warm June sunshine. A few stray geranium petals floated down from one of the balconies, and she glanced up at the hotel. Lakeside was your typical dark brown wooden chalet, four storeys high with pink and white geraniums already spilling over the window boxes on each balcony. Home, and looking perfect, if she said so herself.

The terrace ended by the lawn, and Stacy stood still for a moment to gaze out over the vast expanse of Lake Constance, a handful of metres away. Germany and Austria were hazy green blobs in the distance today and the lake was as blue as she'd seen it, the family cabin cruiser *Lakeside Lady* bobbing up and down in the water. Stacy followed the path round to the landing place, Rico's whistle in the boathouse reaching her ears even before she went inside. Good, he was happy. He'd been pensive about the build at first. In the days before the hotel was so successful, he'd dreamed of opening his own IT business in the boathouse. He was doing a part-time master's degree in IT now, but whether he'd ever start a business was in the stars. Stacy hoped he would, but then what would happen to the hotel? She put the thought to one side – that was future music.

The boathouse door was open and she stepped inside, sniffing the dry, earthy smell of new wood. Rico was in the semi-installed staffroom, bending over plans laid out on the dusty work surface.

He straightened up and waved a hand at the plan. 'We're well on schedule here. The building should be finished by the time we get back from England, although I have a feeling there's a problem with the new landing place outside. They're supposed to start renovating it next week, but I suspect Dad's made a mistake with his measurements – the jetty looks huge on the plan. You'd think *Lakeside Lady* was an ocean liner. I'll call him later.'

'When are we expecting him here?'

'He and Carol are coming on Wednesday, and they'll stay all the time we're away, apart from the three days they'll be in Elton Abbey for the blessing.'

'I'm sure Ralph knows what he was doing with the plans, Rico. Don't forget he works in a boatyard!'

Rico pushed the diagram to one side. 'Useful, isn't he? Ex-hotel manager turned boatyard expert... But I'll call him anyway. And while we're talking about the plans, have a look and tell me what you think about this.' He pulled another folded paper from a folder and spread it out on top of the boathouse plan.

Stacy frowned. 'Another building?' This one was behind the boathouse, closer to the street, and from what she could see it was a large, two-storey house with a cellar and attic, as well as a generous garden back and front.

Rico smirked. 'Not any old building. Our future home. If we have a good year now, we could start building next spring. The layout inside is just my ideas, of course we'd plan the real thing together, but wouldn't it be cool to have our own space? We'll be completely separate to the hotel, with a private garden and everything. Perfect for starting a family later. What do you think?'

Shock rippled through Stacy, leaving her head reeling. *Perfect for starting a family later*. She didn't want to start a family *later*, she wanted to start one as quickly as possible after the wedding, and it had never entered her head that Rico might not feel the same way. He'd said ages ago he wanted kids and at their age, somehow she'd assumed they would start a family right away. Oh, they'd talked about building their own place one day, but they had a lovely home in the flat, and they could easily do the having babies and happy-ever-after bit there too, at least at the start of family life. Living in the hotel would make being a working mum so much easier. And all that was before you even thought about how much a house like this one would cost.

Rico was beaming proudly at his plan, and she put a hand on his shoulder, searching for the right words. 'Rico, love – it looks amazing, but I – I thought we were going to try for a baby sort of, soon? I don't want to be an older mother.'

It was Rico's turn to look blank. 'Good grief, you're not even thirty yet.'

'I'd be well over thirty if we waited until we could move into a house that isn't being started until next year. And yes, I know loads of people have babies much older than that, but... Rico, I really want to start soon. We need to think about a brother or sister or two for the baby, as well.'

He stared at her, then back at his plan. 'I thought you'd be pleased.'

'I am. It looks gorgeous. All I'm saying is we could have a baby while we're still living in the flat.' Heavens, this was surreal. Babies weren't what they should be worrying about in the run-up to a romantic, happy-ever-after wedding.

He folded the plan away. 'Let's talk about it another time. We'll be able to make plans in peace and quiet when we're on our honeymoon.'

Stacy nodded, trying to ignore the apprehensive niggle in her gut. It wasn't unreasonable to want a family soon, was it? Building a house was expensive – could they afford all this, and a baby too? She shivered suddenly; eek, someone was walking over her grave.

Seven days to go...

2

SATURDAY, 1ST JUNE

Flavia Schneider pulled into an empty space outside Denise's block of flats and smiled at the older woman in the passenger seat. Saturday morning at the shops at their busiest was a new high for Alex's mum, who'd spent over a year confined to her solitary flat and refusing to accept help for her agoraphobia. Changed days. As soon as Alex started working at Lakeside and his mum met Stacy and allowed her to help, Denise had managed to get out and slowly increase what she was comfortable doing. So far, that hadn't included going anywhere alone, but hopefully it was only a matter of time.

'Thank you, Flavia.' Denise touched Flavia's jade green T-shirt. 'That colour suits you, you know. It brings out the red glints in your hair.'

Flavia glowed. Her shoulder length mousy-brown hair didn't have a lot going for it, and how kind Denise was. 'Thanks for the compliment. Let's get your shopping inside.'

Denise lifted her handbag and opened the passenger seat door. 'Got time for some iced tea?'

Didn't she just. Flavia opened the boot for Denise to extract her shopping, and followed her up to the first floor.

Denise opened the flat door. 'Have a seat on the balcony, and I'll bring the drinks out.'

She and the shopping vanished into the small kitchen, and Flavia went into the living room. She stopped by the sofa to say hello to

Snowy, Denise's cat, who gave her the usual disdainful glare before graciously allowing herself to be stroked. Flavia fussed over the cat, then a postcard of New York by night on the coffee table caught her eye. Denise appeared with two long glasses and saw her looking.

'Looks amazing, doesn't it? All those lights... Zoe was there with the orchestra. It was the last performance of the tour before they came home to Switzerland. I'll miss getting cards from exotic locations!'

Flavia's mouth went dry. Zoe was – no, Zoe *had been* the love of Alex's life until they split up last December. And the split hadn't been Alex's idea, she knew that for sure. It was more to do with Zoe being a hugely talented violinist in the prestigious Zurich Alhambra Orchestra and having to live in Zurich. Now she was back after a long tour abroad, and not only that, Denise was coping much better with her agoraphobia and was well integrated in the community. Theoretically, there was nothing to stop Alex packing all his worldly goods and going to be a receptionist in Zurich. And the very fact that Zoe had been sending Denise postcards proved – what? That Zoe was still a part of Alex's life, that was what.

Her heart thundering miserably, Flavia followed Denise out to the balcony. The flat was near the top of a hill and the view over the lake was spectacular, but today she saw none of it. Feeling jealous like this was awful. She'd fallen for Alex when he started at the hotel, almost the first time she'd set eyes on him, actually, but he'd been with Zoe then. And nowadays, although he had almost daily opportunities to ask her out, or at least give her some indication that she was more than a workmate his mum was friendly with, he'd never even hinted at a date. And she wasn't the kind of person who went round asking guys out, either. Flavia grimaced. Maybe she should learn.

She cleared her throat. 'Have you seen her yet? Zoe, I mean? Bet she has some great photos, all those places they went to.'

Denise gave her a look. 'No, I haven't. I don't know if I will, either, but there are things a mother should keep well out of. Especially when their children are grown men who left the nest years ago. I know you have a soft spot for Alex, Flavia. But – be careful. I don't think he knows himself what he wants.'

'I will.' Flavia lifted her glass and took a big swallow of iced tea. 'Don't worry about me. We have more important things to talk about – what are you wearing to Stacy's wedding?'

It was an excellent change of subject. Alex's name didn't come up again, and half an hour later, Flavia was on her way home with her own shopping and her aching heart. Hankering after Alex seemed hopeless, but oh... if only it wasn't. He was kind, funny, sweet – a lovely guy, in fact. But to him, she was just little Flavia, the youngest member of staff who got into scrapes and needed a helping hand all too frequently. And she didn't know how to change that.

***

Rico's stomach growled as he sat prodding the keyboard in the office behind reception. Heck, it was almost two o'clock, and he and Stacy hadn't even had lunch yet. Saturdays were always like that, bidding goodbye to last week's guests then preparing for the new influx, which was now imminent. Not such a big influx this time, as they were closing on Friday and as a result, fewer people had reserved rooms. Hopefully, they'd make up the shortfall with a few extra spontaneous cycling tourists, the people who came in for one night on their bike run round the lake. His stomach growled again, but at last – here was Flavia to help Alex man the desk. Rico left them to book in the new guests and took the lift up to the flat for a bite to eat on the run. Sandwiches would be quickest.

He was still making them when Stacy arrived, and she sat at the table opening today's pile of wedding cards and throwing him the odd remark while he organised cheese and pickle on crusty bread for them both. Rico dropped a kiss on the top of her head on his way to the fridge. They should make the most of the next few days home alone here. With Stacy's best friend Emily and her husband Alan arriving from England on Monday, Dad and Carol on Wednesday, and Stacy's parents on Thursday, the flat was going to be bursting at the seams soon. Still, it would be fun to celebrate all together. The usual wistful thought slid into his head. At long last he and Stacy were going to be married, and if only Mum had been here to see it. She'd have loved Stacy.

Rico swallowed. You couldn't change the past, and you couldn't wish people back, not really... but sometimes he did. He pictured Ralph at the wedding, Carol beside him. The pair had met and fallen in love last Christmas, and Carol lived across the lake in Friedrichshafen now, nicely between her son in Munich and Ralph in Lugano. It was all going well for Dad and Carol, but fond as Rico was of her, she would never replace his mother. Not that she wanted to, of course, but–

'Any danger of those sandwiches being ready today?' Stacy twisted round in her chair, her smile fading. 'You look like you're having complicated thoughts, Rico Weber. Spill.'

'Just wishing Mum was here.' Rico slapped the lids on the sandwiches and sat down with them. 'And yes, I know. It's okay.'

Stacy gave his hand a squeeze, then lifted a sandwich and took a huge bite. It was a moment before she could speak. 'Yum. She'll be with us in spirit, Rico. I'll be wearing her sapphire pendant and bracelet, remember?'

Of course he remembered. They chewed their way through the sandwiches, talking about the wedding arrangements, then Rico left Stacy clearing up and went out to the balcony to call his father. Hopefully he was wrong about those plans; an over-large jetty would be expensive as well as unnecessary.

'Rico, son!'

Ralph was in his brother's boatyard in Lugano; Rico could hear Guido's voice booming in the background. He pictured Lake Lugano in the sunshine, high wooded hills on either side of the bay, then realised he was also hearing the drum of rain on the boatyard roof.

'Hey, Dad. Wet day south of the Alps?'

'Set to be a wet week. I'm looking forward to your Lakeside summer sunshine. How's things?'

Rico reported progress on the boathouse renovation, then crossed his fingers. 'Dad – the plan of the new landing place looks biggish to me. It's not a mistake, is it?'

'No, it's fine. Larger than it is now, yes, but we'll be glad of more space sometime, and with the renovation going forward anyway, I thought it was a good opportunity to kill two birds with one stone.'

'It's going to be an expensive two birds we're killing. By the look of these plans we could bring an ocean liner alongside. What are we going to do with all that mooring space?'

Ralph was annoyingly cheerful. 'We'll find something, never fear. You could think about getting some pedalos for the guests to hire.'

Rico sniffed. Pedalos weren't a bad idea, but still... 'I suppose it's too late to change the plans?'

'You suppose right. Rico, trust me. You'll be glad of those extra metres someday, I promise.'

Ralph chatted for a few more minutes, then rang off. Rico trailed back to the kitchen, unable to stop the little thread of worry snaking through his gut. What had his father been thinking? The wedding was expensive – not that he grudged that – but a super-sized jetty seemed surplus to Lakeside requirements. The hotel was doing well, but they still couldn't afford to throw money around as if there was no tomorrow. He'd better get hold of some pedalos the moment they returned from England.

Rico slumped down at the table, mentally totting up their available cash. And it wasn't just the boathouse build, either; Stacy's wish to start a family the moment they were respectably married was another worry. Babies were arguably even more expensive than pedalos, and he'd never even dreamt of having one until he'd finished his master's. Waiting until they had a nice house of their own too would be much more sensible. They were young, and there was a lot to be said for separating your home life and your work. But Stacy clearly didn't see it like that.

The postcard of Zurich on the fridge door swam into view. Bummer, he'd forgotten to ask if Dad knew anything about MJ. Rico sniffed again. Hopefully, MJ would turn out to be some kind of fairy godmother, or the genie in the bottle. They could do with a few magic wishes...

3

Sunday, 2nd June

Church bells were pealing in the background on Sunday morning when Stacy settled down on the living room balcony and opened her phone to facetime her mother. Mum had been born to be mother-of-the-bride; she was loving her role and all the organising it involved. Stacy grinned as she tapped to start the call. It wasn't something she'd say out loud, but it was quite nice being in Switzerland, well away from the daily wedding chaos Mum was happily surrounding herself with.

Janie Townsend's beaming face flickered before it settled on the screen. 'Hello, darling – it'll soon be the big day! The first big day, anyway! Are you ready for it?'

'Yup. If the weather holds, it'll be perfect!'

Janie was rustling papers off-screen. The picture tilted as she waved a handful of cards at Stacy. 'People have been giving us masses of cards and pressies to bring to you. Look, I've got some sample invitations for the reception in Elton Abbey. You can choose which you like best and I'll send them off this week.'

Stacy was taken aback. 'I thought you sent the invites weeks ago?'

'I did, but they were just little 'keep this date free' cards. I want to send the proper ones now, for the church and dinner, and for the dance in the evening, too.'

'Dance in the evening?' Stacy had to stop her jaw from dropping. Last time she'd heard, Janie was planning a dinner at a big posh hotel for family and friends only. Who else was going to come in the evening?

'Yes – for the neighbours, and some of Gareth and Jo's friends, and a few of our shop contacts. Your dad and I were in the hotel to finalise the dinner arrangements last week, and we saw they've opened a big new function suite, so we booked it too. We can move through there after dinner, and the dance guests will join us. It'll be lovely, darling. Have a think if you want to invite any other people.' Janie rustled about in her papers. 'Which of these do you like best?' She held up two wedding party invitation cards.

Stacy's head was reeling. The arrangement was that Ralph was funding the Lakeside celebration, while she and Rico split the cost of the more expensive Elton Abbey do with Janie and John. She didn't want to be stingy, but even with their modest honeymoon arrangements, it was already costing far more than they'd ever thought of spending on their wedding. Now they'd be paying for a party for her brother and his wife's friends and her parents' business associates too, most of whom she didn't even know. And oh, help, she did *not* want to have a sordid falling out over the cost of her wedding. Especially not with her mother.

'Mum – won't that be awfully expensive?'

'Oh, sensible Stacy. You only get married once. Don't worry, darling, your dad and I will carry the extra costs. Which card would you like? I thought the one with the little wedding cake.'

Stacy's heart was hammering under her ribs. How on earth was she to tell Rico that Mum was planning to fork out heaven knows how much more for the wedding? He'd want to pay their way, like they'd arranged. But there'd be no arguing with Janie; that was clear already. They were having a dance after the dinner, end of.

'The wedding cake card's lovely, thanks, Mum. Can I speak to Dad, please?'

'He's playing golf today. I'll get him to call you later. He's looking forward to his trip down the aisle with you!'

Frustration and apprehension rose in Stacy as she chatted for a few more minutes before ending the call. Mum could be infuriating, but then... Stacy leaned back, thinking about Rico's face as he'd spoken about his mother at lunchtime. At least she had her mother. Janie was a mum, that was all, looking forward to her daughter's wedding and wanting it to be the best celebration ever. Stacy gave herself a shake. A big party and a happy family, i.e. a happy mother-of-the-bride – it was what she wanted too, of course it was. The memories would be something for Mum to treasure forever, and if Stacy spoiled that now, it could never be sorted. But oh, my... How many people was Janie inviting to that dance?

Pushing the worry to the back of her mind, Stacy went downstairs and out to the hotel garden. She wasn't working today, and it was lovely. Sunday was usually a quiet day at the hotel, as new guests explored the village and surroundings and made plans for the coming week. She wandered along the narrow side path to the boathouse, tall shrubs on either side banishing the sunshine. She'd called it a 'secret path' when Rico showed it to her on her first visit to Lakeside. What a lot had happened since then.

All was quiet at the building site. Work would start again tomorrow, when the builders came back for the final push before the new fitness room and sauna were ready for action. Stacy tramped round the side of the building and stood looking down the rest of the plot, a narrow strip of land that stretched all the way to the main road. This was where the pie-in-the-sky house for her and Rico would stand, if they ever had the funds to build it after the wedding. In one way, Rico was right – a home that was separate from the hotel would be a more normal place for a child to grow up in, and even last year she'd have said it was what she wanted. But houses took time to build... and money. Stacy folded her arms across her front as thoughts and plans spiralled in her head. Rico would need another year at least before his degree was finished. Then another year to build the house... Suppose he wanted to wait all that time before trying for a family? Stacy's heart ached. A baby wouldn't care if it lived in a flat above a hotel or a detached house with a garden, and she'd wanted to be a mum for so long. On the other hand, Rico was right – they were still young. She had years before her biological clock needed to start sending out alarm bells.

The picture of a little chalet in the middle of the empty plot slid into Stacy's mind as she stood there; a mini-Lakeside with a lovely garden. They could have an apple tree and a swing set. She shook herself, and turned away. Definitely, it was a dream for the future.

***

Flavia printed out the new list of spa shop products she'd put together over the past half hour. Her job was fifty per cent reception and fifty as Stacy's assistant, so the work was varied, to say the least. She leaned back in her chair to see out of the office door to reception beyond; good, Alex wasn't busy with guests. She stuffed the list into a plastic folder and took it out to the front desk, giving Alex a bright smile.

'I've got the new list and the orders for your mum to put together. I'll collect the products for her now.' Part of Denise's work for the hotel involved working at home, assembling gift packs of the spa products so that guests could buy them to take home, or to give their friends and family. The idea had been hugely popular at Christmas, and they'd expanded it since. Guests could order products online, or make themselves a 'pick 'n' mix' basket from the selection too.

Alex barely looked up from the computer. 'You can give them to Stacy to take to Mum. She's going for coffee later this afternoon.'

'Oh. Okay.' Flavia seized the big wicker basket they kept in the office and trudged across the front hall into the small spa area, which housed the manicure and hairdressing booths as well as the storeroom. She piled tubes of creams and gels and bottles of bath additives into the basket, Alex's voice murmuring in the background as he talked to a couple of guests who wanted to know the best places for views of the mountains. He was a whole lot chattier with them than he'd been with her two minutes ago… It was tough when you really, really liked someone, and they took as much notice of you as they would a fly on the wall. Oh, Alex liked her, they worked well together when they were both on reception, and he was quick to spot if she needed a hand with anything. But that was as far as it went. If she could somehow get him to agree to going out with her, just once, then he'd see that she could be every bit as much to him as Zoe had been. Flavia screwed up her nose. That sounded needy, but oh, they could be good together, she knew they could. How on earth was she to move things along?

Suggest going for a coffee next time you're both leaving at the same time, her inner self prompted. Flavia rolled her eyes. She and Alex hardly ever left at the same time, and anyway, doing that would give her a panic attack before she even started. What a wimp she was. Glumly, she checked though the list to make sure she had everything. A better idea would be to bake a carrot cake or something, and bring it in for the staff. She was good at carrot cake. The problem with that was, Rob the chef kept them all well supplied with cake and other goodies, and while a carrot cake might please the others, it wouldn't solve the date problem – and Alex preferred salty or spicy treats anyway. The best thing would be to seize the day and ask him out. It didn't sound hard when you said it quickly.

Her basket full, she pulled out her phone to call Stacy. 'Sorry, I know it's your day off. I have a load of spa shop stuff and a list for Denise down here.'

'Oh, excellent. Put it in the office, Flavia, and I'll collect it before I leave. Well done, we need the new gift sets in the shop.'

At least someone appreciated her. Flavia lifted the basket. Alex was free again; she could start a chat about – something. Go, girl. She started across the hallway, but was still several metres away when Alex's mobile rang. He grabbed it from the desk, his face lighting up.

'Hello, stranger! How's life been treating you?' He caught Flavia's eye, pointed to the desk, and strode out the front door, his phone pressed to his ear.

Flavia's brief moment of hope disappeared like snow in a heatwave. *Hello, stranger?* Could that have been Zoe, calling her ex-boyfriend on her return to Switzerland? Alex had been pleased, no, heck, he'd been delighted to hear from whoever it was. Maybe it was all back on again between those two.

Flavia dumped the basket of spa things in the corner of the office and went back to reception. She was giving the leaflet stand a tidy when an English-speaking guest approached, wanting help with a dinner reservation in St Gallen, and by the time she had organised that and provided information about trains and buses there and back, Alex had returned and was helping a couple of spa-goers who wanted to book massages. And very happy he looked too. Flavia hesitated for a moment, but the sight of him laughing and chatting with the guests, obviously in the best mood ever, was soul-destroying. Oh, it was work-chat, nothing more, but... why couldn't he be as happy to see her, too? *You'd better just forget him, you know. If Zoe's still around you have no chance. You'll only get hurt.* Her inner self wasn't reassuring.

Flavia sniffed, and headed upstairs to see if housekeeping were finished for the day. She was hurt already, but she wasn't going to give up. Not yet. She would have to up her game, that was all. But how?

***

'Did your dad call back?' Rico pulled a chair under the sunshade and joined Stacy on the living room balcony. It was Sunday evening, and a buzz of conversation was filtering up from the guests having dinner on the terrace. He'd spent the afternoon sorting through the boathouse build accounts and paying bills that couldn't wait until after their honeymoon; he could relax now. Except he couldn't – the story of Janie's latest addition to the wedding was weighing as heavily in his gut as it was in Stacy's. He didn't like seeing the worried frown that had settled between her eyes.

'He did, yes. He said he'll make sure Mum doesn't go too overboard, so we don't need to worry about that, but – it's more the thought of dozens of people I've never even met coming to our wedding do. He's sending the details tomorrow.'

Rico couldn't think what to say. Stacy was right; any objection they made would mar the occasion, and knowing Janie, those invitations would be in the post already. It was hard not to feel resentful; Janie seemed to be set on playing at mother of the bride in an old film. Spencer Tracy or Steve Martin could appear any moment... Against that, what he'd said this morning still stood – their wedding was a once in a lifetime occasion. He cleared his throat awkwardly.

Stacy shot him a wry grin. 'Pity we didn't decide on a luxury honeymoon relaxing on a beach somewhere, to build up our strength for the second part of the wedding, huh?'

'Never mind. We'll save the luxury bit for our first anniversary. How about a glass of wine to toast our last weekend as singles?'

'As long as we're not drowning our sorrows about a reception we have no say in.'

Rico kissed her head on his way to the kitchen. 'We'll have a great time, don't worry.' He came back with a chilled bottle and the corkscrew.

'I suppose we will, but I wish Mum hadn't presented us with a fait accompli like that.' Stacy was still looking pensive.

'A what?'

Stacy giggled. 'A done deal. I keep forgetting English isn't your first language.'

'Wish I could say the same about your German. Fait accompli sounds more French, anyway, and I was always pretty dire at that.'

She threw a peanut at him, laughing. 'Your English had a start of over twenty years on my German!'

They clinked glasses, and Rico leaned back. 'Dad called this afternoon too. We talked about the non-fitness and sauna section of the boathouse. There are two small rooms and one much larger one there. I'd wondered about staff accommodation for seasonal summer staff, like we used to have on this floor, but another option would be to have a party-room people could hire for private do's and conferences. What do you think?'

'That sounds good. I'm sure people would go for that. Party plus sauna...' Stacy slumped in her chair. 'I was looking at the rest of that plot yesterday too. Building a place of our own feels like a big commitment, doesn't it? I mean financially.'

Rico leaned across and touched her cheek. 'If I work hard and pass everything, I'll be on the last semester of my course by this time next year. We can start next autumn and move in the following year and have babies.'

She didn't reply, and Rico's stomach plummeted. Stacy wanted their first child to be running around by that time, didn't she? But – the feeling that the wedding was going to be so much more expensive than they'd budgeted was like a ton of bricks in his gut, and he'd have to offer to pay more, no matter what Janie said. His master's course was already stretching their finances, and the boathouse build wasn't going to come in cheap either, especially with Dad's new super-sized jetty.

Rico twirled the wineglass in his fingers. Maybe those pedalos were more urgent than he'd thought. MJ the fairy godmother was going to have his – or her – work cut out.

4

Monday, 3rd June

Today was going to be fabulous. Stacy took a deep breath, determinedly pushing the reception and baby worries to one side. It really was the start of their wedding celebrations, and she was going to enjoy every minute. She started down the wooden stairs to the front hall while Rico locked the flat then ran to overtake her. They arrived at the bottom in record time, laughing and almost bumping into Flavia on her way to the housekeeping cupboard with a large tub of liquid soap.

Stacy swerved round their youngest member of staff, who was wearing a real 'Monday morning' expression. 'Sorry, Flavia, but it's so nice to be officially on holiday! We're off to collect the wedding rings this morning.'

A smile flickered across Flavia's face. 'Exciting! Have a good time!' She went on upstairs, her smile gone already.

Stacy looked after her, but Rico grasped her hand and pulled her to the front door. 'Come on! You can't expect everyone to be full of the joys of summer, even if we are.'

'It's still officially spring,' Stacy told him, but in a way he was right. It wasn't even as if everything in life was rosy, either. The sun had gone AWOL today, and she could push all their worries to the side as much as she liked, but they still niggled away in her head. Mind you, meeting Emily and Alan off the quarter to two train this afternoon would be the perfect distraction. Stacy could hardly wait. Just think, if Emily's dad hadn't won a golf club competition a few years back and donated his prize – a week for two at the Lakeside Hotel – to his daughter, none of them would be where they were today. Emily had met Alan that week, and Stacy met Rico. Stacy smiled, remembering Emily's Easter wedding. Which reminded her, she'd forgotten yet again to ask her parents about the mysterious MJ.

Rorschach, a small town a couple of kilometres up the lake, was pretty quiet. Some of the smaller shops were closed on Monday mornings, but the jeweller's on the main street was open, and Stacy leaned expectantly on the counter while the assistant opened the box with the twin rings, twisted bands of white and yellow gold they'd chosen a few weeks ago. She and Rico were each having the other's name engraved inside, plus the date of the wedding, and two intertwined hearts – corny perhaps, but very sweet. Stacy beamed, twisting her hand this way and that to make the light catch her ring. It was a wrench to take it off again to let the assistant wrap the little box in shiny gold paper.

They celebrated with milkshakes at the supermarket café, the rings stowed safely in the inside pocket of Rico's jacket.

Stacy couldn't help laughing as he patted them for the hundredth time. 'Try not to lose them!'

He stuck his tongue out. 'I'll do my best. Five days to go, Mrs.'

'I know.' Happiness shone through Stacy. This was fun – so what if the wedding was more expensive than they'd planned? They could have holidays at home for the next few years. She pushed away the mean little whisper that was still insisting the evening do was more for her mother than for the bride and groom. That was negative thinking, and it had no place in her life this week. Or any week, come to that.

They were almost back at the hotel when Rico's mobile rang. He was driving, and handed it to Stacy to answer.

She flipped the phone case open. 'It's Carol. She and your dad are both coming on Wednesday, aren't they? I do wish they'd move in together, you know.' She tapped to take the call. 'Hi, Carol!'

Carol's London accent sounded as if she was in the back of the car, instead of all the way across the lake in Friedrichshafen. 'Stacy! Lovely. I have a proposition for you two. How about coming over to mine for lunch tomorrow, and I'll come back with you on the ferry later? It's going to be Wednesday afternoon before Ralph can leave Lugano, and I'd love to have the bride to myself for a day or two before he and your parents get here. Look on it as a kind of un-mother-in-law thing.'

Stacy was touched. 'You're family, Carol, no matter what. And it's a great idea. Let me talk to Rico and get back to you. Emily and Alan'll be here by then too.'

'Okay. We could make it a girls' afternoon, if that would suit you better?'

'A girls' afternoon sounds like a great idea,' said Rico, when Stacy reported the conversation. 'Then Alan and I can do our own thing. I know he has plans for the stag do to discuss.'

***

By twenty to two, Stacy was bobbing up and down beside Rico on the platform at Grimsbach's tiny station, waiting for the little train that trundled up and down the lake bank. Thankfully, the sun had come out, and Grimsbach was at its best. And here was the train.

Emily leapt out as soon as the doors opened and flung her arms around Stacy, hugging her fiercely. 'It's great to see you! I've been homesick for Lakeside – I wish we were staying longer!'

Alan pulled the cases from the train. 'Amen to that. Great to see you two!'

Stacy let Emily go and turned to kiss Alan. 'I'm so glad you could both wangle the time off!'

Emily wrinkled her nose. 'It wasn't easy. But I have job news for you. Stace, how about the two of us walk back to the hotel?'

'Sure.' Stacy slid her arm through Emily's. Emmy's usual one hundred and twenty per cent bubbly personality was subdued today, and her cheeks were pale, too. Something was up. Could she have left her job? It was hard to imagine why she would; she loved teaching her class of primary school children. They took the luggage across the road to the car, and Rico and Alan drove off.

'So what's the news? Nothing bad, I hope?' They wandered along to the main road, then stopped to admire the view of the lake.

'No, but we're looking to the future, as Alan's nearly at the end of his teacher training. I'm giving up my class this summer, and I've accepted a job in a programme providing in- and after-school help for kids who're struggling. We want to start a family soon, Stace!' Hope shone from Emily's eyes.

Stacy held on tight to the arm linked though hers, and oh, she was happy for Emily, she truly was, but wouldn't it be brilliant if she could say the same thing? She injected as much warmth and enthusiasm into her voice as she could. 'Excellent. I suppose the new job means you'll be less tied?'

'Exactly. I want to be a full-time mum for a year at least, if we can possibly swing it, but if we can't, I'd be able to work part time at this job.'

'Sounds like you have it all planned. I wish we were at the same stage, but it won't be too much longer.' Stacy seized the hopeful thought and held onto it. It *wouldn't* be too much longer.

Emily was looking around with a more Emily-like smile. 'Oh, I've missed this place! But tell me your news. How are the wedding arrangements? I can't wait to see your dress!'

Wedding talk lasted them all the way to the hotel, where Emily sighed nostalgically. 'This is such a homey hotel, Stace, even though you've poshed it up so much.'

Stacy laughed. 'It's rosy in your memory because you met Alan here! But you're right. You can tell people have been happy here for decades, if that's not too fanciful.'

She thought wistfully of Rico's parents, Ralph, who she loved, and Edie, who she'd never met. Lakeside had been their child, and now it was hers and Rico's.

Upstairs, Rico and Alan were outside leaning on the balcony railing. Emily joined them, and a 'do you remember' conversation about their first visit to the hotel started.

Stacy inched up to Rico, who had an odd expression on his face. 'Everything okay?'

'Uh-huh.' He raised his voice. 'Okay, gang – how about coffee and cake on the hotel terrace? Our treat.'

'And then a long soak in a hot tub!' Alan rubbed his hands together.

Stacy followed as the others piled downstairs. Something was on Rico's mind, that was certain.

***

Rico forked up Black Forest gateau, gazing appreciatively round the hotel terrace. He didn't often get the chance to relax over cake in his own hotel. It was a good feeling, and having Emily and Alan here meant the conversation was flying around busily; look how Stacy's eyes were shining. There'd be a whole lot more conversation when Dad and Carol and Janie and John arrived, too. It was going to be more than a little crowded in the flat upstairs. Rico swallowed. He saw Stacy looking at him again, the little frown back between her eyes. She'd noticed he was mulling something over. He hurried to make a joke about the summer Alan had spent as barman at the hotel.

After coffee, they moved on upstairs to gather their things for a session in the tubs, and Stacy grabbed Rico's arm as soon as Emily and Alan vanished into their bedroom.

'I can see there's something on your mind. Spill.'

He brushed a stray wisp of hair away from her forehead. 'It's this flat. I've made a decision without you, but please agree, Stace, please. It's fun now, with just us and Emily and Alan. But we seem to take up the entire flat already, so – I want to put your parents into one of the attic floor rooms, along with Dad and Carol. We're not taking any guests there this week so they'll have the place to themselves. Much better than six of us living on top of each other here, and Dad and Carol alone on the other side of the landing.'

He stopped and stood watching her face. The attic floor rooms had previously been another flat, but they'd been converted into hotel rooms last summer. Stacy was taken aback at the suggestion, that was plain.

'Rico, I see where you're coming from, but I don't know what Mum will think about being banished to one of the attic rooms.'

'Stace, you know how much space Janie takes up with that big personality. A little distance might go a long way. And Dad and Carol would be there too, so Janie can't really object, can she?'

Stacy gave a snort. 'You've been taking lessons in tact, Rico Weber. Big personality, indeed. Yes, I know Mum can be maddening, but I want her to enjoy the wedding.'

He kissed her. 'And I want us to enjoy it too. Deal?'

She held on tightly. 'Deal.'

***

Flavia handed over the hotel's map of bike tours in the area, and watched as the pair of guests immediately bent over it before shooting her a quick smile and vanishing round the corner to the terrace bar. It was nice when you could help people so easily, and lucky them, having a partner who shared the same enthusiasm for biking holidays. She stuck out her tongue at the computer. It would be nice if she had a partner who shared her enthusiasm for anything. Come to that, it would be nice if she had a partner. Oh heck, now she sounded like a peeved old biddy who wasn't getting her own way. Not a good look, Flavia.

She clicked to close the folder she'd gone into to print out the map. It wasn't that she was friendless. She had a couple of people at the hotel she did things with – Eva the waitress, for instance, and Vreni from housekeeping. But Eva was married, and Vreni was so obviously on the hunt for a man it was sometimes embarrassing, going out for a drink with her. Then there were the people at the library where she volunteered, and Denise, of course – but they were all older. Flavia went to tidy the leaflet stand. The real problem was, none of her old school and college friends lived anywhere near Grimsbach. She'd taken the job at Lakeside on a whim a couple of years ago, and while she loved her work and the hotel, living here could be a touch... lonely.

Rico and Alan came out of the tub room and gave her a wave before heading upwards. Flavia waved back, grinning. She liked Alan; he'd always been nice to her, the summer he'd worked here as holiday barman. Stacy and Emily followed on, deep in conversation. Longing and nostalgia flooded through Flavia. If she'd taken a job in Aarau where she'd lived for the first seventeen years of her life, she'd have had her old friends on tap. Mind you, Stacy and Emily didn't exactly live next door to each other either. She was being silly. Alex barely noticing her existence had jolted her confidence, that was what.

Thinking of Alex reminded her she hadn't done anything to try and attract his attention. She'd never get anywhere as long as he saw her as part of the Lakeside furniture, no more remarkable than the stapler or the printer. Flavia glanced outside, where the sun was splitting the skies in a very inviting way. A summer evening drink in that café by the lake in Rorschach would be nice... She went into the office and tapped on her phone before she thought too hard about what she was about to do.

Alex picked up on the second ring and was his usual cheerful self. 'Hi there! Did I forget something?'

'Hello, ah, I'm wondering...' Her inner voice cast the sentence for her: *if you'd like to come for a drink in the lake café? I was thinking about going tonight.* She opened her mouth to say it, then a sound in the background sent a chill right through her. Music. Violin music. Classical violin music. Oh no. No. He was with Zoe, he must be. Alex wouldn't listen to classical music by himself.

'Flavia?'

She grasped what was left of her confidence. 'I'm wondering if I should ask your mum to walk down to the lake café in Rorschach sometime? It's quite a long way and she'd be in the middle of strangers when we got there.'

'Nice idea. Why not ask her to walk down to the lake first, then see how busy the café is. They sell ice creams to go as well, so you could always suggest one of those. I think she'd be up for it. She's so much better now.'

'Okay. I'll see what I'm doing this week, then.' Flavia ended the call, the strains of what might have been Mozart still in her ear and dismay heavy in her stomach. Alex saw her as his mother's friend, nothing more.

That had to be the worst conversation she'd had all year.

5

TUESDAY, 4TH JUNE

Stacy pulled on her new capri trousers. Today was going to be another scorcher, and oh, if only the weather stayed like this for the wedding on Saturday. The forecast was stable; she could hope to be a bride the sun shone on. Okay, now to pack her bag for their trip to Friedrichshafen to collect Carol. Which reminded her, she'd need to take some euros with her.

'Can I come in?' Emily peeked round the bedroom door, and Stacy waved the purse she kept her euros in.

'Sure. What would you like to do before it's time to go for the boat? Rico and Alan will be poring over plans in the boathouse all morning, if I know them.' Stacy hugged herself. It was great the two men got on so well. She and Emily had been close friends forever, but it didn't follow that their partners would automatically be bosom buddies too – they were lucky.

Emily plumped down on the bed and stared expectantly at the wardrobe door. 'What I want to do? That's a no-brainer. The dress in real life, please. And what else are you wearing? Nice hat?'

Stacy reached into the wardrobe and pulled out a hanger. The dress was blue-tinged white silk voile, sleeveless and figure-hugging to a high waist while the skirt floated more generously around the legs. It had a lower neckline than she would normally wear, but both her friend Kim and the shop assistant had assured her it was perfect for a summer wedding, and it set off Rico's mum's sapphire pendant beautifully.

She held the dress against her front. 'Here you go. I've got a fascinator with tiny blue and white silk flowers, and white lacy gloves and a shawl, in case it's chilly.'

Emily clasped her hands. 'Stace, it's gorgeous. I love the little blue shimmer on it. Knee-length, is it?'

'A touch below. You don't think it's too revealing?'

'Not at all. It's June, you're a bride – go for it! Shoes?'

Stacy produced a pair of white stilettos with open toes. 'They're comfier than they look, and the dress needs a bit of a heel. I don't often wear heels this height, so I've been practising.'

'Fab. Flowers?'

'White roses and cornflowers. And some greenery.'

Emily came over to hug her. 'You'll look amazing. Hang on, I'll fetch mine and we can admire them together.' She dived down the hallway and returned with a sea-green dress on a hanger.

'That's fabulous. I love the boat neckline, and those lacy sleeves are great.'

'I could have had long sleeves, but I reckoned elbow-length was better for the heat you get here at this time of year.' Emily pouted at the dress. 'It's quite clingy around the waist. I hope we're not having a big pud at dinner!'

Stacy laughed. 'Steamed syrup sponge with custard!'

Emily snorted, then hung her dress on the wardrobe door and flopped onto the bed again. 'We'll all contrast beautifully. Your mum's wearing powder blue, did she tell you? And you should see her hat, Stace.'

'She showed me on Zoom – talk about a wagon wheel!' Stacy hesitated. 'She wasn't happy I didn't go for a traditional long white dress, though.'

Emily gave her a humorous look. 'That's typical your mum, isn't it? She'll be fine on the day, don't worry. I'll make sure of it.'

Stacy put her dress back into the wardrobe, still conscious of the niggly little worry inside her. Oh dear – she shouldn't be worrying about her own mother's reactions to the wedding arrangements on this side of the English Channel, should she? But she was.

She pushed the thought away and took Emily's arm. 'Come on – I'll treat you to a cold drink on the terrace. Plenty of time before we go for the boat.'

Alex was sitting at the staff table when they arrived on the terrace, a half-empty glass of iced tea in front of him. Stacy pulled Emily over to join him. She hadn't had time for a chat with Alex for a while, and it would be good to know he was okay about Zoe being back in Switzerland. This might be the last chance she had for a quiet question before the lovely chaos around the wedding started properly. What with Carol arriving today, Ralph tomorrow and Mum and Dad on Thursday, things were going to be more than a bit busy from now on in.

He grinned at them. 'My mum's looking forward to the wedding. She'll know nearly everyone, and the meal being right here helps too. It'll be a real confidence-booster for her.'

Emily sipped her iced tea. 'She's making good progress, then? Agoraphobia isn't easy to get past.'

They spent a moment enthusing about Denise's progress, then Stacy asked her question.

'Have you seen Zoe since she's been back?'

'Only on my phone. She sent Mum a recording of some of her solos while they were on tour, but – oh!' He put a hand to the back of his neck.

Flavia was standing behind him, a glass of orange juice in one hand and a horrified expression on her face. 'I'm so sorry, Alex – my hand jerked. Did I splash you?'

Alex wiped his hand on his trousers. 'Two drops.' He turned back to Stacy. 'I did listen to it with her, though I'm more of a rock or metal guy, to be honest.'

He had the usual cheeky grin on again, but his eyes were pensive. That music must have been a poignant reminder of the days when he and Zoe were together.

She patted his arm. 'The orchestra'll be doing something at the classics festival in Zurich this summer, won't they? Any plans to go and see Zoe play?'

He bowed his head. 'They have a couple of concerts, yes. I'd like to persuade Mum to go with me, but…'

His phone pinged, and he stood up. 'That's my cue to get back to the desk. Have a good day, ladies.'

Stacy drained her glass too, seeing two of the housekeeping staff approach for their break. It was time she and Emily weren't here.

Half past ten saw them join the queue of foot passengers boarding the ferry *Euregia*, one of the boats that shunted cars, lorries and passengers between Romanshorn on the Swiss bank and Friedrichshafen on the German side. Stacy started up the stairs to the passenger deck, where she led Emily to the back of the vessel. 'Let's sit outside. We'll be out of the wind here, and we'll have the views of the Säntis as we go. I'm so glad Carol came to Friedrichshafen. It's lovely having her just a boat ride away.'

The ferry slid out of the harbour and set course across the lake. It was a mild, sunny day, though not as warm as it had been at the weekend, and Stacy pulled on her sweatshirt. It was blowy even here at the back of the ship. They sat watching as Romanshorn retreated and the Alpstein range, slightly hazy today, came into view.

'Still a few patches of snow on the Säntis,' said Emily. 'But this is a gorgeous place, Stace, and the work you and Rico are doing with the hotel is amazing. You're lucky.' Her voice was wistful.

Stacy touched her friend's arm. 'What's up?'

Emily heaved a sigh. 'It's silly. Part of me wants to be a mum as quickly as possible, but another part is dreading being stuck in Elton Abbey with a baby and no job to go to. And what if I can't cope? We don't have family nearby to help out if I was up all night with the baby.'

'Oh, Emmy. You'd meet other new mums, and you'd be able to help each other. And you'd only have to say the word "babysit" to my mum and she'd be round like a shot. She was saying just the other week she misses the tiny baby stage.' She pulled out her phone to show Emily the latest photo of Gareth and Jo's little Tom, who was now crawling all over the place. Mum was revelling in being Grandma, and as Gareth and Jo lived around the corner and were co-owners of the family stationery shop, babysitting was an almost daily event.

Emily smiled at the photo, then stood up. 'He's lovely. Let's grab a coffee, shall we?'

It was a pretty abrupt change of subject. Something else was bothering Emily, but a busy ferry wasn't the right place for a heart-to-heart.

Fifty-five minutes after leaving the Swiss bank, the *Euregia* slid into the harbour at Friedrichshafen, veered right before executing a smart left turn, and shuddered to a halt at the jetty.

Stacy peered out at the people on the quay. Dozens of tourists were milling around in front of the Zeppelin Museum, and the usual crowd of foot passengers was waiting to board whenever all the vehicles had left the boat.

'There's Carol!' Stacy waved, and a small figure in bright turquoise waved back.

Half a minute later they were on the jetty and hurrying to meet Carol.

'Stacy! Lovely to see you, sweetie, and you must be Emily.'

Carol grabbed Stacy for a hug, then patted Emily's shoulder. Stacy beamed. Carol with her ear infection had been a real problem guest at the hotel last Christmas, but there was no sign of that today; the older woman was positively blooming. They started along the lake promenade, which as usual in summer was bustling with multiculti tourists. Stacy heard French and Italian as well as High German, Swiss German and English, plus a few other languages she didn't recognise.

'So what's the plan today?' she asked Carol, who was leading them up a little alleyway to the old town centre.

'Lunch, I thought, then a walk by the lake and back to mine for coffee and to pick up the car to go over to Romanshorn.'

Stacy whooped. 'You've bought a car! Well done. It's scary at first, isn't it, driving on the right?'

Carol made a wry face. 'Tell me about it. Ralph had me drive round and round Lugano until I knew it better than the taxi drivers. I'm not what you'd call a keen driver, but I do need wheels to whizz up to Munich and down to Tessin.'

Stacy nodded. Carol appeared to be very much at home here. Tessin was the German name for the Ticino, the Italian-speaking part of Switzerland where Ralph lived.

Carol showed them into a garden restaurant, and they sat down under a sun umbrella. 'Tell me the latest about the wedding plans. What did your brother decide?'

'They're not coming to the Swiss ceremony, with the baby, but you'll meet them at Elton Abbey,' said Stacy. 'And in spite of Mum's pleas, Jo and Gareth got their way and baby Tom isn't going to be a page boy after all. And Mum's extended the reception after the church blessing, so I'm not sure who's coming to that.' She remembered the postcard. 'Carol, I don't suppose you know anyone called MJ? They sent Rico and me a postcard from Zurich at the weekend, but we can't think who it is, and it sounded as if they might be coming to the wedding.'

'MJ?' Carol rummaged in her bag and fished out a tissue. She dabbed her nose as the waiter came to take their order. 'I don't think I know anyone with those initials. Have you asked Ralph?'

'Not yet. We'll see him tomorrow.' The drinks arrived and Stacy sat back, pondering. Two things were odd here. Firstly, had Carol been a wee bit evasive about MJ? But then, as Ralph's relatively new partner, she didn't know all the family connections. And secondly, Emily was being unaccustomedly silent. She would have to get to the bottom of that, too, once they were alone again.

The waiter returned with their quiche and salad, and the rest of the meal was spent chatting about wedding dresses. Stacy heaved a happy sigh. Hotel life was great, and being married was going to be even better, but sometimes it was just so good to be out with your girlfriends.

6

Tuesday, 4th June

Rico led the way out of the boathouse, where the plasterers were finishing work on the walls today. The afternoon without the girls was going well; he had shown Alan all around the new additions to the hotel as well as the build. As an ex-employee, Alan was in a good placc to discuss future plans and Rico's vision for Lakeside.

'Pretty impressive, Rico.' Alan wandered along to the landing place and gazed over the lake, sparkling blue in the sunshine today. 'You've got the business well in hand. What a difference to two years ago, huh?'

Warm pride flushed through Rico. Two years ago, Lakeside had been a mess. So had he, for that matter, and his father had been a bigger one. Today, they were all in a good place, and the hard work they had put in was paying off.

Alan kicked a stone and it plopped into the lake. 'The only thing I'm left wondering about is – what are you planning to do with this master's degree? I know IT's your subject and I'm sure you're enjoying your course, but do you really see yourself with a future away from Lakeside?'

Rico thrust his hands into his pockets, moving to the side to let two of the guests wander along the lake path. 'That's the million dollar question. Let's take *Lakeside Lady* out. We'll have more peace to talk on the water.'

He stepped down into the cabin cruiser and lifted the tarpaulin covering the deck and cabin. Alan scrambled in beside him, and Rico started the engine while the other man unclipped the moorings. They set out towards the top end of the lake, water slapping against the hull.

Rico went back to Alan's question. 'To be honest, I'm not sure what I want any longer. IT was the dream for so long. It was a hard decision to postpone the master's while we were getting the hotel up and running. But now...'

He glanced over his shoulder. The boathouse was almost invisible behind trees, but he could see the hotel, standing proudly on the lake bank. Lakeside had always been his home, but now it had turned into something of central, vital importance in his life, right up there with Stacy. It was their future at Lakeside Rico spent his time thinking about and planning for nowadays, wondering how this or that would work, what would be most popular with the guests, how they could best advertise, etcetera, etcetera. And of course, he saw every day how Stacy loved the place too. The dream of today was the hotel, not an IT business.

He said this, and Alan grimaced sympathetically. 'Would you leave your course, now you've started?'

Rico spread his arms. 'I've thought about it, but it seems a pity. Another plan could be to do the course even more part time, take four or five years over it. Stacy knows it was what I'd always wanted and she's worked hard to make it possible for me. I'd feel I was letting her down if I gave up on it.' He heaved a sigh. On the other hand, if he went back to working full-time in the hotel, they'd be in a better place financially to start a family. Not that cash alone would solve the accommodation problem, but still...

He slowed the cabin cruiser down to let Alan stand up with the binoculars as they approached Altenrhein, where there was an airfield. They were right on the border to Austria here. Not it that mattered on the lake, and all three countries were in Schengen, anyway.

Alan watched as a little Cessna plane landed, then turned back to Rico. 'Sounds like the two of you need to have a proper chat, mate.'

Rico could only agree.

They arrived back home late that afternoon and found the girls and Carol sitting round the kitchen table, all wearing big smiles. Stacy got up and pulled a jug of iced tea from the fridge.

'We saved you a glass each,' said Emily virtuously as Stacy poured.

Rico kissed Carol and introduced her to Alan, then raised his glass. 'Day two of the wedding week, and our third guest is here! Cheers!'

They clinked, and Rico stood with an arm around Stacy, happiness coursing through his veins. It would all work out in the end. With the quota of family guests increasing every day this week, they wouldn't have many private moments until after the wedding, but they'd have plenty of time on their honeymoon to have that chat about his future career. Not to mention all the house and baby discussions Stacy had lined up.

Carol was sitting beside the fridge, and Rico saw her glance at the postcard from MJ. A tiny smile flickered over her mouth, then she saw him looking and quickly asked Stacy about the wedding cars.

Rico frowned. Did Carol know something about MJ?

***

Flavia hurried into the staff cloakroom for her things. It was after five – she'd have to hurry to get to Grimsbach library in time to start her volunteer shift at half past. Normally, she tried not to have a library shift after a full day at work, but it was holiday time and the library was juggling staff as much as the hotel was. They always needed at least two people on duty – one to deal with visitors at the desk, the other to return books to the shelves and generally keep an eye open. The library was in an older building and consisted of three separate rooms – fiction, non-fiction and children's books.

Mona, the head librarian, was at the computer checking out a little boy's picture books while he stood there with his father. She gave Flavia a slightly harassed grin.

'Reinforcements, great. Could you start with the trolley, please? It's overflowing.'

Flavia locked her bag in the cupboard under the desk and gripped the book trolley, which was parked behind Mona. Overflowing was no exaggeration; she had to stop twice on her way through to the fiction room to save books from sliding off. She parked the trolley at the end of the room, and hesitated. Heck, the books on here were nowhere near organised. She'd be running up and down for ages...

'Want a hand?'

A familiar voice came from behind her, and Flavia wheeled round. 'Denise! I didn't know you were here today!'

Alex's mother was on the volunteer team too, but she usually only came in for book sales or to help with stocktaking, or the like.

Denise pushed her chest out. 'I had my first solo outing, coming here! I called Mona to say I was on my way, then I got the bus to Grimsbach and walked through the village. It feels as if I've turned the corner, Flavia. Here, let me help you with these.' She seized a couple of books from the trolley.

Flavia's mind was racing as they sorted the books into piles according to the rooms. Alex hadn't mentioned Zoe today – should she ask Denise what was happening with them? If she had no chance with him, it was better to know now and get on with the rest of her life. It wasn't an easy thing to ask without sounding like the worst gossip ever, though.

Flavia compromised. 'Have... have you seen Zoe since she came back from the tour? She must have loads of photos to show off.' Heck, she'd said something like that before, hadn't she?

Denise gave her a shrewd look. 'No, she's been in Zurich since her return. She sent me a lovely recording of one of her solos, though I had to get Alex to help me download it in a version I could listen to. You should ask him to send it to you. It's Mozart.'

Flavia's mind was racing. The thought that had crashed into her head on the terrace this morning was right – that *was* what she'd heard when she called Alex yesterday. Not Zoe come to stay with Alex, but Alex at Denise's flat, being a good son and helping his mother. Hope swelled painfully all over again, but she managed to answer Denise.

'I will. It must be wonderful to be so talented.'

Denise handed her a couple of books for the shelf. 'I think it has as many cons as pros. Zoe doesn't have a normal life, and for a long time that stopped Alex from having one too. And you know, it's the ordinary people living ordinary lives who are happiest, in the end. You don't need to feel inadequate, Flavia. Not in any way.'

Tears shot into Flavia's eyes, and she gave the older woman a spontaneous hug. 'You're a wise lady, Denise Berger. Thank you.'

She went back to the pile of books, but thoughts were still whizzing through her mind. That had sounded as if Denise was telling her not to give up hope with Alex. They were two ordinary people, weren't they? Maybe all he needed was time to get used to Zoe being back in the same country before he started another relationship. Flavia crammed three Agatha Christies onto the shelf. There was no rush; she could give Alex as much time as he needed.

Or... A darker thought loomed up. What if Denise simply didn't want her only child to be hurt again, and a new relationship with Zoe would mean a risk for Alex. He'd need to move to Zurich, too, where Denise couldn't help him as easily, nor he her. Tears burned unshed in Flavia's eyes. Life could be complicated sometimes.

7

WEDNESDAY, 5TH JUNE

Stacy poured second coffees all round and took them out to the living room balcony, where Emily and Carol were lounging on deckchairs, admiring the view of the lake. It felt odd, this week before the wedding when she didn't have to work and, truth to tell, didn't have much to do either. Everything was organised; all they had to do was wait for the day. Stacy plumped into her chair and squinted at her friend. Emmy seemed happy enough right now, chatting to Carol about the new job she was starting after the holidays, but whenever there was a break in the conversation, Emily's features settled into a much weightier expression than she normally wore. Stacy pressed her lips together. She still hadn't managed to grab Emily for a private chat, but it was going to be a priority today. They wanted everyone to have a happy week.

Her mobile buzzed in her pocket, and Stacy pulled it out to find a message from Flavia, on reception duty today. *Parcel here for you.* She abandoned her coffee and ran downstairs, where a shoebox-sized package was sitting on the front desk, a pile of cards on top. Stacy took the lift back upstairs and left the parcel on the kitchen table to open when Rico and Alan were back from their run, then took the cards out to the balcony.

'I thought we'd had cards from everyone we know already, but they're still coming.'

'Weddings are a bit like Christmas, aren't they?' Carol nodded at the pile of cards in Stacy's hand. 'You get cards from people you've barely thought about all year, but then it's lovely they're thinking about you now.'

Stacy opened the first one. 'Nail on head, Carol. This is from Marj and Fred who used to live next door to Mum and Dad. And as you say – it's lovely they're thinking about us.' She went on to open more cards, and shades of Saturday – here was a postcard from the elusive MJ, from Berne this time. *Not long to go! MJ xx*

Stacy gaped. True enough, if MJ was talking about the wedding, but...

'I wish I knew who this person is,' she said, handing the postcard to Carol and squinting to see how the older woman reacted. 'I don't suppose you've had any flashes of inspiration about him – or her?'

'Apart from remembering an old school friend called Melanie Jameson, no,' said Carol. 'A mysterious stranger coming to the wedding! How exciting!'

'Hm.' Stacy wasn't convinced. 'I hope Ralph can shed some light on the mysterious bit. You can have too much excitement.'

'Stacy Townsend – wait until you're middle-aged at least before you start being so sensible,' said Emily, wagging a finger. 'A mysterious stranger is *exactly* what you want at a wedding!'

Carol handed the postcard back. 'Yes – and think what a good story it is to tell your grandchildren one day.'

They were all laughing, but a shadow crossed Emily's face at Carol's words, and Stacy grimaced. Oh to have a few minutes alone with her friend...

A few minutes later, her chance came. Rico and Alan returned from their run and went to shower in the en suite and family bathrooms respectively, and Carol went over to her room on the other side of the fourth-floor landing. Silence fell on the balcony.

Stacy leaned forward and gripped Emily's hand. 'What's up? And don't say nothing. I can see something's bothering you, and it must be more than worrying about your new job, or cold feet about having a baby at some point in the future.'

Emily heaved a sigh. 'That's just what it is, though. My family has a history of losing babies. Mum had three miscarriages before having me, and my aunt had five altogether. I'm scared the same thing could happen to me.'

'Oh, Emmy.' Pity surged in Stacy's heart. How many times had she come across tragedies like that in her previous job as a nurse? 'I'm sure antenatal care has progressed since your mum was at that stage, but in the end, there's never a guarantee – that's me as a nurse telling you. As your friend I totally get it, but hang on in there. You're worrying about something that hasn't happened, and that's not like you.'

Emily sniffed. 'You're right, but I want a family so much and, Stace, it could happen anytime.' Tears in her eyes, she put a hand on her stomach, flat under the blue cargo pants she was wearing. 'Once I get past twelve weeks it'll be better. Mum and Aunt Isabel lost all theirs before that.' She blinked at Stacy, her chin wobbling. 'I'm sorry – I didn't mean to tell you until after the wedding! We didn't want to steal your thunder.'

Stacy jumped up to hug her close. 'You daft thing. How far along are you?'

'Ten weeks. I'm at the all-day nausea stage, and I've never been so tired, but at least I'm still pregnant. I've never actually *been* sick, but I don't know how the baby's still clinging on inside with me feeling so grotty.'

'I wish you'd told me. Emmy – morning sickness is a good sign, whether you throw up or not. It's caused by one of the pregnancy hormones, and it means you're less likely to miscarry.'

Emily's eyes widened. 'Wow. Thanks, Stacy, that helps a lot. I'll need to ask Mum if she had morning sickness. But keep quiet about this, huh? Alan doesn't know I'm so worried. I didn't want to stress him during his exams.'

'More coffee out there?'

Rico's voice floated through from the kitchen, and Stacy went back to her chair, giving Emily a double thumbs up. That was one mystery solved, but oh for the day she could give her friend the same news. Talk about a bittersweet pill... but she *was* glad for Emmy, of course she was.

***

Now that she knew Emily was pregnant, Stacy was careful to steer the day's activities away from anything too strenuous. She and Carol left Emily having a massage in the spa, and did a big supermarket shop for Ralph's arrival that night, and Mum and Dad's tomorrow. It would be family all the way here for a day or two and oh, fingers crossed Ralph and Carol were going to turn into a properly permanent thing and find a home of their own together soon. Carol was such fun, and hopefully she and Mum would get along. Stacy pursed her lips. Her mother and Julia, Rico's aunt, ruffled each other's feathers every time they met, which thankfully wasn't often, but it would happen at the weekend, when Guido and Julia, as well as their son Michael and his daughter Salome, were coming to the wedding.

In the afternoon, the five of them rambled along the lake path to a café just outside Rorschach, and Stacy rejoiced when she saw more colour in Emily's cheeks – sharing her fears appeared to have helped the other girl. Back at the hotel, they found Ralph's Nissan in the staff section of the car park.

'He's early!' Carol dashed off inside while the others were still wandering through the gates.

Rico's eyes followed her. His face was vulnerable, and Stacy slipped her arm through his. It must be weird, seeing your only parent in the loved-up stage of a relationship.

His sigh nearly blew her away. 'Oh, Stace. Every so often it hits me how different things could have been – but they're not, are they?'

'Nope. You can't wish the past back, Rico love. Cherish the memories. I guess it's easier said than done.'

'Most days it's fine, don't worry.' He grabbed her hand and ran to catch up with Emily and Alan. 'Okay, team, how about an aperitif on the terrace before we go up? We should give the older lovebirds a moment together before we attack!'

Stacy was quick with her reply. 'Great idea – Rob has some fab new pineapple juice mocktails on the bar menu, did you see? I'm going to try one of those.' She caught Emily's eye, and they both giggled. Alan looked startled, then smirked, and Stacy winked at him. He'd worked out that she knew about the expected baby, hadn't he?

Rico wheeled round and stared at them each in turn. 'Pineapple juice mocktails... Anything you guys want to share with me?'

Emily patted her middle, then took his free arm. 'Yes, but early days, and all that. Not a word to anyone. It isn't official yet.'

Rico kissed her. 'Well done you. Pineapple juice mocktails all round, then.'

***

Wednesday was a busy day on reception, and Flavia started a quick tidy before Alex came in to replace her until the desk closed for the evening at nine o'clock. After that, the restaurant staff would deal with anything. She stuffed a couple of pens back into the holder beside the keyboard and checked the spa bookings – all okay. She was ready, and the big question was, would she be able to ask Alex about the violin recording Denise had mentioned, and sound natural? It wasn't so much the recording she wanted; it was to feel she was a tiny part of his world outside of work, not just of his mother's world. She gave the desk a polish with her sleeve.

'All quiet? Anything I need to know before you get off?'

Help, he'd sneaked up while she still had her head in the clouds. Flavia grabbed her courage with both hands.

'Nope, we're all good. Hey, your mum was talking about a violin recording you'd sorted out for her – any chance of a share?' There – she'd done that beautifully.

His eyebrows rose, but he whisked his phone out and tapped. 'Here you go. It's Zoe's Mozart solo. I didn't have you down as a classical music fan?'

There was a reason for that... Flavia grimaced inwardly. 'Oh, I don't mind the lighter stuff. Mozart, and so on.' As long as he didn't ask what 'and so on' comprised of.

'Yeah. They're doing a set of Mozart for the summer festival at the moment. Zoe prefers the more avant garde stuff, though.' He leaned on the desk, a tiny frown between his eyes. 'I'm kind of hoping to get Mum to Zurich for one of the festival concerts. What do you think? I don't want to push her too far out of her comfort zone.'

Flavia heaved a happy sigh. This was brilliant, they were having a proper conversation and he was asking her opinion. 'You'd need to plan it carefully – and keep it casual. If you don't make it too important, then she can opt out if necessary without feeling she's letting you down bigtime.'

He frowned thoughtfully. 'Casual... That's a great idea. Thanks, Flavia.'

Flavia told him about Denise's solo outing to the library, and his frown vanished. 'That's brilliant! I'll call her later.'

A car drew up outside, and Flavia jerked upright. It was now or never. 'I wish I could help her more. Hey, how about going for a drink sometime? Have you been to the new café in Rorschach yet?'

Alex froze, his gaze fixed on the computer screen. Flavia could almost see the 'how do I get out of this' thoughts whizzing through his mind. Oh, no, no. Silence hung in the air for an interminable second, then the front door zished open and two guests came in.

Alex smiled vaguely in Flavia's direction before his eyes slid away. 'Nice thought. I'll get back to you about that.' He gave the approaching couple a big grin. 'Hello, can I help you?'

Flavia fled, her cheeks burning. That could absolutely not have gone worse. She would never be able to look him in the eye again.

***

The sun was low over the lake as Rico walked down to the boathouse renovation beside Ralph. His father was bounding along, clearly delighted to be at Lakeside, but were those bright eyes down to the prospect of the wedding – or was it Carol? Rico had his suspicions that his son's wedding alone might not have put such a spring in Ralph's step. It was great to see Dad happy, of course, but it meant that Rico was a little lonely with his memories.

Ralph wandered round the ex-boathouse, nodding approvingly. 'Looking good, Rico. I'll get on with the finishing touches while you're on your honeymoon, and we'll move the fitness room over here right away.'

'Good. They're dismantling the sauna in the cellar on Monday. The Alpstein are taking it.' Rico waved in the direction of the Alpstein Hotel further along the lake bank.

'Excellent.' Ralph led the way out to the tiny jetty where *Lakeside Lady* was moored. 'We'll need to find another place for her when work begins here next week. I'll stick her ten metres out on the lake attached to an anchored buoy, shall I? We can use the rubber dingy to get back and forwards to her in the meantime.'

Rico rubbed his chin. 'Fine. But, Dad, I'm still worried about the finances of enlarging the jetty so much. It seems a bit extravagant.'

Ralph slapped his back. 'Don't worry. I've come into some investment money and I'll cover any shortfall you have until things are back to normal. And you know what your mum would have said – it's short-term pain for long-term gain. This is about the bigger picture. Just enjoy your wedding, Rico.' He looked up and down the jetty with a very cat-that-got-the-cream expression.

Rico started back along the path to the hotel, not sure he believed the part about coming into money. But the long-term thing did sound like something his mother would have said. Talking of the wedding reminded him of something else. 'Dad, do you know anyone with the initials MJ? We've had a couple of postcards from them but Stace and I can't think who it is. They seem to be about to descend on us, though.'

Ralph shook his head. 'Well, it isn't Michael Jackson, and I can't think of a single other person I know with those initials.'

There was a ring of truth in his voice, and Rico gave up. MJ must be one of Janie's additions to the English do after all. 'Dad, Stace is worried about her mum fitting in with the family here. Any suggestions?' Rico thought back to the Townsends' visit last year, when Janie had rubbed several people up the wrong way.

Ralph laughed. 'I'll look after Janie, don't worry. Carol will help, bless her. Okay, let's have a look at your MJ cards.'

He led the way up to the flat, where Rico produced the two postcards.

His father chuckled. 'A mystery wedding guest! I like her choice of Swiss cities, though! You should stop off in Berne for a day on your honeymoon. I don't think Stacy's been there, has she?'

'She hasn't. Berne's on our list of places to visit.'

Stacy came in to make coffee for everyone, and Rico opened the cupboard for mugs.

'Dad doesn't know who MJ is either – so it must be someone from your side.'

'That's right, blame me.' Stacy lifted the panettone Ralph had brought from Lugano. 'Shall we start this?'

Ralph took the panettone box. 'I'll take it out, you two bring the coffees.' He started out to the balcony, where the others were lounging in the evening sun. 'Who's for a slice of Italian sweetbread?'

Stacy's mobile rang while she was still pushing buttons on the coffee machine. Rico took over, listening idly to her side of the conversation.

'Hi, Mum ... yes, everything's ready ... No, no show of presents. Do people still have those? ... Yes, but most of ours are monetary ... Yes ... Not many – the hen night's you, me, Emily, Carol, Flavia and my friend Kim ... No, Guido and Julia & co are driving up on Saturday ... Yes, they'll be in plenty of time ... I'll meet you at the airport tomorrow ... See you then. Love to Dad.'

She ended the call and grinned wryly at Rico. 'Mum thinks we're not being nearly traditional enough. Are we missing out any important Swiss traditions too?'

Rico swallowed his indignation. Janie could be more than a little overpowering. 'Not that I'm aware of, but as I've never been married before, I wouldn't know. It's our wedding, Stace.'

She blew him a kiss, then lifted two of the coffee mugs. 'We'll tell her that. Come on, while there's still panettone left.'

The evening passed companionably on the balcony, and it was nearly midnight when Ralph and Carol left and Alan and Emily adjourned to their room. Rico took the cups and plates through to the kitchen and was stacking them in the dishwasher when he noticed the cards from MJ, now side by side on the fridge. He touched the new one, realisation thudding into his head. What had Dad said? *I like her choice of Swiss cities...* 'Her' choice.

'Dad does know something about MJ,' he said to Stacy, who had followed him with the remains of the panettone. 'He called her "she".'

Wide-eyed, she slid the panettone onto the table. 'How very odd. Do you think she's a surprise guest?'

Rico shrugged. That wasn't impossible, but for the life of him he couldn't think who it could be.

8

Thursday, 6th June

Flavia slid the final two bottles of scented massage oil into the spa shop cabinet in the entrance to the tub room, and ticked them off on her list. With Stacy on holiday this week, she was doing more spa things than she normally did as Stacy's assistant. Not the nursing parts, of course, but there were a lot of admin and organising tasks too, and it was fun. The spa was a good place to work.

She glanced enviously to her left, where Sabine, one of the spa attendants, was talking to a woman in the largest tub. It would be so cool to know enough to be a spa attendant, and chat to the guests as well as giving them advice. Flavia scowled at a handful of bath salt sachets before arranging them on the shelf. Could she work towards that, do a Red Cross diploma and apply for the job next time one became vacant? She could find out about it, anyway. Something in her life had to change; she hadn't felt this unsettled since... actually, she'd never felt this unsettled, and most of it was down to her unreciprocated feelings for Alex. The thought that all he saw was little Flavia who so often needed help was the worst feeling ever. Correction, worse was what he'd thought when she'd as good as asked him out. Well, she wouldn't be doing that again in a hurry.

Stacy came up behind her. 'The shop's looking good, Flavia! I'm sure my mum will buy up most of it, so you'll be kept busy refilling the cabinet.'

Flavia pushed the negative thoughts away. Stacy was her boss, after all. 'Your parents are coming today, aren't they?'

Stacy held up a car key. 'I'm about to pick them up at the airport. You look a bit down – are you okay?'

Impossible to tell Stacy what had happened. Flavia mumbled, 'Fine, thanks,' then was saved by a message pinging into Stacy's phone. She stepped away to read it, then dropped her phone into her bag and came back to Flavia.

'I was talking to Denise earlier. Alex has asked her to one of Zoe's concerts in Zurich, and she said she'd think about it. She's apprehensive about being so far from home, though, with her agoraphobia only recently improved – I thought it might help her if another woman went along too. I'll be on my honeymoon then, but we can organise a day off for you to go with her and Alex. Denise is all for it. What do you think?'

It was the last thing Flavia had expected – or wanted. A whole afternoon – or worse still, a whole evening – with Alex, knowing he'd most likely be wishing her a million miles away. But if Denise already knew about the plan, she'd have to agree, and of course Stacy would think she'd be delighted at the prospect of an afternoon off with Alex, even if his mum was there too. And Denise would be thinking the same thing. The pair of them were probably matchmaking away as hard as they could. Did Alex know about this?

She fixed on a smile. 'Oh – yes – all right. Denise can let me know when it is.'

Stacy patted her arm. 'Good. Ralph will see to the time off for you while Rico and I are away.' She moved away to speak to Margrit, the spa nurse, then headed back to the front hall. Flavia went back to her basket of spa shop items. Somehow, she'd need to find an excuse to get out of that concert.

Five minutes later she'd finished filling the cabinet, and left the tub room. Unusually at this time of day, reception was empty of guests, though Ralph was at the desk with Alex. They were talking in low voices and laughing, but the conversation broke off abruptly as Flavia crossed the hall. Ralph slapped Alex's shoulder and headed for the lift, leaving Alex grinning broadly. He saw her looking, said, 'Wedding talk, that's all', lifted the phone and turned away, still grinning.

Flavia's cheeks flamed. Wedding talk... she didn't buy that. What was so funny about Stacy and Rico's wedding? Nothing at all. Could Alex have been telling Ralph about her drinks suggestion? No, because that would be a mean thing to do, and Alex wasn't unkind. Or maybe she didn't know him as well as she thought she did. Flavia rushed into the staff cloakroom to recover her composure. This was awful.

***

The weather matched her up and down mood as Stacy drove to the airport, with grey clouds chasing across the sky and interrupting the sunshine. Her parents' flight was due in at half past one, and she was planning to take them for lunch at the airport before driving back to Lakeside. And while it would be lovely to see them, she had all her fingers crossed her mother wasn't going to make a fuss over the lack of poshness about the wedding. Two things especially were making her uneasy: one, Mum was a great traditionalist, and two, she liked to be in charge. Having Stacy and Rico organise their own wedding in a foreign country went against everything Janie had dreamed of. Was being in full control of the blessing in Elton Abbey enough to compensate for that? Stacy slowed down as she left the motorway. She'd soon see.

She found a space in the Parkhaus – which, come to think of it, for a two- to three-hour stay was going to cost as much as the airport lunch would. It might be better to find a restaurant on the way home instead, and it was dreadful, the way the price of stuff kept jumping into her head all the time now. Rico was still unhappy about the new landing place, and Stacy could understand his frustration. Why should a few pedalos need a metres-longer jetty? It was unlikely that hiring out pedalos would pay for the reconstruction in a useful time frame, too. But then, Ralph had been in the hotel business for decades, and he wasn't about to do anything that wouldn't be profitable in the long term. Stacy locked the car and headed for the lifts up to the airport. Roll on the long term.

Five minutes later, she stepped off the escalator into a packed arrivals hall, her heart sinking when she saw the board. Oh – Mum and Dad's flight was delayed by fifteen minutes. That wasn't long enough for her to fight her way through the crowd to have a coffee in comfort, so she strolled up and down, mingling with people waiting to greet loved ones as they came through the sliding doors from customs. At last the flight was blinking 'Landed' on the board, and Stacy took up position between the two sets of sliding doors, staring expectantly every time one of them swished open. After a while she heard some English accents as a young couple stepped out and wheeled their trolley towards the exit to the train station. This would be the Manchester flight now.

Five minutes later the stream of emerging passengers slackened off, and Stacy crossed her fingers mentally. Hopefully Mum and Dad hadn't been stopped on the way through. They were bringing a few wedding presents, and Mum would not be amused if any customs officer wanted to unpack them. A vision of her mother berating a uniform-clad officer rewrapping a present sprang into Stacy's mind, and she suppressed a giggle. Did they keep sticky tape at customs? And here were more people. She bobbed up and down on her toes, staring expectantly as more passengers arrived.

For the second time the number of arrivals slackened, then stopped. Stacy stepped back, swivelling on her heels to see up and down the hall. Heck. Mum and Dad must have been on the flight, or someone would have let her know long before this. She was checking her phone to see if she'd missed a message when her name filled the air.

'Will Stacy Townsend please come to the information desk. Stacy Townsend.' It was repeated in German, and Stacy looked round wildly. Where was information–? Ah, there it was at the far end of the hall. And golly, Mum and Dad were there too, with a trolley piled high with bags and boxes. Stacy jogged down the arrivals hall. How on earth had that happened?

'Darling, at last! Where were you?' Her mother's cheeks were flushed.

Stacy hugged both parents, relieved. Actually, it was brilliant to have them here, and fingers crossed she'd continue to think that.

'I was standing by the doors – we must have missed each other somehow.'

'No matter, we've found you now.' Her father was looking strained, and Stacy took over the trolley, throwing the woman at the desk a 'thank you' wave and abandoning the plan for lunch en route. The sooner she had them all sitting round a table, the sooner they could talk properly.

She pointed to the lifts. 'I thought we'd have lunch here before we start for home, but let's put your things in the car first.'

It took a good hour to load the car, find a restaurant and eat their Bratwurst – Dad's favourite Swiss sausage – and all the time Janie barely drew breath, passing on messages from friends and customers and telling Stacy about the plans for the church blessing and the reception afterwards. Stacy's head was reeling as she drove along the motorway afterwards, and she was very conscious of her father in the front passenger seat. He was rigid, staring through the windscreen, his jaw set – and no wonder. Surely Mum had never been so hyper.

It was another hour of Janie's almost-monologue before they arrived at Lakeside and started to unload the luggage and the several dozen wedding presents.

'We'll have a grand present-opening upstairs, shall we?' said Janie, as they squeezed into the lift.

Stacy pressed the button for the fourth floor and grasped her courage with both hands. 'Sounds good. We've put you on the other side of the landing this time, with Carol and Ralph. There are no hotel guests there until after the wedding, so you can spread yourselves out.'

Janie's face clouded. 'We're not in with you, then?'

'Emily and Alan are in with us, so that Emily can help me with my make-up,' said Stacy quickly. 'But you're only ten steps across the landing, Mum. It isn't China.'

Her father guffawed. 'That'll be perfect, love. All the parents together.'

Upstairs, Stacy showed her parents their room, where Janie was delighted to have a little balcony. Relief flowed through Stacy. The new arrangement might have been an issue, as it was plainly a hotel room and not part of their home, but the private balcony had saved them, thank goodness. Rico, Emily and Alan appeared to welcome John and Janie, and thankfully, her mother calmed down when there were more people around to do some of the talking.

'Dad and Carol have gone up to town, but they'll be with us at dinner,' said Rico, accepting an armful of wedding presents from John. 'We'll take the presents over to the flat, shall we, and leave you to unpack and join us for coffee?'

By the time they'd had coffee and panettone and opened all the wedding presents, Stacy was flagging. She could see her father sink further into himself every time Janie started another long story about whoever had sent the gift they were opening. Poor Dad. He preferred a quiet life, and if Mum had been this hyper for long he must wish he had a city job he could escape to, instead of owning a shop below his home with Mum around twenty-four-seven.

'Now,' said Janie, when she'd exhausted the topic of wedding presents. 'Let's have a look at the famous dress. I'm sure it looks even more wonderful in real life.'

Stacy adjourned to the bedroom with her mother and Emily, and produced her dress, fascinator and shoes for inspection.

Janie was silent for a moment, fingering the fabric. 'It's beautiful, darling, even if it isn't a bridal gown.'

Stacy hung the dress in her wardrobe again and grasped both of Janie's hands. 'Mum, we're having the wedding we want, Rico and I. It's not a posh and fancy do, and it's a bit mixed up and higgledy-piggledy, with the honeymoon between the two ceremonies – but that doesn't stop it being our special day. The Swiss part on Saturday is up to us, and the blessing's up to you – except for my dress. I'll wear it for both, of course.'

'Of course,' murmured Janie. 'I'm sorry, darling, I wasn't criticising. I want you to have the best, that's all.'

Stacy gave her a hug. 'That's what we're having, don't worry. Let's all go for a walk before food, shall we?'

***

Rico dropped a handful of teaspoons into the cutlery basket in the dishwasher, then twisted to see behind Stacy as she came into the kitchen. Was Janie–? But Stace was alone.

She leaned on the worktop beside him. 'Mum's gone to get ready for dinner. She enjoyed our walk, bless her.'

'Hm. Your dad thinks she's too overexcited about the wedding.' Rico closed the dishwasher. 'He's worried about her blood pressure.'

Stacy rubbed her head. 'I'll see if she'll let me give her a check-up. She's always been highly strung, and I think that's coming out more now because the wedding's so important to her. I'll have a word with Dad, too.'

'Good. Oh, I forgot – another MJ card arrived while you were at the airport.' He waved at the fridge, and Stacy extracted a postcard of Geneva from under a red magnet.

She read aloud. '*Two days to go! MJ xx* Wow. Has Ralph seen it?'

'Yes – and I'm convinced he knows more than he's saying. But I still can't think who MJ could be. I suppose we'll find out on Saturday.'

Stacy giggled. 'It's probably someone completely obvious who goes by another name.'

'Then why sign MJ?'

'Search me. But Carol was right. We'll tell our grandchildren about it someday!'

Rico found it hard to get his head around the idea of grandchildren. 'Let's have the children first, huh? I was wondering about tomorrow – how about a trip on the ice cream ship in the afternoon? It sails from Rorschach at two o'clock.'

Stacy's eyes lit up. 'What a fabulous idea! I'd been wondering how to keep Mum busy until the hen party in the evening. We'll have a spa morning, the ice cream boat in the afternoon, then our girls' night.'

She danced out of the kitchen, kissing him on the way past. Rico followed on, glancing at MJ's latest card on the fridge. *Two days to go* – this time on Saturday, they'd be married. Husband and wife. Done and dusted. Bring it on.

He punched the air on his way up the hallway, and his arm caught the coatstand, now all but empty as it was too warm to need a jacket when you went out. It wobbled dangerously and Rico dived to save it, sliding on the wooden floor in his socks. His left eye collided with one of the hooks.

'*Aargh!* Jeez...'

'What is it – Rico! What happened?' Stacy was by his side in seconds, pulling at the hand he had clapped over his eye. 'Let me look.'

Rico couldn't tell if it was tears or blood streaming from the eye, and to say it was smarting would be the understatement of several centuries. He wiped his cheek with one hand, the initial relief that the wetness was only tears turning abruptly to panic as he tried frantically to blink.

'I can't open it. Stace, I can't see a thing! That hook – is my eye still there?'

Stacy led him into the bathroom where he sat on the edge of the bath, mopping his eye with loo roll while she fished the first aid kit from the cupboard under the basin. She pushed his hand away and dabbed at his cheek with gauze.

'It's okay, your eye's still there. Let's get something cool on it.'

She handed over a damp pad, and Rico held it against his eye. 'Aren't you supposed to put steak on it, or something?'

'Waste of good steak. Go and sit in the living room, and I'll bring you a packet of frozen peas. Can you see better now?'

Rico removed the pad and blinked unhappily. 'A bit. It's all swimmy, though.'

'We'll give it half an hour, then decide if you need a doctor.'

Her calmness was comforting, and Rico allowed her to propel him into the living room. Stacy went to rummage in the freezer, then he lay on the sofa, holding the peas wrapped in a tea towel to his eye. Imagine if a doctor put a huge dressing on his eye... he'd look a real clown in his wedding photos.

His face was numb by the time the half hour was up, but he could see normally again and the pain was ninety per cent gone. Although – he prodded the area below his eye with wary fingers. Was his cheek swelling up? It was, wasn't it?

Stacy giggled. 'Heaven knows what you'll look like tomorrow. Keep the peas going, my love. They're the only thing between you and a lovely black eye.'

Brilliant. Rico went through and split up the packet of peas so that one half could always be cooling in the freezer while the other was doing duty on his face. What Janie was going to say when she saw him didn't bear thinking about...

9

Friday, 7th June

Rico's heart melted as he watched Stacy spoon up her Coupe Amarena, the breeze from the lake ruffling her hair as the ice cream ship slid through the water. How far they'd come since that day two years ago when Alan, hotel barman for the summer, had called him over to help a pair of guests – Stacy and Emily. He settled his sunspecs more firmly over his eye. It looked better than it felt, but there was still a distinctly puffy area around his eye, and if you gave him more than a passing glance you'd notice a difference in colour, too. He did *not* want to get married looking like a one-sided Panda bear.

The trip on the boat, one of the passenger ferries that looped along the towns on the lake bank all summer with a restaurant full of ices, was a full success, and even Janie was less OTT with a large ice cream in front of her. Stacy'd taken both her parents into the spa this morning, and Janie's blood pressure was all right, but Stace had had a word about keeping calm anyway. John was more cheerful today, too – poor guy, Janie must have been challenging to live with these past few weeks.

The *M.S. Thurgau* sailed on peacefully through the water, heading for Kreuzlingen, and Rico sat back, wondering if he should go and slosh cold water on his eye again while everyone was busy feeding their faces. Emily winked at him, and he grinned back. She was looking better today too; chatting to Stacy about her pregnancy had obviously done her good. Stace did have that effect on people. For the hundredth time at least, Rico's heart lurched. Oh heck, Stace was just dying to start their family and she'd be a born mum, but the finances seemed hopeless this year, and next would be no different. They should have prioritised their own home over the boathouse renovation, that was what, but too late now. Somehow, they had to find a way to afford a baby without taking out a second mortgage on the hotel, almost impossible with both of them working so hard. They'd never find replacements who were prepared to do eighteen-hour shifts like he and Stacy often had to.

Alan started on a series of wedding jokes, and Rico pushed the complicated thoughts away. He stared across the deck to the mountains towering over the soft green of the Appenzeller countryside. The Säntis was grey against a powder-blue sky today, a ring of wispy clouds around the peak, and–

Cold sweat broke out on Rico's forehead. *A ring of...* The wedding rings – what had he done with them? They'd brought them back from the jeweller's on Monday, and he'd meant to put the velvety-brown little box on the chest of drawers in the bedroom. Had he done that? His phone had been charging there overnight; had the ring box been there when he disconnected the charger this morning? Rico racked his brains with no success whatsoever. Heck.

The next hour was lost on Rico as the boat continued towards Kreuzlingen. All he wanted was to get home and make sure the rings were safely in the bedroom. He caught sight of Stacy giving him an odd look across the table, and he managed a grin that must have been more convincing than it felt, because she turned to speak to Emily again. Rico forced himself to breathe normally. This was the pits; he hadn't been so uptight since he'd had to wait for the results of a chest scan a year or two back. He sat fidgeting with his fingers and letting the others' chat wash over him until they could disembark at Kreuzlingen.

The family regrouped on the jetty, Rico dancing with impatience.

'Pity we don't have time for a look around the park,' said Janie, staring at the gardens further along the lake bank.

'If we catch the next train we'll be home by six, in nice time to get ready for the hen and stag parties,' said Rico, trying to sound encouraging. 'And I should get an ice pack on my eye again.'

Stacy took her mother's arm. 'Yes, we want Rico looking elegant in the photos tomorrow, don't we? And it was you who wanted old-fashioned tradition, Mum. You don't get much more traditional than a hen do the evening before the wedding!'

Janie sniffed. 'I suppose so. You're not wearing those sunglasses tomorrow, are you, Rico?'

Rico rolled his eyes behind the shelter of his sunspecs, then regretted it as his cheek twinged. 'I hope not. Come on, everyone – this way to the station.' They would miss the train if they didn't get going...

They drifted along, far too slowly for Rico's liking, but managed to arrive at the station two minutes before the train was due. It was busy with people going home from work and college, and the family had to split up to find seats. Rico ended up in an aisle seat opposite Alan, with the others further along the compartment.

'Rico, are you okay? Is it your eye?'

Alan was staring, and Rico wiped his hand over his brow, feeling the stickiness of dried sweat. 'I don't know where the wedding rings are,' he said in a low voice.

Alan's lips twitched. 'Where did you put them?'

'On the chest of drawers – I hope. But they might be in my jacket pocket, I can't remember exactly. I'm almost sure they weren't on the chest of drawers this morning when I was faffing with my phone and getting out clean socks and–'

'Enough info, thanks. Bet they are there. Or simply fallen down the side, or into a drawer.'

Rico clenched his fists as the train jerked to a halt in yet another little station. 'I guess they must be.'

But what if they weren't?

He made an excuse and dashed upstairs the moment they arrived at the hotel, ostensibly to bathe his eye and conscious all the time that Stacy was staring at him again. Fortunately, the other men gathered round a map of Grimsbach pinned to the wall by reception, planning the stag do pub crawl while the women went to have a look at the spa shop products in the cabinet, so nobody followed him.

The rings... Rico burst into the flat, skidding round into the master bedroom and – the top of the chest of drawers was woefully empty of little brown boxes. Rico peered down both sides – nothing, and there wasn't room for the box beneath the chest of drawers. In his jacket? Nope... It must be in a drawer. He scrabbled frantically through Stacy's underwear and his own in the two top drawers then went on to pyjamas and T-shirts in the deeper drawers. Still nothing, and the winter pullover drawer hadn't been opened for weeks. He had a look anyway, but the drawer held nothing but fleeces and woolly pullies. The flat door banged shut as Stacy, Alan and Emily came in, and Rico sank down on the bed and buried his head in his hands. Where the heck had he put that box?

***

'This might not be the wildest hen night ever, Stace, but it's certainly the most atmospheric I've been to.'

Emily raised her glass, and Stacy flushed with pleasure. It wasn't a huge hen party, just her and Emily, Mum, Carol, Flavia and Kim the hotel manicurist, who was one of Stacy's best friends in the village. Their table was at the edge of a restaurant terrace far above St Gallen. By day, the view was magnificent, but darkness had long since fallen and the party was illuminated by three tall candles and the lanterns at each corner of the terrace. Beyond them, velvety-black night covered the countryside below, lights from distant farmhouses and the odd village twinkling here and there. You could tell by the pool of inky blackness where the lake was, with the far-off houses in Germany mere pinpricks of light on the other side.

Stacy dragged her gaze back to the table. 'It's fab, isn't it? I love it up here in summer, when you can sit outside until midnight.' She checked her watch. Midnight, and her wedding day, were still an hour away.

'How high are we?' Carol swatted a stray mosquito.

'About seven hundred metres above sea. As high as you can get in St Gallen.' Stacy leaned back, happiness flooding through her. This time tomorrow...

Her mother reached for her handbag and stood up. 'Right, girls. As mother of the bride I'm going to settle the bill, then it'll be time to go home. Stacy needs her beauty sleep.' She vanished inside.

'Gee, thanks, Mum.' Stacy dissolved into laughter as she saw Flavia trying to work out if Janie was serious. 'Mum means well, Flavia, but it doesn't always sound like it. I think my poor fiancé's the one who needs his beauty sleep tonight!'

Flavia raised her almost-empty glass. 'It was a lovely evening, Stacy, and I'm sure you'll both look beautiful.'

'Once more with conviction, Flavia.' Fondness warmed its way through Stacy as she swallowed the last of her prosecco. Flavia was always so serious; it would do her the world of good to lighten up now and then. Including her tonight had been a good idea; she worked so hard for the hotel and she was clearly delighted to be here with them.

They wandered down the hill to catch the bus, and Stacy linked arms with her mother. Janie gave her a soppy grin, and Stacy returned it. She was only a tiny bit tipsy, and it *was* her hen night... And at long last, Mum was happy about the wedding. Weddings were all about love and families and making memories and starting on a brand new chapter in your life, and that was what they were doing. Stacy heaved a happy sigh. What were the men up to? Rico'd been unusually quiet this afternoon. Worrying about his eye, probably, bless him.

'Are you and Ralph a permanent thing these days?' Janie turned to Carol, and Stacy giggled. They should have stopped her mother drinking that last glass of fizz...

'Call it semi-permanent,' said Carol, winking at Stacy. 'Oh, I'm sure we'll stay together. The "where" of it all is still up for discussion, though.'

'Don't you like Lugano?' Janie was nothing if not persistent.

'Love it. And Lakeside. And Munich, where my son is. And Friedrichshafen, where all my worldly goods are. Who knows what the future will bring? I could live in any of these places and still be within travelling distance of my grandchildren – though I have to say, Lugano to Munich is a long drive.'

Janie smiled uncertainly, and Stacy thought how different her mother and Carol were. Where *would* Ralph and Carol end up? *Lugano to Munich is a long drive* didn't sound as if a move to the Ticino was on the cards for Carol. Would Ralph return to the north? To Lakeside, even? But he loved being near his brother and working in Guido's boatyard. A little holiday flat there, and a more permanent home in Grimsbach with Carol? One thing was sure: Ralph was head over heels in love. It was so sweet to see the way his eyes kept returning to Carol whenever they were together. These two were together-forever, definitely.

Stacy put the thought away as the bus approached. Ralph and Carol's permanent home was a problem for another day, and it wasn't even her problem, so there was no use stewing over it. And anyway, she had plenty to think about tonight. Like her wedding...

***

The stag night began with a search party. After failing to find the rings, Rico had iced his eye, changed into his stag do gear and gone down to the terrace where the stag and hen party guests were gathering. He bought a round of drinks, then as soon as the women left the premises, he'd confessed what he'd done. The pub crawl round Grimsbach was immediately ditched in favour of 'hunt the rings' in the flat, and Rico hurried into the lift after Ralph, John, Alan and Tobias, Kim's husband and his own good friend.

'They're definitely not in the chest of drawers, but they could be anywhere else,' he said, as they emerged on the fourth floor. 'I've thought about it so much I don't know what I remember and what I've imagined.'

'Okay,' said Ralph, when they were standing in the hallway. 'Rico, you do the bedroom. John, you can fish around in the kitchen, and I'll do both bathrooms and here in the hallway. Tobias and Alan, you're in the living room.'

Rico went into the bedroom. Under the bed... caught up in the duvet? It didn't sound likely, but he checked anyway. Bedside tables... wardrobe. Heck, this would take forever. He rummaged through coat hangers and shirts, then crashed around in Stacy's make-up drawer. Nothing.

Ralph came in to search the en suite while Rico shook out every blessed shoe he and Stacy owned... nothing. And nothing on the shelf above the chest of drawers... or on the window ledge. Wherever the rings were, they weren't in the bedroom.

He joined Alan and Tobias in the living room.

'You've lost them well, Rico.' Alan was rummaging through the wastepaper basket.

Rico flopped onto the sofa. 'Haven't I just. Okay. Worst case, I go to the jeweller's early tomorrow morning and get replacements. They might refund the lost ones, if we ever find them.'

'You'd be able to claim on your insurance.' Alan joined him on the sofa. 'Could Stacy have put them somewhere? Maybe she showed them to her mother?'

Rico clasped his hands, rocking back and forth. They had to find those rings... 'She showed Janie the dress, but I'm almost sure they didn't look at the rings. Did Janie say anything, John?'

John shook his head. 'Not about wedding rings.'

'They must be here somewhere.' Ralph was leaning in the doorway. 'Think, Rico. You're in the jeweller's, collecting the rings. What did you do after that?'

'We walked along the main road and went into the supermarket café.'

'And where were the rings then?'

'In my jacket pocket – but I've looked there already.'

'So you went into the supermarket... Tell us every detail.'

'We had milkshakes, then we drove home. Carol called on the way. Then back at Lakeside, Stace went into the spa to see Margrit about something, and I took the lift upstairs. I went into the bedroom and...' Rico closed his eyes, picturing Monday morning. 'I took off my jacket, and–' His eyes shot open. 'And I noticed it had a stain from my milkshake, so I put the rings into my trouser pocket and hung the jacket up to do something with later. Then I went to make sandwiches for lunch.' Hope flared in Rico's chest.

'With the rings in your trouser pocket? Which trousers, and where are they now?'

Rico leapt to his feet and sprinted through to the en suite. 'In the laundry basket!'

Ralph was close behind him. 'I didn't think to check the laundry!'

'Why would you?' Rico flung the lid of the laundry basket to one side and rummaged for his black jeans. Here they were... He put his hand into the pocket and produced – a little brown box.

Ralph cheered, and slapped Rico's back while more cheers rang out from the living room as the sweat of sheer relief cooled Rico's back.

'Guys, I owe you all big time. Let's get this stag do on the road.'

'Better tidy up here first,' said Alan. 'If Stace and Em see the place like this they'll realise something's been going on.'

'I must say, Rico, you throw an entertaining stag party,' said John, as they put the flat to rights.

Rico nodded sheepishly. It was another story for the grandchildren. But he wouldn't tell Stacy – yet.

10

SATURDAY, 8TH JUNE

Stacy hardly dared open her eyes on Saturday morning. *Happy is the bride the sun shines on...* She covered her face with both hands then peeked through her fingers, and – yes, there it was, warm yellow sunshine streaming through the gap in the curtains where Rico had opened them to see outside. Stacy sat up and stretched. Her wedding day...

The other side of the bed was empty, but the smell of coffee came wafting through the bedroom door, closely followed by her fiancé, a breakfast tray in his hands.

He plonked it down on the bed. 'Grub up! And don't say I don't spoil you.'

'Eek, you've been busy. Omelette for breakfast! I hope this is going to be a regular event in our married life.'

He handed her a plate and fork and joined her leaning against the pillows. 'I reckoned we'd be too busy and too petrified to eat much lunch, so we can stoke up now.' He forked a chunk of cheese and mushroom omelette into his mouth and chewed.

'Who said romance was dead? This is fab. You're amazing.'

Rico smirked. 'I know. Eat your omelette while it's hot, Mrs.'

Stacy squinted at him. His eye was practically perfect this morning, nothing a quick slick of concealer wouldn't cope with. And he was very upbeat for someone whose nerves frequently got the better of him. Stacy waved her fork at the shimmering white dress hanging beside his suit on the wardrobe door.

'No pre-wedding nerves?'

He hesitated, searching for the right words. 'I reckon I feel as if – as if I've come home. To you.'

'Aw, Rico...' Stacy blinked furiously. 'That's just how I feel too.'

It was nearly ten o'clock when they joined Emily and Alan in the kitchen. Emily's eyes twinkled at Stacy from behind her mug.

'Ready for the madness? Your mum's been in twice to see if you're up yet. What's first on the wedding day agenda, then?'

'Nails at half ten. Kim's coming up here to do us both. The flowers should arrive before lunch, and Ruth the hairdresser's coming at one to help with our hair, and Kim again for the make-up, of course. That's about it. We'll exit the hotel at ten past two, which leaves us plenty of time to get to Arbon castle by half past.'

'I can't believe you're getting married in a castle!'

'The photos are going to be fab. The tower's ancient, and the courtyard is to die for.' Stacy flipped her phone open and tapped around. 'And the forecast's perfect.'

Emily blew her a kiss. 'What can go wrong, huh?'

The flat door banged shut as Janie and John arrived, and Stacy met Emily's eyes. The peace was about to be shattered, but this was a special day in Mum's life too. She got up to hug her mother.

By the time lunch was on the table, Stacy was feeling more bride-like – i.e., as if she was about to sit the most important exam of her life. She sat toying with the vegetable rice Carol and Ralph had made. Thank heavens for Rico and a proper breakfast. Nobody else seemed nervous. Janie, Emily and Carol were chatting away about celebrity weddings while Ralph and Rico argued with Alan about football.

Stacy heaved a sigh, and Rico tapped her leg under the table with his foot. 'Don't tell me you're having second thoughts!'

She stuck her tongue out. 'Make sure you remember the rings.' The men all burst out laughing, and Stacy and Emily stared while Janie's mouth fell open.

'Doesn't Alan have the rings? He's best man, isn't he?' Janie's eyes were round.

Stacy put a hand on her mother's arm. 'Swiss wedding, Swiss ways, Mum. Alan's a witness, and Rico has the rings. I hope. And what's so funny?' She glared at Alan and Rico.

'Nothing. I mislaid the rings yesterday, but I found them again, don't worry.' Rico stood up as the doorbell rang. 'That'll be Ruth for your hair, ladies.'

He caught Stacy as she was going into the bedroom with her mother and Emily. 'Relax, Stace. None of this matters, except we'll be married soon.'

Stacy kissed him. He was right, and he was dealing with the nerves better than she was. But then, the bride was supposed to be nervous, wasn't she? She should talk to her mother about that.

***

Flavia pulled up outside Denise's home in Rorschach and glanced up at the flat on the first floor. The balcony door was open, but there was no sign of Denise. They were having a late lunch together here and would go on to the wedding together. Alex was helping with the arrangements at the hotel, but would come later to drive them to Arbon castle for the ceremony. Flavia shivered. She would never feel comfortable in his presence again, but she'd have to say something to get them past her suggestion of going for a drink and back to friendly working relations. This wasn't the day, though, when her main priority was helping Denise through her first real event since the agoraphobia.

Denise was waiting at the flat door. 'Come in – you look gorgeous!'

Flavia pirouetted, enjoying the way her dress – pale pink with a scoop neck and clusters of tiny white flowers here and there – swung around her legs. It was the most elegant outfit she'd worn for a while, and it made her feel as if she'd just stepped out of Hollywood. She grinned at Denise.

'Knowing me, I'll spill ice cream down the front!'

'Not here you won't. We're having plain old cheese and ham sandwiches.' Denise led the way out to the balcony, where the table was set for three.

Flavia's heart gave an uncomfortable thud. 'Is Alex coming for lunch after all, then?'

'He's hoping to. He called an hour or so ago. We're not to wait for him, though.' Denise brought out the food and poured out iced tea, then produced an enormous cloth and draped it over Flavia.

'It's a dust sheet but it's clean, and it'll save your dress from spills. Now tell me all about the hen party.'

Flavia laughed. 'I feel like I'm at the hairdresser's in this. The party was great. We...'

She told Denise all about it, watching as the older woman drank it all in. Denise had been invited too, but she'd been worried that two trips out in as many days would be too much. She laughed in all the right places, though, and seemed determined to enjoy the day. Flavia glowed. Denise was getting better, and she was helping. It was a good feeling, and oh, if Denise wanted to go to the concert in Zurich, she would do her utmost to make sure that happened. One afternoon in Alex's company wouldn't kill her, though it might make her cry later. Unrequited love must be the worst ever.

They were almost finished when Alex appeared in his suit for the wedding. He eyed the remains of their lunch.

'Only two sandwiches left! Good job I grabbed a bite at the hotel!' He took a sandwich and sat down beside his mother.

Flavia had to stop herself staring at him. He was different today, all buoyed up about something. Look at the way his eyes were shining. Was it the prospect of going to the wedding – or was it something else? He winked at her, nodding at her dust sheet.

'Nice outfit, Flavers.'

Flavia rolled her eyes and oh, a week ago that remark would have had her heart racing off in all directions at once. Now, it was making her suspicious that he was acting a part. Or being nice because his mother was here. Or was it to do with Zoe? Or was she overthinking this? He'd always teased her.

Denise brushed a crumb from his shirt. 'I should bring you a bib too! Tell us what's making you so perky.'

He took the last sandwich. 'Concert tickets for next Friday afternoon! They're complimentary so no stress, you can pull out anytime, Ma. They're good seats, on the edge of the side section near the exit. And Ralph said he can easily juggle our shifts at the hotel, so Flavia and I can both be with you. Today will be a good practise run for you, because next week would be less of a challenge, even though it's further away. There'd be fewer people all wanting to talk to you at the concert.'

Denise looked startled. 'I hadn't thought of it like that, but you could be right. Thanks, son. Now, you two can entertain each other while I get my wedding finery on.'

She gathered the empty plates and took them inside. Flavia stood up and removed her dust sheet. Well. This was awkward. But this could be the day to say something after all. She cast around in her head for a way to start the conversation.

Alex poured them more iced tea. 'Thanks again for coming next Friday, huh? You being there will make all the difference to Mum – today too, come to that. Having someone to dive into the ladies with if it all gets too much is a definite safety valve for her, so we owe you one. The catering's all on Rico today, but on Friday I'll treat you to that drink you suggested once, okay?'

Warmth flooded through Flavia. He was reaching out, so maybe he did like her? Maybe he'd had time to get used to the idea? It must have been dreadful for him, loving someone as beautiful and talented as Zoe, thinking she loved him too and they'd spend the rest of their lives together – and then Zoe upped and offed to Zurich. Not only that, she'd been out of the country for months on end with the orchestra. Poor Alex. But this might be the start of something good for them both.

She met him halfway. 'In that case, I'll ask someone at the hotel for an exotic cocktail recommendation!'

He laughed. 'Try Alan. He was barman at Lakeside, wasn't he, before I ever started on reception?'

Flavia sipped her iced tea. It felt as if several decades had passed since Alan's job at Lakeside; time was a funny thing. Denise came back, and Flavia joined Alex in complimenting her on her outfit, and a general get-ready-to-go milling around started. And now she could at least say that she and Alex were friends, and they could definitely work on that. She still didn't know what he'd been laughing about with Ralph that time, but she could let that go. He was buying her drinks on Friday, and that thought alone was enough for today. Enough for all week, actually.

11

SATURDAY, 8TH JUNE

Five past two saw them all assembled in the living room, Rico looking uncomfortable in his new suit and patting the inside pocket every two minutes. Stacy smoothed her dress over her stomach, making a mental note to find out what on earth had gone on when he'd lost the rings. It must have been a bit of an episode; look at the way Alan and Dad were smirking every time Rico's hand moved towards his pocket. And what was Mum looking down her nose at now?

Janie was staring at Stacy's flowers, a charming little arrangement in blue and white, and that would be the problem. Little. Stacy pictured her parents' wedding photo on top of the bookcase in their home in Elton Abbey. The bridal bouquet stretched from Janie's waist to the ground, with roses, orchids, hydrangea and various bits of greenery cascading elegantly downwards. Smothering a smile, she raised her eyebrows at her mother, and Janie smiled weakly.

'The limo's here,' said Ralph from the window.

'Only one car?' Janie had gone wide-eyed again, and Stacy giggled. Poor Mum...

'It's a stretch limo, Mum. It seats twelve. We're all going in it.' Stacy took a slow, steadying breath, gazing round the living room she and Rico had made so cosy together. They'd be man and wife when they came back. It changed nothing, not really, but after the journey they'd had to find each other and set the hotel right, it was definitely a good thing to do. Rico offered her his arm and she took it, laughing. Time to get married.

The long white limousine was waiting in the driveway – and so were most of their friends, as well as the hotel staff. Cheers rang out as Stacy, feeling unaccustomedly elegant, walked down the front steps arm in arm with Rico, who was pulling at his collar. Mobile phones and cameras were pointing from all directions, and good wishes in at least four different languages filled the air. Warmth flooded through Stacy – their beloved Lakeside was celebrating with them on their wedding day. And heavens, they'd barely got started and Mum was mopping her eyes already. It was going to be the best wedding ever.

They all piled into the limo and set off along the main road, a cavalcade of private cars following on. The lake was sparkling blue in the sunlight, tiny white sails racing the wind in the distance, and an excited shiver ran down Stacy's spine. They reached Arbon, and the limo swung up the road to the castle while everyone else branched off to park at the adjacent harbour. Stacy craned her neck to see the top of the tower as they came to a halt at the street end of the castle driveway. This place had been on the lake bank for centuries, the old tower watching out over the water. No enemies were in sight today, though.

The driver switched off the engine. 'We can't get vehicles this long any further up there.' He leapt out to open the door for Stacy.

She allowed the driver to help her out of the car, glad to take Rico's arm for the short walk up the little hill to the lovely old courtyard. Cobblestones were tricky when you weren't used to wearing high heels. The civil ceremony was in one of the smaller rooms, then afterwards they would have drinks outside in the courtyard. Anticipation fizzed through Stacy. They had sent out nearly a hundred aperitif invitations, so it would be a fun do.

Several people had gathered already, and Stacy and Rico stopped to chat.

Janie tapped Stacy's shoulder from behind. 'Are they here for the aperitif already? How long does the ceremony last?'

Oops, Mum had gone a touch querulous again. Stacy put on her most cheerful face. 'It's about fifteen minutes,' she said. 'You can have a longer version, but we gambled on good weather and went for the short one and the aperitif.'

Janie subsided, and Stacy gazed down the castle driveway, now full of family and friends – Guido and Julia had arrived with their son Michael and his little girl, and here were Denise, Alex and Flavia turning out of the main road. Denise was sandwiched between the other two and clutching Alex's arm, but she was smiling. Stacy waved, and all three waved back. No problems there, excellent. Denise deserved some good times.

Ralph winked at her, and Stacy winked back. He had an arm around Carol, and the expression in his eyes brought tears to Stacy's. Ralph was with the woman he loved, and his son was about to get married. She'd never seen him look so happy, bless him.

Someone called for a photo before they went inside, and the bridal party arranged themselves into a suitable pose, blinking into the sunshine as phones and cameras were aimed at them. Stacy squeezed Rico's arm. How lucky they were with the weather, and how lovely this would look – the courtyard with the castle in the background, sunshine dappling through the oak tree in the middle, her flowers setting off her outfit perfectly.

'Cheese again!' It was Alex's voice. More phones pointed, then sudden shouts and barks came from the street below. Stacy gasped as an enormous black dog bounded up the hill to the castle, closely followed by two men waving their arms and shouting.

'Bruno! *Sitz! Fuss!*'

But sitting or returning to heel were obviously the last things on Bruno's mind. Stacy inhaled sharply as he bounded up and danced in front of Alan, dribble flying in all directions, and oh good grief – the dog was soaking wet. If Bruno shook himself now they'd all be spattered with lake water...

Janie grabbed both Stacy and Emily, yanking them backwards away from the dog, and they all toppled over in a heap on the cobblestones. Alan, meanwhile, had kept his head and seized Bruno's collar, pulling him across the courtyard and forcing him to sit. The huge dog didn't seem to mind being stopped so abruptly, and sat there panting and slobbering.

'Are you okay? Up you get!'

Hands came from all directions to help Stacy, her mother and Emily to their feet and dust them down. Stacy stood shaking with laughter. Mum's face...

'We're fine,' she said, after checking the other two had come to no actual bodily harm. Her flowers were none the worse too. 'I hope somebody got some pics of that?'

The dog's owner panted up to reclaim Bruno, then came to stand at a safe distance from Stacy and Rico. 'I'm so sorry! We're with the Water Rescue Dog Club and we were training down at the harbour. It was Bruno's first time, and he panicked when an outboard motor started behind him.'

'No harm done,' said Stacy. 'He's a Newfoundland, isn't he? He's gorgeous – I'd come and say hello to him if he was dry!'

'I hope he didn't spoil your wedding.'

'It'll be something to tell the grandchildren,' said Stacy, exchanging grins with Rico. This was turning into a theme, wasn't it?

'Is no one coming in to get married?' The registrar was standing in the doorway, a bemused expression on her face.

'We'll be right with you.' Rico waved to the dog handler and ushered the bridal party inside.

Stacy's heart began to race. This was it. In a few minutes' time, she'd be Stacy Weber.

***

Rico gripped Stacy's hand as the registrar led the way across a wide hall and through a fat oak door. They found themselves in a charmingly old-fashioned room with panels of polished wood on the walls and the ceiling painted a muted shade of green. Rico breathed out. This was amazing; what a historical place to get married. This room must date from over a century back. He sat down on one of the four chairs facing a long and highly polished wooden table that might have been mahogany, Stacy on his right. They were flanked by Emily and Alan, with the parents behind and everyone else in rows at the back. Rico turned to see their guests. They'd asked for seats for twenty, and a couple of people were standing at the back, but everyone was in, good.

The ceremony began, and Rico didn't let go of Stacy's hand as the registrar spoke, in German, of what marriage meant legally, and about commitment and becoming a family. Every now and again she paused, to give Ralph time to summarise for the English speakers.

Rico breathed in deeply, aware that Janie was blowing her nose in the background. The promise to help and support each other came, and the exchange of rings. He pulled the brown velvet box from his jacket, and Alan cleared his throat.

Rico locked eyes with Stacy. 'Stacy, I promise to love, honour and cherish you, no matter what lies before us, for as long as we both shall live.' He pushed the ring over her knuckle, then she repeated the vow as cool gold slid down his finger.

The registrar beamed. 'I can now pronounce you man and wife. I know in England they always kiss the bride, so please do.'

Rico obliged – their first kiss as a married couple – then they signed the register, and for the first time Stacy was writing Stacy Weber. Rico winked at her, and they watched as Emily and Alan signed too.

Then they were being hugged and kissed, first by Emily and Alan and the parents, then by everyone in the room and yet more people outside. Friends, hotel workers past and present, everyone connected with every hotel in Grimsbach and beyond was in the castle courtyard, all with big happy smiles and flower petals to throw at them. Waiters appeared with trays of brimming champagne glasses, and to Rico's intense embarrassment Janie insisted on re-touching the skin below his eye with concealer.

'People will be taking photos of you, even filming your speech, Rico.'

He managed a smile for her, then stood under the old tree and made his first toast as a married man – to his wife. The crowd cheered, then Stacy pulled at Rico's hand.

'Rico, look!'

A small procession of dogs and owners was walking up the hill to the courtyard, the dogs with large blue bows on their collars. The Water Rescue Dog Club had come to congratulate them, and by the looks of them they'd raided the haberdashery shop on the market square first.

'Photos!' The cry came from all directions, and next set of wedding photos was of Rico, Stacy, and fourteen assorted dogs with their owners standing beside them.

'Best wedding ever, Mrs,' whispered Rico, as they mingled with the guests.

She raised her eyebrows. 'It's not over yet. Hey – do you think MJ's here?'

Rico stood on tiptoe to see round everyone in the crowded courtyard. He hadn't given MJ a thought today. 'If she is, she's being pretty quiet about it. We can only wait and see.'

***

The castle aperitif lasted until five, when most of the guests departed, leaving the bridal party and a collection of others who were going to the dinner at the hotel to return to Lakeside. Some of them were staying at the hotel for the weekend. Rico leaned back in the limo and circled his shoulders. That had been fun, but intense. It was nice to have ten minutes' peace.

'Hey, Dad – did you see if our mysterious MJ was at the aperitif?' He loosened his tie.

Ralph chuckled behind him. 'Whatever makes you think I'd know?'

'Don't be mean, Ralph.' Carol was smiling.

'Rico, I genuinely don't know when MJ will be here, but I promise you, you'll notice when she is.' Ralph's expression was all innocence, and Rico had to be content with that.

The dinner at the hotel passed in a blur. Afterwards, Rico barely remembered eating the Beef Wellington that formed the main course, though dessert was more memorable because he dropped a spoonful of raspberry pavlova on his trousers and had to make a quick exit to remove the smears of cream. The evening ended on the terrace, where he and Stacy mingled with their guests – no dancing, which disappointed Janie, but she'd get enough of his two left feet at the party in England, so Rico didn't feel too bad about it. And this time he was the one who grabbed Stacy and pointed.

'Look!'

Three men emerged from the darkness at the end of the terrace, all wearing lederhosen and each carrying a long alphorn. One was Hans, the owner of the Alpstein Hotel further up the lake bank, and the other two were Peter, manager of the Lakeside restaurant, and one of the Grimsbach town councillors. They set up their instruments and the guests leaned back while a haunting melody quivered around the garden, echoing over the lake, now in darkness.

'Wow – this is incredible!' Stacy was entranced, and Janie was smiling dreamily while John leaned forward to get a better view of the musicians.

Rico put his arm around Stacy, glad that Alan and Emily were both filming the musicians. Peter had played for them before, but it was even more dramatic with the other two adding to the melody. The wedding guests clapped and cheered when the performance ended, and several went up to have a go themselves.

Rico laughed aloud as various burps and toots sounded. He knew from personal experience how hard it was to get a sound out of an alphorn. He was about to suggest John went to try when a waiter approached and handed him a card.

'I have to give you this – it came this afternoon.'

Rico murmured his thanks. The postcard of St Gallen was addressed to Mr and Mrs R + S Weber – their first post as a married couple. Stacy hung over his arm as they read. *Hope your day was fabulous. Be with you soon! MJ xx*

12

SUNDAY, 9TH JUNE

Flavia checked her watch, and stood up reluctantly. She'd had her twenty minutes break, but it was a wrench to leave the staff table on the sunny terrace, especially when the hotel was so quiet it was almost running itself. Officially, they were closed until next week's guests started arriving at two o'clock, but quite a few wedding guests had stayed overnight, so a skeleton staff was manning the restaurant and the spa this morning. And that reminded her, she should make sure the spa shop was well filled. Stacy'd been right; her mum bought half the contents every time she walked past.

She marched into the spa, where Alan and his wife Emily were lounging in a hot tub. Flavia remembered the cocktails she'd wanted to ask Alan about. She was heading their way when Margrit came over from the smallest tub, her white nurse's tunic stained with something green.

'Oh good, Flavia. Can you hold the fort here for five minutes? A soap dispenser in the changing rooms exploded on me and I haven't had a minute to put on a fresh tunic.'

She hurried out, and Flavia gaped round the room. Yikes. There was no spa assistant on this morning, so she was in sole charge. She drifted up to the back where she would notice immediately if anything terrible happened, and stood mentally tapping her feet. This was scary. Nobody looked as if they might collapse before Margrit came back, but stuff happened when you were least expecting it, and oh, what a wimp she was.

Emily called over from her tub. 'Stacy was pleased about how well Denise managed the aperitif yesterday.'

Flavia gathered her best English to reply. 'I didn't think she would stay until the end, but she did. Alex is pleased too. We're taking her to Zurich on Friday. I hope.'

'I heard about that. She's lucky to have you, and everyone here at Lakeside as well.'

Margrit reappeared, and Flavia left Emily to enjoy her soak. Back to her own work now. She would replenish the shop cabinet first, then check the spa orders for next week on the reception computer. Stacy and Rico were leaving at lunchtime to drive to the Bernese Oberland, and it would be nice to be in reception to see them off on the first stage of their wedding trip. And you never knew, maybe one day she'd be leaving to start her honeymoon too. Flavia screwed up her nose. Chance would be a fine thing. Okay, she'd found someone she wanted to spend the rest of her life with, but persuading him he wanted to spend the rest of his with her would be more difficult – unless of course a major miracle was waiting to happen in her life. Alex might realise she was the one for him, and that would be that. It might even happen on Friday. A girl could dream, couldn't she? She made a quick note of what was needed in the shop cabinet and went to collect the basket from the office behind the desk.

Ralph and his brother Guido were there, hunched over the computer and muttering to each other in Italian. Ralph blanked out the screen as Flavia went in, then tapped his nose at her and spoke German.

'I don't know if you saw that, Flavia, but if you did, forget it immediately. It's a surprise.'

'I didn't see it.' Flavia lifted the basket. 'A surprise for Stacy and Rico?'

'Yup. But you know nothing, okay?' He tapped his nose again.

Flavia left them to it. Keeping a surprise secret was easy when you had no idea what it was.

By the time she'd restocked the shop, the front hall was buzzing. Flavia went over to stand in her usual place at reception. Stacy and Rico must be leaving; she'd timed that well. The lift doors pinged open, and the crowd surged forward to surround the bridal couple. Flavia hovered in the background, then Alex slapped her shoulder and she nearly fell over with shock.

'Come on, Flavia – let's wave the happy couple off.'

He spoke lightly, but there was an edge to his voice that stung Flavia even as she complied. She knew what it meant; he was impatient because she'd been hanging back and not 'going for it' like everyone always said you should. But all those people were better friends of Stacy's than she was, so it didn't seem right to push forward. She followed on as they all went out to the car park, where Rico's car was decorated with ribbons and cans tied on the back bumper. There were hugs and kisses for all the parents, including Carol, blown kisses and waves for everyone else, and then they were off. Flavia waved madly too, then they all stood listening as Rico's car, cans rattling behind it, moved off down the road.

Ralph laughed as the din stopped before it had died away. 'He's pulled in at the Alpstein. Oh well, I suppose they can't go on the motorway like that. Coffees on the house all round, folks, and Alex, don't forget we have a job to do later.'

Alex grinned broadly, and Flavia watched as he and Ralph went inside together. Ralph went upstairs, but Alex headed straight for the office. The door closed behind him. Okay. This must be to do with Ralph's surprise, the one she wasn't allowed to know about.

Flavia went to get the desk ready for the expected influx of guests. It was back to business now.

***

By four o'clock, all the wedding guests were gone and next week's hotel guests had checked in, apart from two couples who were flying from England and wouldn't arrive until this evening. Flavia stood at reception, fielding the usual queries about the spa, attractions in the area and booking for the tubs. Ralph had taken Stacy's parents and Emily and Alan to the station earlier on, and was now shut in the office with Alex. Whatever the surprise was, it seemed to need a lot of planning. Flavia pouted. It was silly to feel left out; no one else on the staff knew about it either. She heaved a sigh, rubbing at a felt pen mark on the desk. Truth was, she was apprehensive about the next two weeks without Stacy. It was fine being someone's assistant when they were around most of the time to lend a hand if you needed it, but she was going to have to do the job all by herself for the next two weeks. At least Margrit was here to help.

Luis, one of the waiters, arrived with two cups of coffee and two chunks of banana cake on a tray. He jerked his head at the office door. 'The boss and the receptionist have ordered in.' He tapped on the door and handed the tray in to Alex. The door closed again.

Luis leaned on the desk. 'Is it just me, or are they being mysterious?'

'It's not just you. But they're saying nothing.'

'Well, you know what they say. The best way to encourage anyone to tell you something is not to ask.'

Flavia giggled. Luis was good fun; he'd been here as long as she had and oh, why was she quite happy kidding around with him, and so tongue-tied with Alex? And talking of Alex...

'Hey, I'm going to Zurich with Denise on Friday and Alex is standing me a cocktail. Any suggestions?'

'Are you going for exotic, expensive or fancy paper umbrellas and fireworks?'

'Fireworks? In your drink? I don't know a thing about cocktails.'

'Some have sparklers on them. I'm no expert either, but tell you what. I'm off at six. Why don't we meet in the bar and try out a few? I'm sure they'd do us mini-cocktails at staff rates.'

Flavia didn't hesitate. There was no reason on this earth she shouldn't go for cocktails with a friend, and it was odds-on Alex would see them. If he thought another guy was interested in her – which Luis wasn't, so it wasn't as if she was using him for her own gain – it might spur him on a bit faster. You didn't want to be too available... A girl could be tactical while she was dreaming, couldn't she?

13

MONDAY, 10TH JUNE

Stacy relaxed back in the passenger seat as they joined the queue to exit the car park at the Brienzer Rothorn Railway. They were staying in a hotel at Hasliberg, a lovely mountainous area to the east of Lake Brienz, one of the twin lakes that dominated the region and brought in thousands of visitors every year.

'It's a bit touristy, but you'll see most of the important sights here,' Rico had told her.

And it was true. They hadn't been here two days yet and already she'd seen the Jungfrau, Mönch and Eiger mountains, and Interlaken, the little town nestling between Lakes Brienz and Thun. Today they'd been on the Brienzer Rothorn mountain, going up in a mountain train pulled by a steam-engine – and the views from the top were to die for. The higher peaks of central Switzerland soared in the background, and far below, the vibrant blue-green waters of the twin lakes shimmered. Apparently it was glacial particles in the meltwater running down into each lake that made them more vividly coloured than their own much larger Lake Constance. You could walk for a long way on the summit, and Stacy had taken dozens of photos. And after all the excitement of the wedding, it was lovely to be doing their own thing, just the two of them.

Rico drove along the lakeside – a very different lakeside to their own, with the road nestling by the bank beside richly wooded hills that rolled down to the lake. There was even the odd short tunnel.

The waters of Lake Brienz behind them, they continued up the valley to Meiringen, famous for meringues. Stacy sighed happily. This was fabulous; she should have a honeymoon more often.

'We can go and see the Reichenbach Waterfall one day, if you like. I've never been there either,' said Rico. 'It's where Sherlock Holmes is supposed to have leapt to his death.'

'Really?' Stacy was intrigued.

'Yup. There's a Holmes Museum in Meiringen. We could have a look there after coffee, and do the falls another day.' He drove into the little town, and Stacy pointed out a café with a garden restaurant.

'Let's go there. There's lots of leafy shade under those trees.'

Ten minutes later they were sitting with cappuccinos and enormous creamy meringues in front of them.

'What could be more perfect?' Stacy waved her cake fork at Rico. 'But at this rate, we're not going to fit into our wedding gear by the time we get to Mum's.'

He rolled his eyes. 'Let's just enjoy the day. We can worry about calories when we start back at work. But talking about parents, I had a thought about MJ in the shower today.'

'You know who she is?' Stacy sat up straight. 'Spill.'

'Not exactly, but I wondered if she was someone on Mum's side of the family.'

'I thought Edie only had cousins in Canada?' Stacy tried to remember. 'And one in the States?'

'That's right. But if one of them was visiting Europe, they might well come for a visit but not to the actual wedding, in case that would be awkward for us.'

'Hm.' It didn't sound likely to Stacy. 'Does one of them have the initials MJ?'

Rico scratched the back of his neck. 'I know one of them is Melanie, but, Stace – we didn't have much contact with them even when Mum was alive. And if it was a woman who'd got married, I wouldn't know the surname. It isn't impossible.'

Stacy still wasn't convinced. 'If it was Melanie, then surely she'd sign her full name? MJ sounds more like someone who's familiar.

And think of the postcards – don't you think she'd be more worried about the awkwardness of being as close as St Gallen and not coming ten kilometres further to see us get married?'

Rico waved his cake fork. 'MJ exists all right, but I reckon these postcards are a spoof. Dad and Carol sent them. I bet if we examined the postmarks, they wouldn't match the pic on the front. Dad might be trying to make a bit of a joke to give us something to talk about in the first few minutes of cousin Melanie's visit when we're home again.'

'I'm pretty sure you're overthinking this massively, but I suppose you could ask Ralph.'

'And he'd say, wait and see. So I guess that's what we'll have to do.'

Stacy scraped her plate clean. 'Is the museum far? We could leave the car here and walk.'

Rico pulled out his wallet and signalled to the waitress. 'Stop worrying about calories. If you can't get into your wedding dress–'

'If I can't get into my wedding dress, Mum will have forty fits. Come on – let's get walking.'

***

'Bet you're glad you don't have to bring up a family in this place,' Rico whispered in Stacy's ear, and she nodded. It was Tuesday, and they were at Ballenberg, an open-air museum in a huge woodland park containing examples of original old farmhouses and other buildings brought in from all over Switzerland. After a couple of days of wall-to-wall sunshine, today was cloudy, but this was something they didn't need good weather to enjoy.

Stacy took Rico's hand as they wandered on through the 17th century farmhouse. Golly, how life had changed since then. She stood in the kitchen with its huge fireplace and enormous soup pot hanging there, comparing it to her own kitchen at Lakeside. Imagine trying to feed a large family plus farm workers here – life had been tough in those days.

Upstairs, she stopped at a half-door, looking over into the room beyond, set up as a bedroom. The checked bedspread was cute, but it didn't look like a bed for a good night's sleep.

'I'm glad I don't have to sleep here, too. Think of everything we have now that people back then didn't – good healthcare, fridges, enough food – and yet even today, so many people in other countries don't.' It wasn't a comfortable thought.

Rico put his arm around her. 'You can't save the world, Stace. But how about we donate to something when we're home again? As a "thank you" because we're lucky, and happy together. You can choose a charity.'

Tears came into Stacy's eyes. He was kind, was Rico; he cared about stuff. 'That's so sweet. How about–'

Her words were drowned by a shrill scream and a series of thuds coming from the dim and narrow wooden staircase she and Rico had negotiated – carefully – a few minutes beforehand. A man's voice boomed through the building. '*Eva!*'

Stacy rushed to the top of the stairs, Rico close behind her. A young woman was half-sitting, half lying over several treads in the middle of the staircase, her face drawn in pain. A dark-haired young man bent over her from above, then jumped down nimbly to kneel on the step below.

Stacy pulled out her best German and called from the top of the stairs. 'Are you okay? I'm a nurse, can I help?'

Her stomach lurched as the woman twisted round to see who was calling. Eva, whoever she was, was pregnant. Very pregnant, in fact.

'I've twisted my ankle.' The woman stretched a hand down to her left foot. Stacy recognised the clipped High German as coming from the north of Germany. These people were tourists, like them, and Eva was pressing a hand on her belly.

Stacy stepped over the woman and touched the sandal-clad foot. There was no obvious abnormality, but that didn't mean the ankle was merely twisted. It could be broken.

Eva flinched. 'I'm not sure I can stand,' she said, tears in her eyes.

Stacy peered up to Rico, still at the top of the stairs.

'Call an ambulance, Rico,' she said in English.

He pulled out his phone. 'I'll see if I can find someone with a first aid kit, too.' He spoke briefly into his phone, then climbed over Eva and vanished outside.

The young man, who introduced himself as Markus, was clutching Eva's hand. He looked as shocked as she was, and obviously had no idea what to do.

Stacy took Eva's pulse – it was fast, but not alarming. 'When's the baby due?'

'Five weeks.' Eva's hand circled her bump. 'He's moving. I think he's okay.'

'Good. Any other injuries, or just your foot?'

'Just the foot,' said Eva, her voice shaking. 'I didn't really fall; I missed a tread and stumbled down a few stairs.'

'Right. Let's get you off these stairs. There are stools in the kitchen.'

Markus helped Eva to her feet, then carried her downstairs and into the kitchen, Stacy supporting the ankle all the time. He deposited Eva on a hard wooden stool, and she leaned back against him. Stacy pulled over more stools for the injured leg, and examined her patient in the better light. There didn't seem to be a fracture, but Eva was pale and her skin was clammy. Where the hell was Rico with help?

The thought had no sooner entered her head than he returned, a Ballenberg employee clutching a first aid box striding into the kitchen behind him.

Stacy fished out a bandage and bound up Eva's foot while the museum employee ushered three other people viewing the farmhouse back outside. Eva was still leaning on Markus, her eyes closed. She moaned, breathing out through pursed lips, both hands clutching her bump.

'Was that a pain?' Stacy rubbed the other woman's arm, worried. Thirty-five weeks wasn't dangerously early, but the baby should stay in there for a little longer to have the best start in life – and no matter what people had done in the seventeenth century, this farmhouse was no place to give birth today. She straightened up, and Eva gripped her hand.

'Don't go away! I've had a couple of practice contractions this week. The doctor said it was normal, and this one didn't feel different.'

'That's good,' said Stacy encouragingly, her fingers on Eva's pulse again. It was still pretty fast, though in the circumstances, that was to be expected. But what Eva needed was a doctor and an ice pack for her foot, and neither was anywhere in sight in the old farmhouse kitchen.

A siren sounded in the distance, and the museum employee went outside to greet the ambulance. Two male paramedics manoeuvred a wheelchair into the kitchen, and Eva allowed them to help her into it. She reached for Stacy's hand, her eyes frantic.

'Please – can you come too? My baby–'

'Of course. I'm sure your baby will be fine, but I'll stay with you until we get to the hospital.' Stacy gave her a hug. Poor Eva.

'Interlaken hospital,' said the paramedic, when Rico asked where they were going. 'Less than half an hour away, driving normally – and don't worry, we'll get her there a lot quicker than that,' he added to Markus. 'You can follow on in your car.'

Stacy gave the young man her most reassuring nursey smile. Markus was evidently one of those people who weren't great in an emergency. He was almost as pale as Eva.

'On you go. I'll come and find you there,' said Rico, kissing Stacy as she walked behind the wheelchair.

Stacy got into the back with Eva and clicked on her seatbelt, then the ambulance crawled through the park before zooming along the highway on the south bank of Lake Brienz, blue lights flashing. Well. It was a long time since she'd been in an ambulance travelling at speed. A hospital was the one place she hadn't expected to visit on her honeymoon.

14

MONDAY, 10TH JUNE

The ambulance containing the German woman and Stacy disappeared into the distance as Rico drove out of the car park back towards Interlaken. Eva's partner overtook him in a black Porsche as soon as they were on the highway, and he followed on more sedately. Interlaken hospital was in Unterseen, once a separate little village, now caught up in the spread from the most visited tourist destination in the Oberland – or that's what it looked like today, anyway. Holidaymakers were thronging the streets of the town, which were touristic in a rather kitschy way. Rico found an expensive place to leave the car and hurried through the main hospital entrance. Stacy was sitting in the waiting area at A&E, fishing in her bag. He edged up from behind and trailed his fingers across her neck.

'Heavens, Rico – you scared me half to death! I was about to call you.'

She was laughing, and Rico made an educated guess that all was well with Eva and her baby.

'They don't think she's in labour, but they're keeping her under observation for a few hours, to be sure,' Stacy confirmed when he asked. 'The ankle's sprained, but it's not a bad one. I gave her one of my hotel cards, and she's going to let us know what happens.'

'Good thinking. And good advertising, too, for Lakeside.' Rico put his arm around her as they walked outside. The sun had come out, and they mingled with a steady stream of visitors going to and from the car park. 'Where to?' he said, stabbing the key into the ignition. 'Back to Ballenberg? Another walk through Interlaken, as we're here? Or we could drive up the other lake, Lake Thun, to Spiez. It's a lovely little town, and it would show you something new.'

'Is it far?'

Rico grinned. *Cup of coffee* was written all over Stacy's face. 'Quarter of an hour. Twenty-five minutes to *Kaffee und Kuchen*, how's that?'

'Perfect.' She blew him a kiss, then sat back to enjoy the view as he drove along the banks of Lake Thun, small and slim like its sister lake.

The rest of the afternoon passed without any extra excitement. They had coffee and lemon meringue pie in Spiez, then drove on, going all the way around Lake Thun then back to Hasliberg and the Hotel Alpensicht, which, as the name suggested, delivered spectacular views of the mountains.

'I'll be glad to have a shower,' said Stacy, as Rico parked in their designated space. She sniffed her arm. 'I'm sure I can still smell Interlaken hospital!'

Like Lakeside, the Alpensicht was a small, family-run affair, though privately Rico thought they weren't making the most of the place. Shabby carpets were a theme everywhere, and while the hotel was comfy, it was old-fashioned. If they were strapped for cash, it was hard to see why; the area was an absolute magnet for tourists. The staff were pleasant, though, and Rico was thinking aperitif- and dinner-shaped thoughts as they walked through the main door.

To his surprise, the receptionist and the manager, both bent over the computer screen on the desk, didn't look up as they went in. He and Stacy were right in front of the pair before anyone noticed them, and Rico frowned. Something was up. The young receptionist was red-eyed and blinking back tears, and the close-to-retirement manager's brow was shining with sweat as he jabbed at the computer keyboard.

Rico exchanged a glance with Stacy. 'Problem?' he asked, and the manager banged both hands on the desk.

'Anita has clicked on something she shouldn't have, and the entire system's frozen.' He sounded desperate, and heavy resignation spread through Rico's gut. Bang went a speedy glass of fizz and a lovely shower with his wife...

'Can I help?' he said, as the receptionist handed Stacy their key. 'I'm in IT.'

He was welcomed with open arms on the other side of the desk, and Rico could only watch as Stacy headed for the lift.

***

It was over two hours later before he arrived in the hotel room, where Stacy was sitting with her feet up flipping through the channels on TV, a glass of juice from the minibar by her side.

Rico collapsed on the bed, and she clicked the TV off.

'Hard work? I saw on the news there's been some kind of buggy scam thing on emails. Seems pretty widespread throughout Switzerland.'

Rico sat up and helped himself to a swig of her juice. 'That's it. It's one of those ransom malware attacks, and the receptionist clicked on the link without realising what it was. I've got them secure, and running provisionally on a laptop that wasn't affected, but they'll need their own support team to re-access their files. Fortunately, everything was backed up. The good news is, we're getting dinner on the house, so I'll grab a quick shower and let's go – I'm starving!'

They were enjoying a starter of garlic mushrooms when an uncomfortable thought slid into Rico's head. Those malware emails – would Alex, or whoever was on the reception at Lakeside, know not to click on anything suspect?

'I'm sure Alex is well up to speed on things like that,' said Stacy, when he told her what he was thinking. 'He's a trained receptionist. And your dad would be careful, too.'

Rico wasn't convinced. 'It's nearly eight... Suppose Carol's minding reception? Or Flavia, or one of the non-trained staff? I think I'll give Dad a quick call.'

Stacy cast her eyes heavenwards. 'Talk about a busman's honeymoon – we've both worked hard at our professions today!'

She was smiling, though, and Rico wrinkled his nose at her as he connected to his father's phone. Oh. Voicemail. 'Hi, Dad, give me a call when you get this, will you? I'm worried about the malware thing that's going around.'

Their steaks arrived, and the waiter topped up the wine glasses. Rico lifted his knife and fork. He was ready for this...

Making plans for the rest of the week kept them talking through the main course, and the plates were being cleared again before Rico realised his father hadn't called back. Odd. What could Ralph be doing at this time of night that he couldn't take five minutes to reassure his worried son?

'Cinema in St Gallen?' suggested Stacy. 'He'd have his phone switched off, there.'

Rico shrugged. 'Could be, I suppose. I know, I'll call reception.' He tapped to connect, and Alex's voice spoke in his ear.

'Lakeside Hotel, Alex speak– oh, Rico! Anything up? You're on honeymoon!'

'I know. Have you seen the dodgy emails going around?'

Alex was trying not to laugh, Rico could tell by his voice. 'I have a large-sized notice stuck to every computer screen in the hotel, Rico, and two others in three languages in the lift and on the desk to warn guests. Barring a slip-up, we're onto it. How's the honeymoon?'

Rico relaxed. 'Great. And well done. I tried Dad earlier but got no reply, so I was a bit worried.'

'Ralph's gone down to Lugano. I can give you Carol, if you like?'

'*Lugano*? He's supposed to be–' But Alex was gone; Rico could hear him calling for Carol in the background. And what on earth was so urgent in Lugano that Ralph had swanned off to the other end of the country while he was acting manager? Rico's mouth went dry.

'Hi, Rico, how are you two?' Carol sounded her usual cheerful self. That was a good sign, wasn't it?

He assured her they were having a lovely romantic honeymoon – or they had been, until today – and asked about Ralph.

'It's some business stuff at the boatyard that needs a signature, that's all. He was supposed to sign it before he left, but it wasn't ready in time. He'll be back tomorrow.'

Rico was only half-convinced. Ralph's job at his brother's boatyard was important to him, but wasn't Lakeside more important? And why couldn't Guido have signed? Come to that, why hadn't Guido brought it with him for Ralph to sign? But then, Guido and family had gone back south on Sunday, and the document could be new since then. But what on earth was that urgent? Dad would say, 'wait and see, Rico', wouldn't he? Rico gave up, and chatted to Carol for a minute or two before ending the call and turning back to Stacy.

'Dad's left Alex and Carol in charge while he signs stuff in Lugano. Seems – odd.'

She handed him the dessert menu. 'Rico. Honeymoon. Now.'

'But if anything–'

She interrupted him, and this time there was a definite edge to her voice. 'Nothing will happen that couldn't happen if you were there manning the desk twenty-four-seven and opening every email personally. This is the last week off we'll have for a long time, and it's the calm before the storm when we arrive in England next week, and Rico – *we are on honeymoon*. Forget Lakeside for a day or two.'

'But–'

'*Rico!*'

She was glaring now, and people at the nearby tables were staring. Rico swallowed, then laughed, gripping her hands across the table.

'Well, that's our first fight as a married couple behind us. Sorry, love. What's for pud?'

'I'm having orange sorbet.' She passed him the menu, and the rest of the meal passed without a mention of Lakeside. Rico hugged Stacy to his side as they went for a post-dinner stroll around the village. The mountains were dusky-hazy in the background, he was in a lovely alpine village with his wife, and everything in his world was all right. He hoped.

15

WEDNESDAY, 12TH JUNE

Flavia heaved a new tub of the scented additive they used in the tubs onto a trolley and wheeled it through to the large spa. A substantial delivery had come that morning, and it was her job to put everything in the correct place. Storage space was still at a premium at Lakeside, but that would improve when the new boathouse build was open. Bring it on.

She was wheeling the trolley back through the tub room when a shriek followed by laughter came from – was it the changing rooms or the loos? She and Margrit looked at each other, then Flavia parked her trolley and rushed to investigate. A woman was standing in the ladies dabbing at her swimsuit with a paper towel while green liquid soap oozed down her front. Another woman, giggling madly, was trying to help.

The soap-covered guest laughed at Flavia. 'Your soap dispenser's a little, um, temperamental! It spat about a gallon at me the moment I went near it!'

Flavia grabbed another handful of paper towels and handed them over. 'Oh no – I'm so sorry! Are you all right?'

'It's only soap, love, and I'm about to have a shower before I go into the hot tub. No harm done.'

Flavia leaned out of the door to give Margrit a thumbs up, remembering that the nurse had had the same problem. Someone should have dealt with the dispenser before this, and in the absence of Stacy, that someone was her. She should channel her inner Stacy; her boss would have been right onto it after the first incident. Several minutes spent prodding the soap dispenser had no result except to waste a lot of soap, so she wrote a large "Defekt" sign on a card and stuck it to the dispenser. English speakers would understand that too. Come to that, she could probably write it in Chinese and people would get the message. A sign on a machine usually meant one thing only.

Back in the office, she tapped into the computer and opened the folder with the details of which companies had installed what in the spa. Here were the bathroom fittings, and help – over two hundred francs for one single soap dispenser? That was pricey... Okay, these were special, motion-activated and matching-the-décor dispensers, but maybe she should wait until Stacy was back to decide if they wanted an expensive replacement. But then, those dispensers were used multiple times a day; they were necessary pieces of equipment. Oh, dear – decisions weren't her strongest point.

She trailed out to ask Alex for an opinion. 'Faulty soap dispenser. Do you think I should order a replacement? Or–'

He'd been poking glumly at his keyboard, and to Flavia's amazement, he turned on her. 'I think you need to learn how to do your own thinking! What do I know about soap dispensers?' He marched off towards the restaurant, leaving Flavia open-mouthed at the desk. What had got into him?

Kim the manicurist was coming out of her treatment room. 'I heard that. I wouldn't worry, Flavia, he's been snapping everyone's head off today. Not the guests, of course, but everyone else.'

Flavia sniffed. Alex was feeling the pressure of being more or less in charge of the whole hotel while Ralph was away, that was what. She repeated the story of the soap dispenser for Kim. 'What do you think? They're over two hundred francs.'

Kim considered. 'I would put an ordinary one on the basin in the meantime and wait for Ralph to get back. It might be something he can fix.'

Kim went back to her room with her next client, and Flavia hesitated. She wasn't on desk duty today unless there was a rush, but someone should be here. After the way Alex had spoken to her, though, she wasn't inclined to do him a favour and stay. His voice approaching gave her the excuse to leave, though, and she scurried into the storeroom for a normal soap dispenser which she plonked down on the basin in the ladies. There, sorted. And now she was going for lunch. It was a gorgeous day; she'd treat herself to a restaurant salad on the terrace, then she'd go for a walk to calm her nerves. People being horrible to you was upsetting no matter what reason they had.

A cheese and ham salad and a walk by the lake with Vreni from housekeeping did a lot to cheer Flavia up, and she tramped back across the terrace ready to get stuck into her next job. She glanced through the open office door as she passed the desk, and oh, no. Alex was there, his phone pressed to one ear and the other hand clutching at his shirt. Flavia folded her arms across her middle, her heart thudding all the way down to Australia. Something *was* wrong. His expression... it was broken-hearted, tender, longing, and the only person she could think of who would make him look like that was Zoe. Beautiful, talented, unattainable Zoe, and why the woman wasn't grabbing Alex with both hands was a mystery.

Flavia clenched her fists, hovering in the hallway. This was gut-wrenching. If any man – especially Alex – talked to her with a face like that, she wouldn't leave his side again. But this had to be the end of any dreams she had about her and Alex ever getting together. Fumbling for a tissue, she stomped into the storeroom, unshed tears almost choking her.

A voice spoke from the doorway. 'Flavia? Have you got a moment?'

It was Luis. Flavia blew her nose quickly, then turned round.

He stared at her uncertainly. 'You okay? I was wondering if you'd like to try a few more cocktails after work? We had fun last time.'

Flavia stuck her chin in the air. Why shouldn't she? Alex had made it plain as you like he wasn't interested. She clasped a box of body lotion and bath oil that was en route for the spa shop to her front. 'Sounds good. We still have plenty of cocktails to try.'

He was still gaping at her. 'See you at reception later, then? Are you sure you're okay?'

Flavia rolled her eyes as dramatically as she could. 'It's not worth mentioning. Alex gave me grief about soap, that's all.'

His mouth twitched. 'Want me to punch his nose?'

Flavia managed a smile. She'd have to get used to covering the heartache. 'No! His mum would never forgive me.'

Luis laughed, and left her to it. A short queue had formed at the desk when she left the storeroom, and Flavia joined Alex to deal with a waiting guest. This was turning into one of those days when you kept having to stop doing something to do something else.

The woman was wearing a worried frown. 'I've lost my glasses. Has anyone handed them in?'

Flavia switched on her efficient-receptionist smile. Thank goodness, this was something she could deal with easily. 'I'll check the lost property box. What colour are they?'

'Red frame, and the lenses are squarish.'

Flavia went into the office and yanked the lost property box out of the cupboard. It was heavy; people did seem to lose books in summer. They should keep these separately. She fished out the plastic container holding breakables, and yay! The woman's specs were right here. Flavia replaced the container and was lifting out a couple of books when she noticed a small cream-coloured cloth with something dark and shiny half wrapped inside it. She pulled it out too. Oh – this was a block of rosin, the stuff violinists used on their bows. It must be Zoe's. Did Alex know it was here? Flavia stuffed it into her overall pocket, returned the specs to their delighted owner, then pulled out the rosin.

'Alex, I found this in the lost property box. I guess it must be Zoe's?' If he snapped at her again, she would punch his nose herself.

He gaped at the rosin, his cheeks going white before flaming. 'Oh – I guess it is. That's weird; I've never noticed it there.'

'It was right at the bottom. I wouldn't have seen it if I hadn't taken out a couple of books to put them somewhere else.'

Alex wasn't listening. He picked up the rosin, holding it as if it was not only breakable but infinitely precious too, and hopelessness pierced through Flavia. She loved him, and he loved Zoe, and Zoe loved her music. This couldn't end well for any of them.

She moved away; there were no guests waiting now. 'I'll leave it with you, then.'

He was still staring at the rosin. 'Thank you. I'm sorry I snapped at you earlier, Flavia. I was stressed, but that's no excuse.'

Flavia managed a smile. 'Forgotten already.' Not true, but what else could she say? They were taking Denise to a concert on Friday; they couldn't have an atmosphere in the car.

'Hello, you two! Any problems since I left?' Ralph strode through the front door looking very pleased with himself.

Alex answered before Flavia could open her mouth. 'Nothing important. Did you have a successful visit?

Ralph guffawed. 'I did! I'll show you. Flavia, you don't mind if I borrow Alex for ten minutes, do you?'

Flavia shook her head. This would be about Ralph's secret surprise for Stacy and Rico. The two men trooped off into the terrace bar, and she turned to deal with a guest who wanted to settle his minibar bill. Carol appeared while she was still searching for coins.

'Oh, Carol, can you mind the desk for a moment? We don't have enough change in the cash box.'

Flavia sped out to the terrace and handed her note to Robin behind the bar. He opened the till and started counting out a selection of coins while she waited, looking out over the lake. A snatch of talk from Ralph and Alex floated over from a nearby table, where the two were hunched over a plan of – was it the landing place?

'...boats? Is there space for all that?' It was Alex, and he sounded incredulous.

Ralph shushed him, and their conversation continued inaudibly. Flavia accepted a handful of change from Robin, and went back to reception. Boats? Someone had mentioned pedalos last week – was that the surprise?

She finished with the waiting guest and moved closer to Carol. 'I overheard half a sentence on the terrace. Is Ralph getting pedalos for Stacy and Rico?'

Carol gave her a huge grin. 'I couldn't possibly say... Better not spread anything around, though. Ralph wants it to be a surprise.' She smiled brightly, and left Flavia alone at the desk.

Well. This was interesting. However many pedalos was Ralph getting? They must be coming from his brother's boatyard in the Ticino. Hopefully, the staff would be allowed to hire them too. A vision of sharing a pedalo with Alex slid into her head, and Flavia pushed it away. Not going to happen, was it? But maybe she could share one with Luis or some of the others. This was a fun place to work, faulty soap dispensers and crabby receptionists notwithstanding.

16

THURSDAY, 13TH JUNE

Stacy sauntered across the square in front of the Swiss parliament building in Berne, fanning herself with the brochure she'd picked up on their tour around the building that morning. Rico had teased her for wanting a paper souvenir, but it was coming in useful now, in the midday heat. Enviously, she stood watching a little group of children as they danced among the jets of water shooting up in the middle of the square. It would be kind of nice to join them…

Rico jogged up, fumbling with his phone. 'Want a pic of us with the Bundeshaus in the background? Then a wander through the old town, and lunch by the river?'

'Only if you promise me shade!' Stacy posed, and he slung an arm around her and held his phone at arm's length.

'Cheese!' He clicked.

Stacy's head was swivelling from right to left and back as they left the square, imprinting it all in her memory. Berne was an imposing sight, in spite of the swathes of multiculti tourists – sand-coloured buildings and domes everywhere you looked. And all this culture had given her an appetite.

'Look, Rico, there's a street market. Let's buy some lunch and eat as we go. We can do the river later.'

They found a stall with Zwiebel Chuechli, a kind of mini onion quiche, and walked along munching. Swallowing her last mouthful, Stacy wiped her fingers and reached into Rico's rucksack for the water bottle. This was lovely. Literally hundreds of tourists were doing the same kind of thing, enjoying the sunshine and exploring the city. And Rico hadn't mentioned the hotel once today. They were having a real, proper honeymoon now, no accidents or blue lights and sirens or faulty computer systems.

'I love all the fountains they have here,' she said, dipping her wrists into the cool water of one and tilting her head to see the figure at the top of the colourfully painted pillar. 'Heavens, is that a bear in armour?'

'Yup. This is the Zähringer fountain, commemorating the founder of the town.' Rico had his phone out again. 'Stand there and I'll take your pic.'

Stacy posed again, shifting right and left to allow Rico the best shot of the old clock tower behind her. Golly, there was history all over the place here.

He put his phone away. 'Let's head for the bear garden. It's on the river bank, further along here and over the bridge. We can grab a coffee somewhere on the way.'

'How about in there?' A moment later, Stacy pointed to a shady pavement café under the arcade that swept all the way down the street. 'I feel as if I've been on my feet all day.'

'Yeah, that's a real change for you,' said Rico, laughing, nonetheless following her over to a table. 'Okay, Grandma, what's it to be?'

'Latte, please.' Stacy picked up a paper someone had left on the table, and leafed through it while Rico went to place their order. Nothing much was happening in the world this week – politics and other daily news retreated into the background when you were on holiday, somehow. She came to the Events page, and scanned what was going on in Berne that week. An open-air concert they could go to tonight, perhaps? An article in the middle of the page grabbed her attention.

Exhibition of Modern Art at the Rosen Gallery. Martina Johanna Jahn shows her latest collection. Opening times...

Stacy froze, then read the text with more attention. *Martina Johanna... Martina Jahn...* She was a Swiss artist, and she lived in the Ticino, in Lugano, in fact. Where Ralph lived. Stacy lifted the paper to see the photographs in a better light – the artist was an older woman, and one of her paintings was there too, a stark, mountainous landscape, but both pics were tiny and in black and white so it was hard to judge anything. But *Martina Johanna Jahn...* Could this possibly be their MJ?

Rico slid a large mug across the table and sat down. 'Here you go. And a chocolate brownie, and don't say I don't spoil you. What's up? You look as if you've seen a ghost.'

Stacy handed over the paper. 'Look. There in the middle.'

Rico scanned the article, and she could almost see the penny dropping. He leaned back in his chair, frowning. 'Wow. I wonder...'

'Has Ralph ever mentioned meeting her, or going to an exhibition in Lugano?' Stacy nibbled her brownie. 'Our MJ won't be Martina Johanna in person, of course, but it seems too much to be coincidence, doesn't it?'

'It does.' Rico was frowning. 'And now I'm thinking about it, that little picture he has in his hallway could be one of hers. You know, the very colourful one of a stone house and a bridge at sunrise. I wonder if Dad's bought us one of her pictures, and that's what's on the way to see us.'

Stacy thought about that. 'It's still weird. If it's a picture, why go to all that trouble to be so mysterious about it? He could bring it in the car.'

'Unless it's too big. We have a hotel full of largish walls, remember. He could have bought an enormous piece of artwork for reception. And it could well be that Martina Johanna is coming in person too – Dad and Guido know masses of people in Lugano, and she looks around their age. Heck, one of them could have been at school with her, back in the day. They grew up in the Ticino, remember.'

Stacy finished her coffee. 'Why don't we go to the exhibition?'

'Good idea.' Rico smoothed the paper out to see the address. 'This isn't far from the bear park – we'll do the bears first, then go up the hill to the gallery. Lucky you spotted this – we'll have to think of a way to get back at Dad for all those MJ postcards!'

***

Stacy stood on tiptoe and to see over the bridge. The waters of the Aare were blue-green shimmers as the wide river moved swiftly past the most ancient part of the old town below. They were looking down on the roofs of these riverside houses; it was a picture that would have looked good on a swanky calendar – and that was an idea. She would have her best honeymoon pics made into a calendar for next year, then she'd have lovely holiday memories every day.

'These houses look like they're growing out of the river. You'd think they'd be damp inside,' she said, remembering the problems they'd had at Lakeside when the lake flooded last summer.

Rico joined her leaning on the stone balustrade. 'I think those might be the houses they have to evacuate some years, if the Aare's carrying too much melt water. I once saw people on the news, being plucked from the roofs by helicopter. Come on. We're nearly at the bear park.'

Rico took her hand and they crossed the road, and Stacy leaned over the opposite balustrade to see the park, a green rectangle on the sloping riverbank far below, where – wow – fat brown bears were meandering around among the trees and bushes. Or running around like wild things, in the case of three small shapes chasing each other.

'They used to be in round pits. You'll see those when we go past them in a moment,' said Rico, pulling her on. 'They were poor things in there, though. The park's much nicer.'

They strolled around the bear park perimeter, and Stacy took photo after photo. The babies were so cute... and they did have a better life here than in the stone pits she'd seen on the way round from the bridge.

Back at the entrance, Rico fanned his face with his sun cap. 'I need some air conditioning – let's go to the exhibition, then we can always come and see the bears again on the way back, when it's cooler.'

The Rosen Gallery was a short walk away, and Stacy was glad to get out of the sweltering summer heat. She dived into the loos at the entrance to wash her sticky hands and touch up her make-up. That was better – you couldn't walk round an art exhibition covered in lunch smears and the entire morning's dust and sweat. Would Martina Johanna Jahn be here in person? She went on into the foyer, looking round for Rico.

He was standing blinking around the entrance hall, and Stacy's jaw dropped when she saw the three paintings on display there. All were huge, well over six feet tall, and the colours... Slashes of deep blue and black with crimson streaks and daubs of purple and an occasional splash of green and white covered all three canvases. Seen from a distance, you could tell they were mountains, lakes and sky, but oh, they weren't her kind of thing at all. These paintings were sombre, moody. Funereal, even. Surely they were nothing like the picture Ralph had in his flat?

Rico's expression was as grim as Martina Johanna's artwork. 'I don't know about you, Stace, but I wouldn't give these house room,' he whispered.

'Perhaps she does, um, milder ones too. Let's go and see. And for heaven's sake, don't criticise the pics out loud near anyone else. We still don't know if she's here in person.'

He handed her a flyer. 'According to this, she's not. She'll be here for the last few days of the exhibition in August. Stace, Dad wouldn't give us something like this – would he?' He waved one hand at a particularly lurid canvas.

Stacy pictured Ralph's flat in Lugano, her heart sinking. He did have a taste for the colourful, and his clothes selection was more often vivid than not. These paintings didn't look his style, but you never knew...

'Rico, what'll we do if he has? Imagine if he appears at Lakeside with Martina Johanna and a huge painting like this one?' She stood in front of a giant purple and blue Matterhorn.

Rico took her hand. 'Maybe her older work is in a different style. Come on. It can only get better.'

Wrong, thought Stacy, as they ambled around the first of three exhibition rooms. Martina Johanna's paintings were undoubtedly striking, but – not to put too fine a point on it – they were hideous. She stood in front of a full-wall painting of Lake Lucerne and Mount Pilatus. Art was a matter of opinion, of course, but waking up to a view like that opposite her bed every day would give her a permanent headache.

'Can't we leave now? I think we've seen enough.' Rico stood still at the end of the second room.

Stacy wasn't slow to agree. She stuck her head into the third room, saw more of the same, and followed Rico back to the entrance, where they reclaimed the rucksack Rico had handed in and fled the building.

'Okay,' said Rico, when they were calming their nerves with iced tea in the café by the bear pit. 'Worst case, Dad appears with Martina Johanna and gives us a painting. We can put it in the relaxation room in the spa and tell him that's where most people will see it.'

Stacy snorted. 'A pic like that in a room where people are supposed to chill would be self-defeating. We'd give all the guests high blood pressure. And supposing we get back to Lakeside and he's hung it up already? Martina Johanna might be waiting by the front door when we arrive back home.'

Rico's shoulders sagged. 'Aw, heck. Cross your fingers as hard as you can, Stace.'

Stacy pushed her empty glass away. 'Crossing all fingers. And toes.'

17

Friday, 14th June

Flavia stood back admiringly as Denise fastened a string of multicoloured beads around her neck. They were doing things in style today – salmon steaks and salad for lunch, and now the theatre.

'You look lovely, Denise.'

'Thank you, Flavia – so do you. Just think, here we are for the second time in a week, lunching together before jetting off to another glam event! And my first time in Zurich for I don't know how long.'

Denise was laughing, but Flavia wasn't fooled. Alex's mum was nervous, but she was hiding it, which was a good sign. The old Denise would simply have claimed the outing was impossible, and that would have been that.

The doorbell rang, and Denise hurried to the window and peered down to the street. 'Alex is here.' She picked up her handbag. 'We'll go straight down, shall we? We don't want to be late.'

Flavia followed her out and down the stairs. 'We're in good time, don't worry, and the traffic won't be heavy at this time of day.' She crossed her fingers while Denise wasn't looking. Going to Zurich would be no problem; the concert started at half past two, but the journey home at half past four would be busier. They'd be in the thick of the Friday rush hour traffic most of the way.

Alex was waiting beside his yellow mini. He grinned cheerfully at his mother and winked at Flavia – he seemed his usual self, but all Flavia could think of was the way he'd looked when he answered his phone on Wednesday. He must have been talking to Zoe, and what would he be thinking now they were setting off to see her perform with the orchestra she'd left him for?

'You go in the front with Alex, Flavia,' said Denise, opening the back door and tossing her bag in.

Flavia's stomach lurched. That was the last thing she wanted. 'No – I thought we could both go in the back, then I'd be company for you.' She looked at Alex for support, but he made a 'don't ask me' gesture.

Denise was having none of it. 'Exactly, you'd be babysitting me again. I want to see if I can do this. I'll let you know the moment I'm not happy alone in the back, don't worry.'

Reluctantly, Flavia settled down in the front passenger seat. Brilliant. Now she had a good hour's journey sitting next to the guy she wanted to spend the rest of her life with, but his phone call with Zoe had made it all too clear that he didn't care two hoots about her in that way. Hopefully Denise would keep up her end of the conversation, that was all. She pulled on her seatbelt feeling as if she was at the dentist.

Alex stabbed the key into the ignition. 'Zoe texted before I left the hotel. She'll meet us in the foyer before the concert, to say hello. She's looking forward to seeing you, Mum.'

Flavia slumped in the passenger seat. Better and better, she was going to have to chat to the girl Alex loved, the one who was breaking his heart. This was like being in some kind of TV drama. Any moment now they'd crash and end up in hospital, then a hunky doctor would appear and she'd fall madly in love with him, and meanwhile, Zoe would visit Alex and realise he was the only one for her...

Denise was rustling in the back seat. 'Here, have a caramel. Flavia can unwrap yours, Alex.'

Flavia complied and dropped the sweet into Alex's outstretched hand, sudden tears burning in her eyes when he didn't even look at her. This was so crap, and it was degrading, feeling like this about a guy who'd probably never stopped being in love with someone else. Okay, he'd tried to get over Zoe, but he'd been kidding himself, and maybe he still was. She was going to have to think long and hard about what she was doing with her life. But not right this minute.

Fortunately, Denise wanted to talk. 'Have either of you heard anything from Stacy and Rico yet?'

Alex swung onto the motorway and the car leapt forward. 'Rico called on Tuesday, all worried about the email scam that was doing the rounds. Otherwise, nothing.'

Denise chuckled. 'No postcard or photos yet? They must be having a good honeymoon!'

She went on to chat about various family holidays they'd had when Alex was small, and Flavia pulled herself together and chipped in with her own stories. She was here for Denise, after all. An hour later, they swooped past Zurich city limit, and Flavia relaxed. They'd arrived, and Denise had managed magnificently.

They left the car in a multistorey car park near the theatre, and Flavia glowed as Denise turned her head right and left while they walked, drinking in the special atmosphere of the Bahnhofstrasse, the famous shopping street in Zurich. You could see Lake Zurich down at the bottom of the road, tourist boats moored at the harbour, while far beyond, sun-soaked mountains soared in the distance, some still with a sugar-coating of snow. It was a perfect day for Denise to be here.

Alex sent off a message to Zoe as they neared the theatre, and they arrived to find the girl waiting in the foyer, dressed in her musician's black that in no way subdued her sparkling personality.

'Denise – I'm so, so happy to see you here! I could hardly believe it when Alex said you were coming. Hi, guys!'

The last part was aimed at Flavia and Alex, who stood by dumbly as Zoe admired Denise's outfit, presented her with a programme and waved to a theatre employee who rushed up with three glasses of – was it champagne?

Flavia stole a glance at Alex as they clinked, Zoe with a bottle of water. She beamed at Flavia. 'I can't drink before the concert. Daniel would have a fit. He's the conductor, you know. I have to go now, but I'll see you all later!' She kissed Denise, waved at Alex and Flavia, and ran off, her dark hair swinging in its ponytail.

Denise took Alex's arm, and Flavia saw the concern in her eyes. He was pale, but he took a large swallow of champagne and managed a grin. 'She doesn't change, does she?'

'She never will. She's a lovely girl,' said Denise, and Flavia winced. That was undoubtedly what Alex thought too, and pointing it out to him was like rubbing salt in an open wound. Or did Denise hope he was over Zoe now? Flavia sipped her champagne, pondering. It might be an idea to tell Denise about Alex's face when he was on the phone to Zoe, but that would have to wait until they were home. This outing was complicated enough as it was.

They took their seats, Denise between Alex and Flavia, and the concert began. It was short one, an hour and a quarter with no interval, ideal for Denise's first major outing. The music was popular extracts from the most famous Mozart works, and Flavia recognised most of them. A lump came into her throat when she saw how rapt Denise was, her head moving with the music, a little smile tugging at her mouth. Think of all these months – years, even, when Denise had missed out on things like this. She would have to make sure that didn't happen again. No matter what happened with Alex, Denise was her friend.

Zoe had a solo right at the end, and Flavia watched the slight figure on the stage, swaying in time to her music. This one wasn't a piece she recognised but Zoe brought it to life, and applause crashed down at the end. The orchestra was given a standing ovation, and Daniel Marino led Zoe forward to bow three times before the final curtain fell and the lights in the house went up.

An immediate buzz of talk filled the theatre. Denise jerked, and stared around wildly as people surged towards the exits.

'We'll wait until the rush is over, shall we?' Flavia took Denise's hand. This was the first time the older woman had shown how nervous she was.

Alex cleared his throat. 'I'll go and collect our jackets, then we can get straight back to the car. Wait here, I'll text you when it's quiet in the foyer.' He vanished into the crowd.

Denise flopped back in her seat and fanned herself with her programme. 'It's all right, Flavia, I'll be fine. It was just a moment. Like suddenly waking up in a strange place.'

Flavia moved to let the last few people squeeze past to leave the row. 'We'll be in the car soon.' She switched her phone back on, and sat clutching it. Was Alex going to text her, or Denise?

'I left my phone at home,' said Denise, when Flavia asked. 'But he'll come and get us if he sends a text and we don't appear.'

The auditorium was almost empty now, with only a group in wheelchairs still making their way to the back exit.

Denise stood up. 'Let's go and find him.'

She took Flavia's arm, and they walked along a deserted passage to the foyer. Alex was nowhere to be seen, and Flavia was about to phone him when Denise pulled at her arm.

'Over there. Oh, Flavia, what am I to do about that boy of mine?'

Flavia stood still, her heart thumping. Alex and Zoe were half-hidden in the dimness of another passageway leading off the foyer, but it was plain that they were arguing. Zoe was gesticulating wildly, and Alex was holding up both hands and backing away. And there it was again, that heartbroken expression. And it was mirrored by the one on Zoe's face.

Flavia pulled Denise back a few steps. 'I'll text him we're on our way out.' She tapped, then pressed send and swallowed. 'He's an adult, Denise, and so is Zoe. They have to sort it out for themselves.'

'I'm sorry, Flavia. This is hard for you.'

Flavia managed a smile. 'You're the important one today, and you've done brilliantly, so well done. Alex is going to be pleased about that.' She took Denise's arm again, and they went out to the foyer for the second time. Alex and Zoe were on their way over, all smiles now.

Zoe reached out to touch Denise's arm. 'Alex said you enjoyed it – I'm so glad. You'll come again, won't you?'

Denise took the girl's hand. 'Of course. I'm sorry we can't take you out for dinner, Zoe, but I need to get home again.'

'I'll come and see you next time I'm in St Gallen.' Zoe kissed Denise, smiled dreamily at Flavia and Alex, and was gone.

This time, Denise didn't object when Flavia sat in the back with her. They sat holding hands, and for the life of her, Flavia didn't know who was comforting whom. It was a silent drive home along the busy motorway. All Flavia could think was – why? Alex and Zoe were so much a couple, even when they were apart and arguing. Why had they let Zoe's job get between them? Denise might have been the reason at first, but there had to be more to it now.

18

FRIDAY, 14TH JUNE

Rico dipped both feet in the fast-flowing waters of the Rhine, enjoying the cool tug of water around his legs and the view of the riverbank opposite, where the rooftops of Basle's old town were silhouetted against a pale blue sky. Friday evening, and they were sitting on the long, high steps that stretched along this section of the riverbank. Tourists and locals alike were gathered here, and this must be the best way ever to end a busy afternoon. He glanced at Stacy. She was watching a little group further along the riverbank, two small boys and a tiny girl with their parents, and oh, the expression in her eyes. Broody didn't come into it. Rico swallowed panic – this wouldn't do; he was on his honeymoon.

A boat full of holidaymakers chugged past, most of them waving at the crowd on the bank, and Stacy waved back. 'I think Basle is my new favourite Swiss city. I wish it wasn't so far from Lakeside.'

Good, she was distracted from the family now. Rico cleared his throat. 'It's perfectly possible to have a day trip to Basle, don't worry.'

'We definitely should do some day trips. Isn't this fab? I can't believe how quickly the river's flowing.'

'And I can't believe how cold the water is, even in summer.' Rico pulled his feet onto dry land.

Stacy did the same, and wiggled her toes in the sunshine. 'Odd to think this water has passed by Lakeside, gone right along Lake

Constance and back into the Rhine, down the Rhinefalls and all the way here!'

Rico poked her. 'Now you're being a geography lesson. Honeymoon, Stace. But talking about work – which we weren't, I know, but there's a quirky little Pharmacy Museum I thought you might like to see tomorrow before we go for the Paris train. It has everything from ancient Chinese meds to ceramics. I've never been, but I've heard about it.'

'Let's do it. Oh, Rico – imagine, we'll soon be in Paris! The city of lovers. The romantic part of our honeymoon.' Her eyes were soft.

Rico shoved his feet back into his sandals. Hopefully, the romantic part wouldn't include talking about babies... 'Come on. Let's go back to the hotel and freshen up, and I'll show you what romance is before we go for dinner. Want to try that Italian place we went past this morning?'

The hotel was two streets back from the river, and Rico swung their shopping bag as they went. They'd bought some lovely souvenirs of the honeymoon – an enormous wooden bear in Brienz, two silk scarves and a top for Stacy from a tiny shop underneath one of the arcades in Berne, three tourist T-shirts for him, and four tins of Basler Leckerli, spicy biscuits traditional to the area. One of these was going to England with them, and everything else could stay in the car until their return. This time tomorrow, they'd be on the fast train to Paris, where they'd do some whistle-stop sightseeing before getting the Eurostar to London on Monday morning, then another train to Manchester. It was a long-winded way to get there, but he'd wanted to see more of England and the train was a good way to do it. They'd leave the car at Basle Airport, then fly back there from Manchester at the end of the honeymoon.

'Hello – did you have a good day?' The receptionist at the Feldberg Hotel leaned over the desk as they went through reception, and Rico smiled at her. That was what you wanted in your receptionist – polite, friendly, and approachable.

'Great, thanks.'

The girl reached under the desk. 'A card came for you.'

She handed it to Stacy, who was nearest, and Rico leaned over her shoulder to see. Locarno, in the south of Switzerland. Stacy turned the card, and they read: *I'm on my way! See you soon! MJ xx*

***

Stacy took her seat at a corner table and accepted a menu from a beaming waiter. The restaurant was like Italian restaurants everywhere – warm and friendly and smelling yummy. They ordered water and wine, and wow – how odd it was to think that tomorrow, they'd have been married for a whole week. The honeymoon was half over; in fact it was nearly all over because the moment they arrived in Elton Abbey, Mum would whirl them into the church blessing preparation and all the – she shouldn't call it stress – all the arrangements to do with that. The ceremony was a week today and they were flying home a week on Sunday, and after that it would be back to business as usual.

Rico lifted his glass. 'I'm not sure you're thinking suitably honeymoon-like thoughts, Stacy Weber.'

Stacy clinked. It still felt odd, to hear people call her Stacy Weber. And one day, she'd even have a Swiss passport – you could have dual nationality, and it made sense to have the passport of the country you lived in as well as your own nationality. And when they had kids, it would be nice if all their little family had the same passports.

She put down her glass. 'Just thinking about passports. I have to do complicated things to get two passports, but our kids can automatically have British as well as Swiss ones.'

Rico laughed. 'That's a problem that'll keep for a year or two. Let's enjoy the novelty of being married first!'

A shadow spread over Stacy's evening as alarm bells shrilled. He was serious about not starting a family soon, wasn't he? Yet it was – yes, it was vital to her. Was she being selfish?

She took a deep, steadying breath. 'I'd like to think I was at least expecting our first child by this time next year, Rico.'

He took her hand across the table. 'We need to talk properly about this, Stace. I think we should wait until the new house is built before we have kids. It won't be more than a year or two.'

The waiter came to take their order and Stacy sat back, gloom settling heavily over her. If they weren't starting the build until next year, it would be way over a year. He couldn't have understood how important this was to her. As far as she was concerned, there was no reason why they shouldn't have a baby soon. Rico was six months into his degree, so he'd be almost finished before any baby was born – and a baby wouldn't care where it lived. And anyway–

'I don't want a big house.' She had blurted it out without even consciously thinking it. A real gut reaction.

His mouth tightened. 'It's about living somewhere future-proof, love. We have three bedrooms in the flat, one of them tiny. We can't live there long-term with two or three kids, can we? By building our own place, we can easily have five bedrooms, generous ones, and all the mod cons you want.'

'I don't want us to spend all our free time doing housework, for heaven's sake. It would be a full-time job cleaning a place like that, and anyway, kids can share rooms. I do see that building the house would be an investment and if we can afford it, then it's a good idea. But I'd want to make it two flats, not one detached house. Four bedrooms is plenty.' Their starter arrived, and Stacy prodded unenthusiastically at her garlic mushrooms.

Rico took a large swallow of wine. 'It doesn't need to be a large house. But what would we do with the second flat, if we did that?'

'Rent it out. Sell it. Maybe your dad and Carol would like it.'

Rico gave her a look. 'Do you really want to live next door to your in-laws for the rest of your life?'

'I don't see why not. We all get on, don't we?'

'Well, yes, but...'

'Or you could use part of it to open an IT business, when you have your master's degree. There's so much about this we have to talk through, Rico.'

'You're not wrong there. Can I make a suggestion before we start flinging plates? Let's put the subject – all of them – to bed in the meantime. We can commence peace talks when we're at home with time and privacy for a good discussion, and waiting eight days won't make a difference to either the family planning or the future build, will it? We're on honeymoon, as you so often remind me.'

Stacy speared her last mushroom and glared at him. 'Excellent idea. But I'm not backing down.'

He refilled their glasses. 'Neither am I.'

Their risotto arrived, and Stacy touched his hand across the table. Rico stuck out his tongue, and she gave him a small smile, reassured. Until now, their honeymoon, in spite of the busman's holiday parts and the brief interlude in Martina Johanna's exhibition, had been everything she could have dreamt of. They shouldn't let minor details like the number of kids they wanted and the size of their future home spoil the rest of it. Paris here they came, and if the city of lovers didn't get them back on track, nothing would. Meanwhile, it wasn't as if they didn't have other things to talk about. They still didn't know what on earth was going on with MJ...

19

SUNDAY, 16TH JUNE

Carol sank down on a fallen tree trunk and rummaged in her rucksack. 'Uff! This is hard work! Let's have a breather.'

Flavia joined her, and accepted a slug of now lukewarm iced tea from Carol's flask. They were having a Wandertag, a day out hiking in the Appenzellarland. After taking the train to one of the tiny alpine villages dotted around the countryside, they were heading along a narrow trail that led through hilly woodland and eventually emerged at a little lake further up. The path was steep in places, but on such a hot day it was lovely to be among the trees, with glimpses of the mountains here and there. The plan was to have lunch at the lake, then take a different track back to the village they'd started in. Ralph was going to meet them there with the car and whisk them off for coffee and cake in Appenzell, the main village in the canton.

Flavia inhaled the special, earthy smell of trees and old wood. It was nice to be out with Carol. Their friendship dated from last Christmas when Carol was a hotel guest and had helped Flavia gift wrap an impossibly large number of orders from the spa shop. Carol was one of those people who saw what needed to be done, and got stuck right in to help you do it.

Flavia watched as the older woman slid the flask back into her rucksack. Some neutral advice about her love life would be good... But then, what could anyone possibly say except 'move on, Flavia, anything more than friendship with Alex isn't going to happen'.

And in her head she knew that, but there was still a tiny part of her heart that was hoping. Hoping against hope... Flavia heaved a sigh, then covered it by standing up and dusting herself down.

'Come on. The sooner we're there, the sooner we'll be in the lunch queue at the restaurant.'

Carol gave her a sharp look but said nothing, and Flavia led the way along the narrow trail. The woods were cool and shady, with muted green light flickering through the trees. It was peaceful. They tramped on, munching the nut and sultana chocolate Carol produced from her rucksack.

'Flavia, tell me if I'm poking my nose in, but are you okay? You've been a little distracted recently.'

This was Carol getting stuck in to help her again. Flavia grimaced. 'I guess I'm trying to come to terms with not getting what I want. I'll live, don't worry.'

Carol passed her another chunk of chocolate. 'Alex? Oh Flavia, you don't want to be with someone who's secretly hoping to be with someone else, do you? I had a chat with Denise last week at the wedding. The poor woman doesn't know what to wish for him.'

Heck, did everyone in the hotel know about it? With an effort, Flavia managed a smile for Carol. 'You and Ralph are lucky. He's nuts about you.'

'I know. But I also know you can never take anything for granted. Life has a habit of surprising you – and shocking you, too.'

'Words of wisdom from the older and wiser, huh? But thanks.'

Carol shot her a grin, then peeled back her sleeve to see her watch. 'Are we nearly there yet?' She lifted an eyebrow at Flavia.

'Half an hour more. Come on, Grandma!'

Carol laughed. 'Cheeky!'

A few minutes later, the path crossed a patch of scrubland with fewer trees, and Carol took some photos of the mountains peeking above the green of alpine meadows. Flavia waited while she sent one off to Ralph, then snapped her phone shut and waved at the view.

'Isn't it lovely? We should do this more often. Ralph is many things, but an enthusiastic hiker isn't one of them.'

'I'd like that. There's a hiking club in Rorschach, we could join that.' Flavia rubbed her arms as the trail re-entered woodland. After being in the full strength of the alpine sun for the last few minutes, the sudden shade was chilly. She was about to unpack her jerkin when Carol, now in front, stopped so suddenly that Flavia bumped into her.

'Flavia – listen!'

A few seconds passed while Flavia strained her ears. 'What? I can't hear anything.'

'That's just it. The birds all went silent, didn't you–'

She grabbed Flavia as a roar filled the air and the ground beneath them vibrated. Flavia cried out, clutching at Carol, and they gaped ahead, where – oh my God, where a hundred metres or so further along the path the trees were – hell, no, the trees were sliding downhill. And still the air roared, and the ground shook.

Flavia held on tight to Carol's hand, and pulled her back the way they'd come. 'Quick! We have to get away from here!'

They stumbled along, out of the shady woodland back into the sun, past the place where Carol had taken her photos, on into the woods again, further and further away, surely they'd be safe now; they could–

Another roar, more vibration, and oh, no... the path in front of them was sliding, sliding. Flavia grabbed Carol's hand – or tried to. Her arm jerked upwards as she tumbled back, no, no... She was sliding downhill. A scream split through the roar of ground rent asunder: Carol's scream, but Flavia couldn't see her, couldn't see anything apart from thick, flying dust. It was choking her; she couldn't breathe and – no! Something hard struck her shoulder, and Flavia sank into darkness and noise as the earth beneath her fell away.

***

Rico gripped Stacy's hand as they strolled along the bank of the Seine, listening to the chatter of different groups of tourists as they went. With so little time here, they had to prioritise, so this morning they'd gone up the Eiffel Tower, where Stacy had taken dozens of photos. Now, they were heading for the Louvre and the Mona Lisa, which Stacy had declared was a must-see, especially after the MJ exhibition in Berne. Art had played a part yesterday, too, as their hotel was near Montmartre and they'd spent the evening wandering around there when they arrived yesterday. Tonight was the Seine Cruise plus dinner that Stacy's mum had booked for them. It was all very cultural and both his and Stacy's bucket lists had been ticked several times, but right now, lunch was looming in his mind.

'Shall we grab a sandwich from over there, and find a bench somewhere?' He pointed to a boulangerie on the other side of a busy crossing.

'If we can make it across the road without being killed,' said Stacy. 'Busy, isn't it?'

'City life in Paris. We'll stick to the pedestrian crossing, don't worry.' He pulled her across the first set of white stripes on the road and then the second, and they stood at the shop window, where baguettes of every imaginable size and filling were displayed. The place had a handful of tables on the pavement, and Stacy bagged one while Rico went in to buy their lunch. His French wasn't brilliant – theoretically, children in the German-speaking part of Switzerland were supposed to leave school with adequate, if not fluent, French, but school was a long time ago. He stammered his way through ordering baguettes with Brie and salad, and OJ, aware that his phone in his inside pocket was vibrating. He'd put it on silent in the restaurant they'd had dinner in yesterday, and forgotten to turn it back up.

'Grub up.' He dumped their lunch on the table, and accepted a wet wipe from Stacy. You got a lot dirtier in Paris than in Grimsbach, somehow. He took an enormous bite of his baguette, then pulled out his phone.

Stacy gave him a pointed look, and he swallowed hastily. 'Sorry. But someone called while I was ordering the – oh! It was Dad.' He scowled at the missed call notice. His father was the last person who'd interrupt anyone's honeymoon unless it was absolutely necessary.

'Call back,' said Stacy. 'It'll be some business stuff about the boathouse build. Maybe you need to call someone before we go to England.'

Rico hesitated, his heart thumping. Dad would be able to clear any business problems without his input. He cleared his throat. 'More likely something's wrong.'

'You're overthinking before you know what he wanted. Bet you MJ's arrived, and wants to talk to you.'

She was smiling, but a little frown was nestling between her brows. Heck, she thought it was odd too. Rico tapped to connect.

Ralph answered on the second ring. 'Rico, I thought you should know in case you saw anything on the news. There's been a huge landslide up in the Appenzellerland. Thing is, Carol and Flavia went hiking there today and we're having problems getting hold of them. I've given their names and details to the police and the mountain rescue, and they can pinpoint where they were because Carol sent a photo shortly before the landslide happened, but…'

'Oh no. What do you want me to do?'

'Nothing. Mountain rescue say there's probably no signal up there and all we can do is wait. They're surveying the area now. I'm going to drive up to Appenzell, and I'll let you know the moment we hear anything. I didn't want you to get a fright if you see it on the news. I don't know if any names would be mentioned. I'm leaving now – I'll be in touch.'

He disconnected, and Rico sat taking shaky breaths. Dad's voice had been much higher than usual and clipped, brittle. He was holding himself tightly under control, but he was clearly terrified and who wouldn't panic, in that situation? And Carol and Flavia… his poor father. Mum's cancer death had knocked the feet from under Dad; it was years before he'd found happiness again with Carol – and now she was missing.

Stacy's eyes across the table were huge. She gripped his arm and shook it. 'Tell me what's wrong.'

He stumbled through an explanation, all the time searching for news reports on his phone. There wasn't much, but apparently the area was cut off from the road, and helicopters and drones were out assessing the situation. Stacy came round the table to sit beside him, and they looked together.

She put an arm around him, feeling the tremor in his body. 'We'll hope with everything we have that they're okay, Rico. It doesn't bear thinking about... They'll find them, because they must.'

Rico put his phone back into his pocket. 'I'll give Dad an hour to drive up there, then I'll call him again.'

Stacy stood to pack up the remains of their lunch. 'Come on. We'll walk back to the hotel. That'll fill the hour, then you can call Ralph in peace and quiet.'

She took his hand, and they walked in silence, Rico trying to fight back the sense of impending doom. If Carol was – if anything had happened to Carol, that would the end of the honeymoon and the end of the church blessing too. And the end of Ralph's happiness.

***

Flavia inched closer to the young fir tree she was clinging to. This was what she'd collided with when the ground started to slip, and they'd crashed down the wooded hillside together at a terrifying speed, the roar of trees and earth fracturing all around her while that thick, smothering dust covered everything. All she could do was close her eyes and cling to the tree. After a minute or an hour it had stopped, gradually, the roar first, then the movement, and then – now – the dust was settling too. She was alive.

'Carol? Are you there?'

Silence, an odd silence on top of the odd little slither of sliding earth and stones every time she moved.

'Carol?' Huddled beneath the tree, which was tilted at an impossible angle, Flavia turned her head as far as she could in both directions without moving her body. Rays of sunlight were piercing through the treetops. They were sparser treetops than before. No sign of Carol, no answering cry. Oh no, no. That scream...

More silence, or stillness would be a better word, and Flavia sat there, her heartbeat loud in her ears. Somehow, the air felt different – thicker, and she was struggling to breathe, struggling not to panic. Every few moments she heard the sound of more earth moving, far away to her left. She shouldn't move; she could only wait and hope this particular piece of ground would stay put. Any movement at all could set it off again, and she was still a long way above the valley. Flavia closed her eyes again and held on for dear life.

After a while – a long while – there really was stillness. No movement of earth, no trembling of air, and the birds were singing again. Did that mean it was over? Moving slowly, slowly, Flavia inched one arm out of her backpack, then the other, then put it on again across her front, fastening the strap to her trousers in case she let it go. Her phone... was her phone still working? She rummaged for it in the side compartment and flipped it open. It was working, but there was no signal. A text? Would that work? She was about to tap when a sound overhead set her heart beating wildly. A helicopter! But they wouldn't see her, among all these trees. She didn't have a flare; who took flares when they went out on a normal Sunday hike? But she did have her phone. She switched on the torch and shone it upwards, making little circles and squiggles – such a thin, shaky beam of light, this couldn't compete with the sunlight still streaming down. It was all she had, though. *Oh, please see me, please help, please...*

20

SUNDAY, 16TH JUNE

It was after one o'clock when they arrived back at the hotel. Stacy's heart ached for Rico – and Ralph. And Carol, and Flavia, please, they must be safe. The walk through the sunny Paris streets had been never-ending. Every so often she'd checked the map on her phone to make sure they were going the right way. It had been a silent hour for the most part, with Rico clutching her hand in one of his, and his phone in the other, ready to react instantly if it rang. But it hadn't.

In their room, he pulled out the chair by the tiny table that was more of a shelf on the wall, breathing fast. 'Can you see what news you can find on the iPad? I'll call Dad now.'

For a long moment he sat clutching his phone, then he tapped. Stacy went into the safe in the wardrobe then sat on the bed with the iPad. Not that finding something on a news site would help any of them. She glanced at Rico. The hand that wasn't holding his phone was clenched so tightly on the tabletop that his knuckles were white. Ralph hadn't taken the call yet. Then:

'Dad! Any news?'

Stacy moved to be as close to him as she could get. 'Put it on speaker, Rico.'

Ralph's voice crackled into the room. '...Flavia. The doctor's checking her but she says she's okay. They're still looking for Carol, but at least now they have a more exact location to search.'

Stacy let her breath out slowly. Half good news, but what must Ralph be going through?

Rico was speaking. 'Where are you?'

'In a field a couple of kilometres past Appenzell. They've set up a kind of rescue base here. I wish – Rico, what if they don't find her?'

Stacy leaned towards the phone. 'They will, Ralph. Hang on. They found Flavia pretty quickly, didn't they?'

'She was flashing the torch on her phone. Maybe Carol didn't think of that. She could be lying somewhere, hurt, unconscious...'

'They have thermal cameras that find people by their body heat, Dad. They *will* find her.'

'I didn't think of that.' His voice broke. 'There's nothing I can do to help her, Rico.'

Stacy jumped in again. 'The experts are out looking for her, Ralph. What you can do is be with Flavia – she must be terribly shaken, even if she isn't hurt.'

He cleared his throat. 'She's in an ambulance with the doctor. I'll go and see her again now. I'll be in touch.'

The call ended, and Stacy reached out to Rico. He allowed the hug, but half a second later he shook her off and stood up. 'I have to go back, Stace. Back to Lakeside.'

***

Flavia sat shivering in the back of the ambulance. It wasn't cold, so this must be reaction to what had happened to her. If she'd known when she was having breakfast this morning that in a couple of hours she'd be strapped to an air rescue paramedic, swinging in the air above the woods, a thrumming helicopter above her, she'd have gone straight back to bed, you could bet on that, and oh, oh, where was Carol? The helicopter had returned to the search, and they had dogs out, too. She gripped the blanket someone had draped around her, hot tears running down her cheeks.

The ambulance paramedic, an older woman, handed her a tissue and went on cleaning the scratches on Flavia's arms and neck. 'Now the doctor's signed you off, you can get back to your – is it your dad that's come for you?'

'He's my boss. My parents live in Aarau.'

'Must be a good boss, then.'

Flavia remembered that technically, Ralph was her ex-boss, but it was too complicated to explain and it didn't matter, anyway. 'Have you got a mirror? I must look awful.' The paramedic had practically drowned her with antiseptic, she must look like a scratched tomato and– How stupid to care about that while Carol was... *where* was she?

The paramedic handed one over, and some more wet wipes. 'Fix your face as best you can. I'll go and tell your boss you're passed to go home.' She jumped down from the ambulance.

Flavia dabbed at her cheeks, both of which were scratched, but not as badly as her arms were. She was searching for her compact in her rucksack when Ralph appeared at the open door.

'How are you feeling? I called Rico and Stacy. They're waiting for news of Carol, but they're glad you were found so quickly.'

His voice was monotone; you could tell he was worried sick. Flavia pulled her blanket more tightly around her shoulders. 'I wish they'd found her too. I don't even know if she's further up the hillside than I was, or if she was swept down like me. I think she must have been. Oh, God.'

Now she couldn't stop crying, and it hurt, huge hot sobs that came from deep inside her. Ralph climbed into the ambulance and sat giving her shoulder the odd pat, but the only thing that would help would be Carol's voice saying 'hey, I'm here and I'm fine'.

A knock came on the open ambulance door. 'Hello? I'm from the restaurant up the road. I thought you might be glad of a hot drink. The paramedic said it's okay.'

Flavia blinked up. A young man in the black trousers and white shirt of a waiter was standing at the door holding a tin tray with two beakers of something, and little packets of sugar and cream and biscuits.

Ralph went over and handed a beaker to Flavia. 'That's kind, thank you very much. Which restaurant is it?'

'Die Trauben.' The waiter put the tray on the floor and gave Flavia an encouraging smile. 'I hope you'll be none the worse.'

Flavia nodded bleakly, snuffling into her beaker. It was coffee, and it was strong, and good.

'No bones broken. She'll be fine,' said Ralph. He took a business card from his wallet and scribbled something on the back. 'Next time you're in Grimsbach, come into the Lakeside Hotel for a drink and ask for Flavia and Ralph. It'll be on the house.' He handed the card to the young man, who saluted and turned away.

Flavia sat sipping. And still the helicopter was droning overhead, and still there was no news of Carol.

***

Rico dropped the iPad onto the bed beside him and flopped back. He could search as much as he liked, he wasn't going to find an available flight to Zurich today. It would have to be the train. If he got a seat on the TGV, the super-quick express, he'd be home in... He tapped his phone to see the exact time. Ten past three – on the TGV, he'd be in Basel less than four hours after it started, then he only had to drive the width of Switzerland back to Lake Constance. Six hours in total.

Stacy was making yet another cup of tea on the hospitality tray. She'd made him eat the rest of his lunchtime sandwich, but now Rico felt sick. No matter what he did, it would be hours before he was back at Lakeside.

He lifted the iPad again. 'There's a direct train to Basel at twenty past four. I'll go for that. But you should go to England as we planned, Stace.'

She handed over a steaming cup. 'Whatever we do, Rico, we do it together. I still think we should wait here for news of Carol. They must find her soon, and then Ralph will either be busy looking after her, or he'll be sitting at her hospital bed, or–' She brushed away a tear, the end of the sentence hanging unspoken between them. *Or she'll be dead and Ralph will be gutted and need us.*

Rico stood up. 'I need to go, Stace. Let's get packed.' He was swinging his case from the rack onto the bed when his phone rang. They both froze, staring at each other with blank faces.

***

Flavia stared out unseeingly as Ralph drove through the Appenzeller countryside, heading downhill. He'd only been persuaded to leave the rescue site when the police told him that the helicopter would take Carol straight to the hospital in St Gallen when she was found, as it seemed more than likely now that she was injured. Perhaps seriously. Flavia shifted in the passenger seat, trying to breathe calmly. They were speeding along a country road, dodging through Sunday traffic while she clutched Ralph's phone in one hand and her own in the other. The rescue people would let them know the moment Carol was found.

To her surprise, they swung onto the motorway at St Gallen.

Ralph cleared his throat. 'I'll drop you off at Lakeside. I can be there and back in half an hour, so I'd still be at the hospital on time even if they called right this minute to say she's found.'

Thirty minutes there and back would mean going way over the speed limit, but there was no way she was going to start criticising his driving. 'Thanks. Maybe there'll be news when – when we reach Lakeside.'

He didn't answer, and Flavia closed her eyes to keep the tears in.

At the hotel, he almost literally 'dropped her off'. The car stopped for all of two seconds to let her out, then in another two seconds the brakes screeched as Ralph took the turn onto the main road. Flavia clapped her hands to her face. He was in a state; he shouldn't be driving, but what could anyone do? The only person who could help Ralph now was Carol.

The hotel door opened. 'Flavia! You're safe! Who brought– oh, sweetheart, come here!'

Flavia burst into tears. She was gathered into Denise's arms and cuddled, and Alex was there too, helping them both inside while Luis ran for Margrit, who took one look at Flavia and ushered them all into the medical room.

And oh, it was good to have people here who cared about her and were looking after her. Margrit shooed Alex and Luis out, and insisted on giving Flavia a full examination.

She shook her head when Flavia told her about Ralph's state of mind. 'I wish he hadn't left without coming in. Abandoning you on the driveway is a clear indication he's not thinking straight. You're right, he shouldn't be driving.'

Denise bit her lip. 'He must be worried sick. We can give him half an hour to get well into the hospital, then phone. Oh, Flavia, thank goodness you're safe.'

Flavia's teeth were chattering again. Margrit wrapped her in a blanket and sent for some hot chocolate, holding the mug to Flavia's lips when it arrived. 'Get that inside you, then we'll see what you want to do.'

'She's coming home with me,' said Denise firmly. 'This is no time for her to be alone in her flat.'

Flavia took the mug from Margrit and sipped. The panic inside her was slackening off, but oh, her heart was heavy. Carol...

When half an hour had passed, Margrit tapped on her phone. Flavia listened to one side of the conversation.

'Any news, Ralph? ... Let's hope so ... She's all right, with Denise now – how are you? ... You should have someone with you.'

Denise touched Margrit's arm. 'Alex can go.'

Flavia let the arrangements wash over her as exhaustion kicked in. She allowed Denise to lead her back out through reception and into Alex's car. He drove them swiftly to his mother's home, then sped off again towards the motorway while Denise tucked Flavia up in an armchair and gave her Snowy to cuddle before going to make sandwiches. Flavia forced one down. And still there was no news.

***

Rico sat in their hotel room, swiping through the iPad. They'd heard nothing from home since Ralph's call several hours ago, when he'd insisted that Rico and Stacy stayed put until they knew what had happened to Carol. Rico had called at six to be told there was still no news, except a large-scale search was now ongoing. It was difficult terrain and apparently likely to slide further, so searching was slow work.

Ten o'clock, eleven o'clock, and they were still huddled together on the bed, waiting. And waiting. The Seine cruise was forgotten, of course. They'd decided not to tell Stacy's parents what was going on until they had proper news, and Rico sat cursing himself. He should have ignored Dad. If he'd got that train as he'd wanted to, he could have been sitting with his father now. Wrong decision, Rico.

Midnight. One o'clock, but sleep was unthinkable. Then a shrill ringtone set Rico's heart racing, and Stacy jerked upright.

'Dad?' He tapped on speaker.

'She's here, Rico. Carol. We're still at the hospital. She isn't hurt apart from a broken wrist, but they say it's a simple one, whatever that means. She wasn't swept as far down as Flavia, and she managed to crawl into a cave in the hillside and shelter there, but she didn't dare try to get down to the valley. She's okay, Rico.'

Rico closed his eyes in relief. 'Thank God.'

'Yes. I'm with her now. She was struck by a tree but then it protected her from the worst of the landslide, and she was able to crawl into the cave. Oh, Rico...'

His father was babbling. Rico's throat closed, and Stacy took the phone, tears shining in her eyes.

'You hang on in there, Ralph, and give Carol our love. You've had a horrible day, but it's over.'

'Yes. I'm sorry, I've messed up your day too. I shouldn't have leaned on you two when you're on your honeymoon.'

Rico pulled himself together. 'No point having a son and daughter-in-law unless you can lean on them sometimes, honeymoon or not! And we still have plenty of that left, don't worry.'

Ralph gave an odd-sounding, strained laugh. 'I'm sure Janie has plenty more wedding-like activities planned for you! I'll see you both in England as we planned, and I'll get Carol to send a message when she's up to it.'

He rang off, and Rico dropped back down on the bed. 'Jeez. That was – intense.'

Stacy was tinkling around the bottles in the minbar. 'It was, but we can celebrate now.' She waved a small bottle of Prosecco at him. 'We'll toast the two rescue-ees, and your dad, and the rest of our honeymoon!'

Rico accepted a glass, and they clinked. 'Cheers. At least we don't need to break it to your mum that the blessing's off. Okay, Mrs Weber. What now?'

Stacy sipped. 'We grab a few hours' sleep before we go for the train. England is waiting for us, and so is my mum.'

Rico pulled her close. Panic over.

21

Monday, 17th June

Transfixed, Rico stood at the window as their capsule inched skywards and the city below grew more distant. He'd always wanted to go on the London Eye, and here he was. How impressive were the Houses of Parliament, seen from the air? And there was the BT Tower – Ralph had been up that, before it was closed to the public. And St Paul's Cathedral, and buildings as far as you could see. Wow – London was massive.

And what a difference this was to the angst and suspense of yesterday. After the all-clear, they'd managed a few hours' sleep before the alarm wrenched them awake to dash across early morning Paris. The Eurostar provided another opportunity to sleep, though, and neither of them saw much of England on the way up from the coast.

Rico's phone buzzed, and he whipped it out. It was almost twelve, and Ralph had promised to call.

'Morning, Rico. Just a quickie – Carol's home now with a lightweight plaster, and we're all set to see you in Manchester on Thursday.'

'That's great, but take it easy for a day or two, huh? You had a fright, and so did Carol.'

Ralph sniffed. 'Don't worry. Margrit is barely letting either of us breathe by ourselves at the moment. Carol said tell Stacy she'll call her later.'

'Great. And Flavia?'

'She stayed with Denise last night. I haven't heard anything today yet, but I expect she'll take a few days off too. Enjoy your time in London, son. See you soon.'

The call ended abruptly, and Rico glared at his phone. It was hard to tell what kind of state Ralph was in. His words were upbeat, but his tone of voice was still brittle. Not that you'd expect anything different after what Dad had been through.

Rico reported back to Stacy, then went to look down the Thames in the other direction. They'd decided to spend their time outside, soaking up the London atmosphere before catching an early afternoon train north tomorrow. He and Stacy had both reckoned that after Berne, Basel and Paris they'd have had enough of museums and sightseeing, and they'd been right. A more intensive exploration of the UK's capital could wait for another time. They were planning to walk from the Eye over the bridge to Westminster, then down – or was it up? – the Mall to Buckingham Palace. Tomorrow morning would involve a visit to Covent Garden before heading to Euston for the train.

Their capsule eased back down to ground level, and Rico took Stacy's hand as they stepped off. 'That was brilliant. What's next? I'm hungry – we didn't do a lot of eating yesterday.'

Stacy pointed to a minimarket on the other side of the bridge they were crossing. 'Let's buy some sandwiches and take them with us. We can find a shady tree in St James's Park. I could do with a sit-down for a bit.'

Rico squeezed her hand. Finding normality wasn't so easy after what had happened. They'd read in the news that several small earthquakes had been registered in the Appenzellerland over the past few days, which wasn't unusual, but this time it had been enough to set the woodland slope in motion. Fortunately, Carol and Flavia were the only people who'd been caught up in it.

They meandered along, chatting about the places they were passing. Every so often Rico would catch Stacy glancing at someone's children, a wistful look in her eyes. He chewed his lower lip. It was hard, seeing her like that when he didn't feel the same way. Kids in two years would do him fine, and right now they should be enjoying a lazy day or two in an interesting city before the journey to Elton Abbey and their wedding blessing – after which it would be home to Lakeside and everyday life. And his master's course. And that was his other problem.

Sudden heaviness settled in Rico's middle. It had taken being away for a few days for him to see it, but running the hotel was more fun than uni. It was all he wanted from life, actually. Would he be letting Stace and Dad down if he broke off his course? He could still do IT stuff for the hotel, and friends.

'Problem?' Stacy was peering up at him, and Rico forced the uncertainty back. They'd had enough problems for one honeymoon, and there would be plenty of time to discuss his future when they were home again.

He took Stacy's hand and swung it, grinning down at her. 'I was wondering about fish and chips for dinner tonight. Shall we?' Hopefully Stace would buy that...

Luckily for him, she did. 'Let's do it. You know, it's weird, coming here as a tourist. England feels so familiar – the shops, the language and so on, but the longer I'm here, the more I realise that Lakeside and Switzerland are home.'

Her face was tranquil as they started up the Mall heading for Buckingham Palace, and a lump came into Rico's throat. Stacy was his home as much as Lakeside was. All he needed in life was his wife, and the hotel. Why had he ever started a time-consuming master's course that took him away from them both? IT was useful, but his first degree gave him enough for the job of hotel manager.

'Rico?'

He hadn't realised he'd stopped walking. Rico pointed to a spot under a large oak tree in St James's Park. 'Lunch? There's a tuna sandwich with your name on it in this bag!'

They settled down and ate lunch cross-legged on the grass. Rico chewed his cheddar and pickled onion sandwich, gathering the courage to speak. Now that he'd started thinking about giving up his course, it didn't seem right to be hiding it from Stace. They'd promised each other ages ago, 'no secrets'. Or none that involved anything other than birthday presents and the like. Even if it turned out to be another discussion they'd postpone until they were home again, he should tell her.

Stacy blew him a kiss. 'Spit it out, Rico. I can see there's something.'

'I'm thinking of giving up the master's.' He kept his eyes on hers.

Her eyebrows rose. 'Are you sure? Why? You've been hankering after that course since before we met.'

Rico popped a can of cola open. She didn't look as if she thought he was letting her down. 'I know. But now I've started, I see that being manager of Lakeside is what I want to do, not start up an IT business. I'm sorry if you think I'm being a let-down.'

'Don't be daft – why would I think that? I don't want you to give up a dream for a job that was wished upon you, that's all – especially as I was the one who did the original wishing!'

'Now you're being daft. I guess I've changed. The Rico you met that summer isn't the guy you married.'

'Oh, I think they're both sitting opposite me here in this park. Tell you what. Keep on thinking, and we can talk it over as much as you like when we're home. The end decision is yours.'

Rico swung forward to kiss Stacy. He had a wife in a million.

***

Flavia gave her face a final dab of concealer in front of Denise's bathroom mirror, and went through to the living room for her bag. Staying with Denise had been the right thing to do – not that she'd been given any choice about it. But she was rested now, and the whole nightmare had faded into something like a bad dream in her head. The worst part had been waiting all those hours for news of Carol being found, though she'd fallen asleep on the sofa long before that. Denise had woken her to pass on the good news, then they'd both gone to bed and Flavia had slept until ten o'clock.

Denise came in from the balcony, and glared at her. 'The first thing Ralph will do when you walk into the hotel and announce you're there to work is send you home again, you know!'

'He won't. I'm fine, after all your care. And the spa's short staffed as it is, with Stacy away. Tell you what, though. If you come down to Grimsbach and meet me at seven after my shift, you can cook me dinner at mine.' She raised an eyebrow at Denise. It wasn't too big an ask; the bus stopped outside Denise's flat, and it would drop her just fifty yards from the hotel.

Denise sniffed. 'I'll do that. You know, I've been thinking about moving. Flat, I mean. Now that I'm doing more work for the hotel, it would be good to live in Grimsbach. What do you think?'

Heavens, that was a surprise. 'It's an idea. You'd miss your view, though.'

'Yes, but I could find something with a bit of garden. Snowy would like that. No rush, but I'll start looking.'

They chatted for a few more minutes, then Flavia left to catch her bus. Hm. Denise in Grimsbach would be much handier, for her and for Stacy as well as for the older woman. Flavia's heart lurched. It would make it easier for Alex to join Zoe in Zurich, too. Was that a part of what Denise was thinking?

The day was overcast and muggy, and somehow, the heaviness of the air matched Flavia's mood as the bus meandered down to the lake bank and along in the direction of the hotel. The adrenaline she'd run on yesterday was gone, and in spite of her brave words to Denise, she was tired. And feeling alone, in spite of her mother having called three times since she'd heard the news.

Flavia pulled out a tissue to dab her eyes. Seeing how frantic Ralph was yesterday only emphasised her loneliness – no one here would miss her like that. Denise was lovely, but a friend wasn't the same as having a partner there for you. And Alex didn't seem to be worrying about how Flavia was after her ordeal. He'd called his mother last night, twice, in fact, but he hadn't spoken to her. Come to think of it, they hadn't even talked about Friday's trip to Zurich, apart from saying how well Denise had managed, and it all felt so…

artificial, that was the word. Alex's feelings about Zoe weren't up for discussion, and while this was maybe okay when it came to talking to his fellow receptionist, Denise had mentioned last night that he wasn't talking about it to her either. That was less good. He could be trying not to worry her, of course, but his mum was still hurt. Flavia pouted. Heck, why was life so complicated?

Margrit shot out of the medical room in the spa the moment Flavia arrived. 'Flavia! How are you? You shouldn't be here, you know.' She put both arms around Flavia, and heavens, here was Sabine coming for a hug too – maybe she wasn't as friendless as she'd thought.

'I'm absolutely fine, and work'll distract me from thinking about it all. Please don't say you don't need me.'

'Of course we need you – but we want you to be all right, that's much more important than restocking the spa shop and tweaking the staff rota.' Margrit pulled her into the medical room. 'I'll check you over again. If you're not okay, you can go right back home.'

Flavia allowed her blood pressure, temperature and pulse to be checked, and of course, she was fine. Five minutes later she was whizzing through reception en route for the storeroom.

Alex glanced up. 'Are we on fire?'

Flavia jerked to a halt. He looked worse than she felt, his eyes heavy in a pale face. What was going on there? He'd been up late, waiting with Ralph in St Gallen, but still. She gave him a careful smile. 'Just getting some stuff for the shop. Desk duty okay?' She didn't dare ask how he was in case he burst into tears at the desk. He'd hate that.

'Uh-huh. Can you watch reception for five minutes, please? I need to see Ralph about something.'

Flavia slid behind the desk, wishing there was something she could do to help him. But the anguish he was in was about Zoe, not her, and seeing Ralph and Carol yesterday would have brought it home to him that he and Zoe were miles apart in more ways than geographically. Flavia handed out a new key card to a guest who had managed to break his, then stood drumming her fingers.

There was nothing else for it: she was going to have to forget the crush she'd had on Alex ever since he'd started working here, almost exactly a year ago. A crush was all it was. You couldn't say she'd been in love with him, because nobody could stay in love with someone who barely noticed them all that time, not in real life, anyway, no matter what happened in books and films. It was a pity it had taken her so long to realise that, though, and the problem was, in spite of not being in love anymore – not really – she was still no closer to moving on than he was. It was complicated.

A pair of guests arrived at the desk, wanting advice about an afternoon trip that didn't involve too much walking. Flavia grimaced in sympathy. They were older people from the Orkney Isles, and it was thirty degrees plus today. By the time she'd sorted them out with an airconditioned bus trip to St Gallen and a wander around the textile museum there, Alex was back, looking more cheerful.

'Thanks, Flavia. Um... I was wondering. I still haven't treated you to that cocktail. How about going to the new bistro in Rorschach when we both have an evening off?'

Flavia had to concentrate to stop her jaw from dropping. He was asking her out – what was going on? He could be simply rewarding her for her help on Friday, but a quick drink after work one day would have done that.

She managed not to stammer. 'That would be fun. Thanks.'

He screwed up his nose. 'Wednesday?' He opened the staff rota on the computer. 'We both stop at seven.

'Sounds good.' Flavia smiled nervously and left him to answer the phone. This was very odd...

22

Tuesday, 18th June

Stacy craned her neck as the train slid into Manchester Piccadilly. Yes, there was Mum, bobbing up and down on the platform, flanked by Dad and Gareth, and Jo – and wow, baby Tom was huge! She helped Rico gather their luggage, and they joined the queue to leave the train.

'Stacy, darling! Come here!'

Enveloped in her mother's arms, Stacy inhaled Janie's familiar perfume. How good it was to know she was loved, even if Janie was the most OTT mother of the bride ever. Janie let her go, and Stacy went to kiss her father and the rest of the family.

Gareth winked at her. 'You're looking good, Stace. Married life must suit you. How was Paris?'

'Amazing. Yet another city for the list of places to go back to.' Stacy tapped eleven-month-old Tom's cheek, and he gaped at her, his little face blank. It was his birthday soon; she'd been an aunt for nearly a year, but oh, to be holding her own child.

The tears in Stacy's eyes made the world a blurry place. She linked arms with her mother as they wandered up the station, but Janie's happy expression was enough to cheer anyone up. Although – she was going to have to tell Mum and Dad about those hours in Paris when they'd paced up and down a hotel room, waiting for news of Carol. Not to mention the Seine cruise they'd missed. Stacy grimaced. Carol might well need a bit of pampering and support when she arrived on Thursday. She'd sounded okay on the phone yesterday, but the talk had been more about her broken arm than her ordeal.

John was checking his watch. 'Come on, people. There's less than five minutes left on the meter. See you at home, Gareth.'

The two cars left the city centre in convoy, although Gareth soon pulled away in front as they drove through the stretch of countryside between Manchester and Elton Abbey. Stacy peered out nostalgically as they entered the village. The landmarks of her life were here – her old school, and the park where she'd spent so many teenage evenings with her friends, and the flat she'd shared with Emily. And here they were outside Pen 'n' Paper, Mum and Dad's stationery shop, now run mainly by Gareth and Jo. Jo's gift for arts and crafts, and the courses she ran, had pulled the shop out of the doldrums last year, just when everyone was starting to think Mum and Dad were flogging a dead horse.

'Now, here's the plan,' said Janie, when they were all sitting in the flat above the shop, little Tom crawling around from one person to the next. 'Tomorrow, we should check the wedding clothes. I had your dress cleaned, Stacy, darling, it looks perfect. Emily's coming with hers, too. We can all walk down to the village afterwards to show Rico the church and the hotel, then we have a meeting with the vicar at four o'clock, and a short wedding rehearsal. On–'

Stacy nearly spilled her coffee as Rico twitched violently on the sofa beside her.

'Wedding rehearsal?' His voice was your classic surprised squeak.

Stacy couldn't help laughing. She caught her father's eye and he winked.

Janie was back in full swing. 'It's what we do in England, dear. Then on Thursday, Ralph and Carol arrive and we'll have dinner at the hotel where the reception is, so you'll see it on the inside, then the wedd– um, the ceremony is on Friday.'

Stacy took a deep breath. 'Mum, Dad. About Ralph and Carol.' She explained in a few sentences, relieved when her father told her he'd booked Ralph and Carol into the same hotel the reception was in. Having their own space there would make it easier for the couple to have a quiet moment if they needed one.

And typical Mum, she was concerned, of course, but it didn't take long before she was back to the arrangements for Friday.

'Everything's organised at the hotel, too. Emily has arranged for someone to do your hair and make-up here, and Daddy took the flowers order to the florist yesterday, and they'll arrive on Friday, of course.'

Apprehension flooded into Stacy's head as soon as the word 'flowers' crossed Janie's lips. They should have talked about this beforehand... Knowing Mum, she'd have ordered the contents of an entire hothouse to make a bridal bouquet the size of the Empire State Building. Stacy bit her lip, then noticed that her father was looking sheepishly innocent.

Janie saw it too. 'John, darling, you did put the order in, didn't you?'

Every head in the room turned towards John, even the baby seeming to notice something was afoot. Rico looked nonplussed and Gareth and Jo were barely containing their smiles. John went brick red, and Stacy leaned over and patted her father's knee.

'What have you done, Dad?'

He gave Janie a hunted look, then winked at Stacy again. 'Well, when I went into the shop, there was a lovely little arrangement in the window, not unlike the one you had in Switzerland, Stacy. So I had a chat with the florist and we changed the order to another just like it, and something similar for Emily. But the flowers for the church and the tables are exactly as you planned, dear.' He finished off gazing virtuously at Janie, whose face was a comical mixture of horror and dismay. Stacy could feel suppressed laughter shaking through Rico.

'Thanks, Dad,' she said warmly. 'That sounds perfect.' She beamed at both parents, and Janie blinked back.

'Oh. I thought... But as long as you're happy, Stacy, darling.' She subsided into her coffee cup.

Stacy rose to the occasion. 'What flowers have you planned for the church, Mum?'

Janie launched into a description of sweet peas and roses while John leaned back in his chair, a satisfied smile pulling at his lips. Happiness flooded through Stacy as she listened to her mother rhapsodise about the church flowers. Mum and Dad both loved her, though they had different ways of showing it. And thank goodness Dad's way was different.

Eventually, Janie talked herself out and went to fetch more coffee. John crossed the room, took a thin folder from the bookshelf in the corner, and presented it to Stacy.

'You're not the only ones with building projects, you know. We've taken the advice you gave us last summer, Stacy.' He pointed to an image of a red brick bungalow with dormer windows in the sloping roof. 'It's on a new estate on this side of Elton Abbey, and it'll be finished in the autumn. We move at the beginning of November when we retire officially, and Gareth and Jo will move in here.'

Tears shot into Stacy's eyes. This was what her parents needed. A fresh start, a nice little garden to take care of, and no shop underneath reminding them of everything that had changed in their lives. And with Gareth and Jo here, Mum and Dad wouldn't even need to feel nostalgic for their old home; they'd be visiting regularly. They could even get a dog. And if only her own accommodation plans were as easily sorted. Come to think of it, this bungalow would suit her down to the ground too.

They were still poring over the plans when Stacy's phone buzzed in her bag at her feet. Oh – this was Carol.

'It's Carol. I'll take it somewhere quiet.' She hurried downstairs to the shop, where the call wouldn't be overheard.

'Hi Carol – how are you?' Carol's last words to her yesterday had been 'See you on Thursday,' so a call now might mean something was up. Or was she falling into the overthinking trap again?

'I'm all right, Stacy, love, but I wanted a quick word before we arrive on Thursday, and I'm guessing your mum has a full programme for you tomorrow.'

Stacy's alarm bells were pealing like never before. That low, shaky voice… the last time she'd heard the older woman sounding so vulnerable was back in December, when they didn't know if Carol would be well enough to fly to Australia to spend Christmas with her family there.

She gripped her phone. 'Something's wrong, isn't it?'

Carol's sigh whistled down the phone. 'It's Ralph. He had a terrible fright on Sunday, Stacy. I've never seen him like that. I think he was more afraid than I was. Afterwards, he was so – so clingy, and I was too, it was wonderful to be back safe with him, but now… I don't know. Today it's as if he's angry, too, angry with me for putting him through all that fear. Oh, we're coming on Thursday, don't worry, and I'm sure he'll be all smiles for you, but – I don't know how to deal with him when he's like this.'

Stacy sat down at the big crafts table in the middle of the shop. 'I wish we'd been there to help him on Sunday. He'll need time to get over it, Carol. And you know how complicated he can be.'

'I think he's protecting himself from more hurt, but it feels like I'm being pushed away. Sorry, I shouldn't be unloading all this on you in the middle of your wedding celebrations. Ralph needs distraction, and at the moment, I'm not the person to provide it. I've invited Hans from the Alpstein for dinner tonight.'

'Good idea, and don't worry. I'm glad you've told me. We'll think of something to get him back to the old Ralph.'

'Please do. Even this wretched MJ surprise is only half distracting him today.'

Stacy's thoughts spun back to the hazy figure of MJ. 'I'll get Rico onto it. We can use the surprise to get Ralph thinking about other things. Leave it with me, Carol.'

She ended the call and went back upstairs to Janie's questions about Carol. Stacy answered as well as she could, then beckoned Rico into their room to unpack. He listened while she told him about Ralph, then nodded slowly.

'Distraction sounds like a good idea until it's all less raw in his mind. I'm sure we can do something with MJ and the surprise. Put your thinking cap on.'

Stacy opened the wardrobe and handed him a coat hanger. 'Will do. Meanwhile, get your shirts hung up.'

She busied around, transferring the contents of her case to the wardrobe. This wasn't her old room but Gareth's old larger one, with a new set of furniture and neutral décor, and Stacy smiled. So the flat above the shop had no 'Gareth's room'. Was 'Stacy's room' still the same as always? She tiptoed across the landing and pushed her old door open – and found a well-equipped nursery. Stacy laughed out loud. Her mother was incorrigible.

***

Her shift was over at last. Flavia left Maria, the part-time evening receptionist, in charge of the desk and meandered across the hotel garden and down to the lake. A breath of lakeside air would do her good.

She sank down on the low stone wall by the landing place, which was now a mini-building site as it was extended several metres along the lake bank. Flavia said 'good evening' to a couple of guests who came down to take photos of the lake, glad when they didn't stop to chat. She was more tired today than she'd been on Sunday after her rescue, or even yesterday. Delayed reaction, perhaps.

It was peaceful, sitting here in the evening sunshine, looking out over the water. Small boats were chugging along in the distance, and a couple of sailing ships were scudding up the middle of the lake towards Bregenz. Not many people were on the lake path, though a buzz of chatter behind her told Flavia that the terrace was full of happy holidaymakers dining al fresco. All with their friends and family and partners... and here was she, the only solitary person in the entire hotel. Flavia swallowed, trying hard to shake off the gloomy feeling. She was alive, and she might not have been. A tear escaped and ran down her face; oh, help, this was no good. She should go and see Denise, or pop into the library, see who was there. But Denise had helped her so much already, and the library would close soon.

A loud thud to her right banished her despondency. The builders were long gone – who was in the boathouse? Flavia pushed herself off the wall and crept up to the boathouse entrance, phone in hand in case she had to call for help.

The door was open, and she approached slowly to see inside into the small reception area leading to the sauna and new fitness room. Ralph was there, hunched over the desk, his shoulders shaking with sobs.

Flavia's breath caught in her throat. She'd been wrong; she wasn't the only one alone here, and she wasn't the only one feeling down, either. By the look of things, Ralph was every bit as affected by what had happened on Sunday as she and Carol were. Flavia moved back, retracing her steps to the jetty wall as a low sob emanated from the boathouse. She shoved her phone into her pocket and stood with her hands clasped under her chin. Should she tell someone? Who could help Ralph? Carol, yes, but she needed support too. Alex had gone home, and Rico and Stacy were in England. It was going to be down to her, because she couldn't leave him like that.

Flavia set her shoulders and strode back to the boathouse, but the door was banged shut from the inside before she got there. Oh. Was Ralph...? She hesitated for a few moments, then turned up the side of the building, and yes, there was Ralph locking the top door behind him. He gave her a wave, then crossed the grass to go into the terrace bar.

When Flavia arrived there he was deep in conversation with a couple of guests, his smile stretching from one ear to the other. Flavia ordered a glass of white wine and took it to the staff table, where Luis was sitting with Sabine from the spa. This definitely wasn't an evening she wanted to spend alone.

23

WEDNESDAY, 19TH JUNE

Rico awoke to the sound of voices in the street below. He stretched, glancing at the alarm clock by the bed. Nearly eight o'clock; he'd had a great sleep, considering all the ups and downs of the last few days and the excesses Janie had treated them to last night.

The other side of the bed was empty, and Rico swung his legs to the floor and went for his phone, charging on the chest of drawers. It was nine in Switzerland now. Okay, time to do something to help Dad over his reaction to Carol's accident, and thinking about MJ might just do that. Nothing like forcing someone into thinking pleasant thoughts, was there? At least, hopefully MJ was a pleasant thought. But if nothing else, doing this would give them the opportunity to talk to Ralph today, and they could do it a few times. Rico smiled grimly. He and Stacy had formed a vague plan last night, but whether it would work or not remained to be seen.

'A good time to give Dad a call, do you think?' He buried his nose in the lemony fragrance of Stacy's hair as she came in from the shower. 'Mm. Wish we had the place to ourselves for a while.'

'Well, we don't, and Dad is grilling bacon as we speak. But let's call Ralph and set the plan in motion. Remember, you're worried that I'm not going to like whatever MJ is, and you want to know what Carol thinks. You need to sound perfectly normal about Carol.'

'Got it.' Rico tapped, and three rings later he had his father's voice in his ear.

'Rico?'

Hm, that odd little strained tone was still there. Rico breezed on. 'Dad, very quickly while Stacy's getting dressed. She *is* going to like this MJ surprise, or secret or whatever it is, isn't she? I'm worried it might be something a bit too, um, Swiss for her.'

'Too Swiss? Stacy loves Switzerland.'

Rico gave Stacy a thumbs-up. The strain had been replaced by astonishment. 'I know. Still... what does Carol think about it? Did you get an okay from her before you arranged it?'

'Of course I did, and she's all for it! Rico, you're worrying about nothing!'

'I'm sorry if I sound ungrateful, but women think differently about surprises compared to us mere blokes.'

'Rico, it's fine.'

'Okay. Thanks, Dad. Love to Carol and look after the hotel for me.' He rang off and high-fived Stacy. 'Phase one complete, Mrs.'

She kissed his neck. 'Fab. Get dressed.'

***

Rico emerged from the shower to find Stacy and her father in the kitchen. She handed him a mug and pushed him over to the coffee machine beside the fridge.

'I'll make you some toast, shall I?'

'Lovely.' Rico pressed buttons and inhaled deeply as steaming and aromatic brown liquid trickled into his mug.

He was finishing his toast when the flat door slammed and Janie burst into the kitchen, a well-filled shopping bag in each hand.

'Good, you're all up and ready. I met Alan at the supermarket. He and Emily will be here in an hour and we'll check the clothes, then I thought we could all go for lunch together before the rehearsal?'

Stacy was nodding. 'That would be lovely, Mum. Emily texted me a while ago – she's invited Rico and me for dinner tonight, so you and Dad can relax and, um, deal with any last-minute issues.'

Janie hesitated for the briefest of moments, then lifted her bags onto the work surface.

'Excellent, darling. Now, I'll put these bits away and...'

Rico switched off as she chatted on. A few hours' peace with Emmy and Alan would be great; more than likely it would be the last peaceful interlude before the flight home to Switzerland. He circled his shoulders. All he had to do here was go with the flow. Janie had wanted a big wedding party and she was getting it, and Stacy was happy too, so... Darker thoughts of his bank balance swerved into Rico's brain, and he ignored them determinedly. It *would* be all right.

He was less sure of this half an hour later when Janie produced a few additions to his outfit. His suit had gained a waistcoat, and he, Alan and John – and Ralph too, if Janie had her way – were now wearing white silk ties.

John must have seen his expression, because when Janie and Stacy started a conversation about the impossibility of walking more than twenty yards wearing stiletto heels, he leaned over to murmur in Rico's ear, 'Be happy. I put my foot down about the top hats and tails.'

Put like that, Rico found he *was* happy...

Emily and Alan arrived, and Emily immediately started a complicated discussion with Janie about her bridesmaid's dress. Alan jerked his head at Rico, who smothered a smile. So Stace had roped in some help with phase two of their Ralph plan. Stacy muttered an excuse about needing Rico to check something on the iPad, and the two of them escaped to their room.

'My turn. Breathe quietly.' She plumped down beside Rico on the bed and connected to Ralph's phone, holding it between their heads so that Rico could hear too.

'Hi, Ralph – I won't keep you, but Rico's fretting about your MJ thing. Does he need to? I can't seem to reassure him it won't be anything, ah, drastic, or embarrassing. You know what he's like when he's worried.'

'Good grief, Stacy... Drastic? I don't know, but I promise you it's not the least bit embarrassing. He's going to love it. You both will.'

'I'm sure you're right, but fretting like this is in his nature, isn't it? And it's such a waste of time when you agonise over things like that. He's his own worst enemy sometimes.'

'Yes, ah – Stacy, it's fine, don't worry. Carol loves it too.'

'Does she? Good. Thanks, Ralph. I'll give Rico a good pep talk, don't worry. Oh, and could you tell Carol not to forget her hair straighteners, I'll want to borrow them. See you both tomorrow!'.

Rico held up a hand for a high five. She deserved an Oscar for that one... 'Now he has even more to think about. We'll have phase three this afternoon.' And hopefully Dad would take the remark about agonising over things to heart.

***

By quarter to four, they were all at the church, Janie bustling around showing them the aisle Stacy and John would walk down, and pointing out where the flowers were going. The vicar arrived, and Rico cheered up a hundred and ten per cent. Phil Cameron was in his early thirties and was wearing none-too-clean jeans and a dusty sweatshirt. A smudge of something dark streaked from his forehead up into tousled blond hair.

'Sorry,' he said, shaking hands all round and spreading dust generously around the wedding party. 'I've been in the cellar all afternoon. Bit of bother with the boiler, but the engineer's on his way. Shall we have a quick walk-through, and if you like we can practise the vows?'

And once again, Rico began to feel as if he was in the middle of a decades-old American movie. Slushy music would be starting any second...

He muttered in Stacy's ear. 'Aren't they the same vows as the ones we made in Switzerland?'

She turned to the vicar. 'I think we're okay with the vows, Phil. We don't want to keep you too long when you have an emergency on. A walk-through would be perfect.'

Out of the corner of his eye Rico saw Janie open her mouth to object, but John gave her arm a shake and she subsided.

Phil waved at the front pew. 'Okay. Rico, you and the best man sit here. When the bride arrives at the back – and yes, I know you're already man and wife – you stand up and wait as she comes down the aisle.'

They moved through a practice ceremony with Rico increasingly glad they were doing this. It was quite different to their Swiss version. When they came to the end, Janie mopped her eyes.

'It's going to be perfect, Stacy darling. I'm wondering if we couldn't have little Tom as page boy after all? He'd be so sweet, and he'd manage to walk up the aisle if someone holds both his hands–'

'*No!*' Stacy, Jo, Gareth and John all spoke at once, and surprise flitted across Janie's face.

'Oh – all right. But–'

'Mum, it's amazing the way it is. Thanks, Phil.' Stacy took Rico's hand as he turned to Janie.

'I'm glad you organised this, Janie. I feel much better, knowing where to stand and so on.' It was true, too.

They trailed out of the church with Janie talking non-stop. A black cat was sitting in the doorway having a good wash, and Jo and Gareth stopped to stroke it, showing baby Tom how friendly the creature was. Emily joined them, and this might be a good moment... Rico jerked his head at Alan, who raised his eyebrows, then moved over to talk to Janie and John.

Rico winked at Stacy. 'Phase three?'

She took his arm. 'Go for it.'

Rico tapped. 'Dad, sorry to bother you again. I'm wondering if you've told Carol I was worried? What did she say?'

'Good grief, Rico, would you please stop worrying! You're making much too much of this – there's no problem!'

Rico injected some doubt into his voice. 'I guess I inherited that from you. So you're sure MJ has never been a problem?'

'Well, it was tricky at the start, but it's fine now. You can put the worry away.'

'Good. Let's make a pact to do that as much as we can, huh? Putting the worries away, I mean. Both of us. I'm sure Stacy would call us worrywarts, you know.'

There was a moment's silence, then Ralph cleared his throat. 'Deal. Go away, Rico. You'll see me soon enough.'

Rico stuffed his phone back into his pocket and high-fived Stacy for the third time that day. 'I think we can leave it there, don't you?'

She took his arm again. 'Yup. Well done.'

Rico broke out into a whistle as they walked on. It would be a fantastic wedding blessing, a great party, and the best end ever to the happiest month of his life. The optimism lasted as far as the main road, where a tiny doubt wormed its way into Rico's head. You couldn't compare worrying about an unknown surprise to the worry Dad had gone through about Carol, could you? But surely his father would be all right in the end.

24

WEDNESDAY, 19TH JUNE

Flavia finished her shift in the spa at quarter to seven on Wednesday evening, and hurried through and into the loos for restaurant guests. She didn't want to get ready for her date with Alex in the staff cloakroom in case he came in and caught her checking that her make-up was still concealing the scratches she'd picked up on Sunday. This was so strange – *why* had he asked her out? You only had to look at him when he was talking to Zoe to know he was still in love with her.

Flavia dabbed on more powder, then squirted perfume on her neck. Come to that, why had she accepted his invitation? It was asking for trouble, like picking a scab, and the only excuse was that tonight should help her clarify in her own head what she wanted to do with her life. And now she was ready. Channelling her inner lion, she returned to the front hall.

Ralph's voice boomed across reception as she arrived. 'Alex! Is this a good time to go down to the boathouse for five minutes?'

Alex was handing over to Maria, who was covering reception until it closed. He gave Flavia a worried look. 'Is that okay? We need to organise something before Ralph goes to England.'

'Sure.' Flavia went round the desk to stand with Maria. Maybe the pedalos were arriving? They must be coming soon, and it sounded as if Alex might have to oversee it while Ralph and Carol were away. She watched as the two men vanished across the terrace. Ralph had seemed his usual self today, but he was a hotelier, wasn't he – he was good at acting a part.

It was over ten minutes before Alex was back. 'Sorry, sorry. Ready?'

'Not your fault. Everything all right?'

'Yup, all good.' He held the front door open for her and led the way to the car park.

As interesting conversations went, this wasn't a great one. Flavia wracked her brains for something else to talk about, but neither of them said another word until they were sitting in the car.

Alex reversed out of his space. 'Is the new bistro still okay?'

'Sure. Have you been there?'

He stopped at the gates to wait for a space in the traffic. 'Nope. We'll soon check it out, though.'

Silence again. Flavia fidgeted with her handbag. How on earth were they going to fill the hour or so until she could decently suggest they went home? This was awful. She'd been so... so keen for them to get together, desperate, even, but it wasn't going to happen, and when she thought about it with her brain switched on, she knew that and didn't even want to get together any more. They were friends and workmates, end of, and she would make sure he understood that before she was three seconds older.

'A waiter from a restaurant up near where we went hiking on Sunday was really kind after I was rescued,' she said wildly. 'He brought coffee for Ralph and me. I must go up there soon and thank him properly. I'm going to look him up and buy him a drink.'

'Good they all took care of you. Are you fully recovered now?'

'Yes, thanks, apart from a few bruises. I'm glad Carol can still go to England tomorrow.'

It was more meaningless conversation, but at least talking about Carol and the wedding blessing lasted them all the way to the new bistro, which turned out to be a crowded little café on the main road. Loud music was blaring into the street, and Alex stood still.

'Um... no, thanks. Have you eaten? Let's go for a pizza. On me.'

'Okay.' That sounded as if he wanted to talk about something, so this was going to be about his mother, wasn't it? They retraced their steps and went into the pizzeria next to the station, and Flavia relaxed. Denise was a good topic of conversation. Alex didn't seem to be sharing her feeling of awkwardness, because he was chatting comfortably with the waiter, who suggested Flavia's favourite red wine and some nibbles before their pizza.

Alex clinked with her as soon as the wine arrived, then leaned across the table. 'I need to ask your opinion about Ma.'

Flavia sipped glumly. She'd been right. But this was what she wanted, wasn't it? Friends only. 'She's doing incredibly well, isn't she? Or is there a problem I don't know about?'

Alex speared an olive. 'Indirectly, yes. Do you think she would cope if I went to live in Zurich?'

Wow. Good job she wasn't still hankering after him as much as she used to – a few months ago, that question would have sent her plummeting into the depths of despair. Flavia thought for a moment. A superficial answer wasn't what was needed here.

'I think she would. You could organise some extra support for her, especially for the first couple of weeks – nothing official, she'd hate that, just some friends who were aware that she might be feeling a bit lonely. I'd help, and so would Stacy, and I could mention it to the team at the library.'

'Yes... and there's the people she does cakes for, and sewing. Some of them would help too. And people like Margrit at the hotel. But you don't think she'd be fretting away inside? That would be my big worry.'

Flavia took another sip of wine. This wasn't easy. 'Alex, if Denise thought you were truly happy, she'd be so delighted she wouldn't have space in her head to fret. Are you and Zoe together again?' There, she'd asked that just like a friend would.

He pressed his lips together for a long moment before answering her. 'We do want to try again, and there's an admin vacancy in the orchestra team coming up. It would be ideal. I haven't mentioned it to Ma yet. I don't see how I can leave her here and not hate myself.'

'She'll be absolutely fine. Go for it, Alex.'

The look he gave her was positively vulnerable. 'Thanks, Flavia. It's what I want, and in the circumstances, I'm pretty sure I'll get the job, though I'd be gutted to leave Lakeside.'

'We'd cope, don't worry.' Flavia remembered something. 'Has Denise said anything to you about moving to Grimsbach? She mentioned it to me this week.'

His eyes widened. 'Not a word. That would be great. She'd have everything much closer, and you and Stacy too. Wow...'

Talking about looking for flats in Grimsbach, and other ways to help Denise, lasted them all though the pizzas. They left the restaurant shortly before nine with Alex looking much happier and Flavia feeling rather proud of herself. She'd managed that beautifully, all things considered. And now for the final nail in the coffin for her crush on Alex. She waved a hand at the station, where a small crowd was waiting on platform one.

'There's a train in five minutes, I'll get that. No sense you driving all the way back to Grimsbach when the train's quicker, is there?'

He stared. 'Sure? Okay. And thanks for your advice, and all the help you're giving Ma already.'

'She's my friend. Thanks for the pizza.'

Flavia kissed his cheek – just like a real friend would – and fished out her phone to buy her ticket for the three-minute journey to Grimsbach. Alex waved as the train left, then Flavia flopped back in her seat and heaved the deepest sigh ever.

He would go, wouldn't he? And he and Zoe would make it work this time round, though Denise might not be quite as unaware of what was going on as Alex thought. That sudden plan to move to Grimsbach hadn't come out of nowhere, and Denise would know that living within a short walk of the hotel and several of her friends would make it so much easier for Alex to go.

The train trundled along then pulled up at Grimsbach, and Flavia got out. Two more minutes and she'd be home. She thrust her hand into the jacket pocket where she always kept her keys – and found a large hole that had replaced the tiny one she'd noticed a day or two ago. She stood still, searching frantically, but her keyring was definitely gone, and tonight was getting better and better... Okay, Flavia, think. She'd have noticed if the keys had dropped out while she was wearing the jacket, unless it had happened in Alex's car. But that was unlikely. They'd probably fallen out when she was at Lakeside. She'd try there first, anyway.

Reception was deserted, though there was still a murmur of voices from the terrace bar, where the glow of lamps was illuminating the tables as darkness approached. Flavia went straight to the staff cloakroom where her jacket had been all day – no keys. Bummer. Could she have lost them in the restaurant loos while she'd been faffing around with her make-up? She'd chucked the jacket down on the chair there. A quick search revealed nothing, though, and Flavia sighed. Looked like she was going to have to disturb the neighbour who had her spare key. The one remaining hope was the lost property box in the reception office, which was now closed. Flavia jabbed the button for the lift. Ralph and Carol were the last people she should be interrupting on their evening off, but needs must.

It was Carol who opened the flat door. Flavia explained, and the older woman grinned.

'I think you're in luck. Someone handed in keys at the restaurant earlier, so they're in the office. I'll come down with you.'

The keys in the office were hers, and relief washed over Flavia. She leaned against the table, her keys clutched in her hand. Funny how your legs went all weak when the worst didn't happen.

Carol perched on a chair. 'How are you? I keep wondering when we'll be able to put our escapade behind us and just enjoy life!'

Flavia pulled a face. 'I know. It was worse for you, though, all that time.'

Carol shook her head. 'It wasn't. I was safer in a cave than you were on that slope, and I knew I'd be found eventually. I think Ralph suffered more, not knowing anything.' Her eyes were bleak, and Flavia shifted over to put an arm around her. 'Safer in a cave' was only true if it was a smallish landslide, but she wasn't going to point that out. Should she tell Carol about Ralph being so upset last night? But then, Carol knew him.

'He needs time too. He'll get over it, Carol, don't worry.'

'I do worry, though. He's pushing me away, Flavia. It's as if he can't let me in because if anything did happen to me again, he'd be even more hurt. He says he can't change how he feels, but... I don't know. I don't know what's going to happen.'

Heck... that didn't sound good. Flavia hugged harder. 'You both need to give it time. Go to England, enjoy yourselves, and think about other things. You need a bit of distance from it all.'

Carol mopped her eyes. 'I know. You sounded like Stacy there. Thanks, Flavia.'

Flavia left the hotel with her keys safely in her handbag and her heart glowing in spite of the doleful conversation. She sounded like Stacy, did she? Now that was a compliment...

25

THURSDAY, 20TH JUNE

Stacy spent the first hour of Thursday morning sitting at the kitchen table nursing a mug of coffee. The most positive word you could use about the day before their wedding blessing was – so far – 'challenging'. Her mother had been up since six and was now in a flap due to a mix-up with the hairdresser, and nothing anyone said could convince her it would be okay on the day. A breakfast time text to say that Ralph and Carol's flight had been cancelled was the last straw, as far as Mum was concerned, and although they'd been given an alternative flight which would get them in only an hour or two later than the original one, it was as if her mother enjoyed being stressed out of her mind. None of them were saying the right things, either. There was no right thing to say, when her mother was in this mood.

Stacy met Rico's eyes across the table – poor Rico too, this wasn't what he needed during the countdown to the big do. He wasn't saying much, but she knew he was dreading tomorrow, and with every word Mum uttered, the silence hovering over Rico grew gloomier. Dad was no help either, he appeared to have shrunk into himself as he sat there spooning up his cornflakes, not meeting anyone's eyes.

Stacy got up to make more coffee for everyone. 'Mum – stop it. You'll frighten us all into an early grave if you carry on like this.' She grasped her mother's shoulders and pushed her into a chair. The same look of relief flashed over Rico's and Dad's faces when Janie heaved a sigh and sipped the coffee Stacy gave her.

'All I want is for everything to be perfect for you, darling.'

'And all I need for it to be perfect is Rico, you and Dad, and Ralph and Carol,' said Stacy firmly.

Rico leaned over and kissed her. 'Well said, Frau Weber. Janie, whatever happens, it'll be fine.'

'Exactly. It's not as if we're keeping up appearances, is it?' said Stacy, lifting an eyebrow at her mother.

Rico gave her a 'what are you talking about?' kind of look while Dad spluttered into his coffee, but at least there was comparative peace in the kitchen again. Stacy grimaced round the table.

***

It was early afternoon when Stacy pulled up in the car park at Manchester Airport and heaved a sigh. The traffic en route had been worse than Zurich and Basle combined, but at least Mum and Dad had stayed at home.

Rico clapped her shoulder. 'Well done. I'll drive back, if you like?'

Stacy gave him a push. He'd spent half the journey with his eyes shut. 'It wasn't that bad, was it?'

'Not at all. But it's not fair to let you do all the tough stuff.'

Stacy laughed. 'Liar. Oh, you can drive home. But I bet it takes us twice as long to get there with you behind the wheel on the "wrong" side of the car! Come on, let's get into the rabble.'

The airport was as chaotic as usual, but Ralph and Carol's new flight arrived on time. Stacy was glad to see that both seemed their usual selves, though of course they wouldn't be. But no use thinking like that – distraction was the name of the game for now, then a good talk at some point when they had the peace to talk in.

Rico, true to his word, settled into the driving seat. Stacy was glad to sit in the back with Carol – it gave her chance to get a proper look at the older woman. You could see where scrapes and scratches on Carol's face had been skilfully covered up. Ralph was in good form in the front, joking with Rico, but he was an expert at hiding what he was feeling. It would take something truly momentous to make Ralph lose control, and Stacy knew he'd been closer to doing that last Sunday than at any time since she'd known him. They inched through the afternoon traffic with Ralph teasing Rico about his driving, and Stacy met Carol's eyes and pointed discreetly to Ralph, her eyebrows raised. Carol gave her a thumbs up behind the passenger seat with the hand that wasn't in plaster, then made a 'more or less' movement. Stacy nodded. It was likely to be more 'less' than 'more', but Carol wouldn't want to worry her.

Rico braked to avoid a van that pulled out in front of him. 'Jeez! Does nobody indicate here?'

'You're not used to north of England traffic.' Stacy reached out to rub his shoulder. He'd driven in England last year, but there was no comparing the streets of Elton Abbey to Manchester. Poor Rico's shoulders stayed up by his ears until they pulled up in front of Pen 'n' Paper.

The family were gathered upstairs, and Janie handed round glasses of fizz to toast the new arrivals.

'To the happy couple,' said John, raising his glass.

'To all the happy couples.' Stacy looked round their little group. Mum and Dad, her and Rico, Ralph and Carol, Gareth and Jo... they were all happy, weren't they? She wanted everyone to be happy at her wedding. And heck, she was as bad as Mum. At her wedding *blessing*.

Afterwards, Gareth and Jo went home to get ready for dinner at the hotel, and Stacy drove Ralph and Carol the three minutes through town while her mother chivvied Dad and Rico into a few glad rags. Both men listened to her instructions about looking their second best – presumably their best was to be saved for tomorrow – with hangdog expressions, and Stacy left the house grinning from ear to ear.

She was less amused when she pulled up at the Abbey Hotel. A year or two ago, it had been a comfortable family hotel set in rambling gardens, but it hadn't half had a facelift. It was now as different to the previous homely atmosphere as it could possibly be. Pillars by the door, marble steps with alternating red and white begonias regimented on either side – no wonder the reception was the price it was.

'Very swish,' said Ralph, manhandling the cases from the boot.

Stacy grimaced. It was a bit too swish to be comfortable, but hopefully the staff were good at their jobs and would make everyone feel at home.

She pulled Carol to one side while Ralph took the luggage in. 'He seems okay, Carol – I'm sure it'll be fine in the end, you know.'

Carol sniffed dolefully. 'I'm hoping this weekend will be good for him, Stacy, though we'll have to talk more about coping with stress together, instead of him shutting himself away from everyone. For a day or two there, I wasn't sure we'd make it as a couple, he was so scared and so closed off from me. I'm going to whisk him off to Friedrichshafen after, ah, um – when things settle down again, and have a good heart-to-heart. And now that we're well away from home, I'll have a word about enjoying ourselves in England.'

Stacy squinted at her. Carol had gone a bit pink, and she was gabbling now, what was that about? But a porter arrived for the rest of the luggage, and the private moment was over.

Back home, the family were almost ready to leave, and Stacy rushed to change before her mother offered to help her. Ten minutes later, she arrived in the living room only slightly out of breath.

Janie jumped up immediately. 'Good, you're here. Come along, everyone. It's a lovely evening, so let's walk over to the hotel, then we can all enjoy a glass of wine.' Without waiting for an answer, she bundled John into his jacket, and half a minute later they were outside in the warm summer air.

Stacy seized the opportunity for a quick word with Rico while her parents were locking up. 'Be warned, the hotel isn't the small family affair I remember from last time I was there.'

He barely had time to nod before Janie was behind them, steering them along the street. They took the short route through the park, then Janie pulled John firmly to the front of their little procession to lead the way up to the three-storey whitewashed house.

Rico was frowning, and Stacy gripped his arm. She could sympathise with the waves of negativity coming from him. This hotel wasn't the kind of eatery her parents usually went to – so why now? Then she caught sight of Janie's proud, happy face, and her heart melted. A wedding blessing was special, after all, a once in a lifetime thing, and Mum was trying her best to make the day as perfect as possible, that was all. The fact that they might not want something so ostentatious wouldn't have entered Janie's head.

Ralph and Carol were waiting in the bar, and Stacy nudged Rico. There was no sign of stress about Ralph tonight; judging by his grin and the way he was bobbing up and down, looking from one person to another, something was entertaining him hugely. It was unlikely to be the prospect of dinner with his son's in-laws, so... was it whatever he was planning about MJ? And please, please, that mustn't be a huge and horrible painting. Ralph's purple shirt leapt into sudden focus, and Stacy's heart plummeted. Yikes...

Rico pulled her over to his father while John and Janie were talking to the restaurant host, and spoke in a low voice.

'Like to share, Dad?'

Ralph winked at him. 'Nope.'

Stacy accepted a glass of prosecco and sipped glumly. One – nil to Ralph.

Janie joined them, and peered down at Carol's usual stilettos. 'So elegant, Carol, dear. I'm glad you don't have to walk far tonight, though. It's all too easy to lose your balance when you're older, isn't it?'

'Oh, I'm used to them, don't worry.'

Carol's eyebrows were hitting the ceiling, and Stacy turned a laugh into a cough then sipped her prosecco again. This was turning into an episode of Fawlty Towers... Rico sidled over to his father and spent the next few minutes trying to get the latest news about Lakeside and a hint about MJ out of his father, but Ralph only laughed.

'You're on honeymoon, Rico. Leave the work until next week. Lakeside's fine.'

He exchanged a grin with Carol, and Stacy gave up. Two – nil to Ralph, and something was definitely amusing him – but possibly the quickest way to be told about it was to pretend not to notice.

'Mum's got a lovely tie and waistcoat all ready for you for tomorrow,' she told Ralph, enjoying the apprehensive expression that immediately crossed his face.

'Yes – you'll all look perfect,' said Janie happily.

Stacy giggled. It was two – one now. Gareth and Jo arrived with baby Tom just as the restaurant host swooped up.

'Mr and Mrs Townsend – your table's ready when you are.'

Stacy took her seat between Rico and her father at the round table, feeling grudging admiration for the shining glasses, the immaculate and bewildering array of cutlery and perfectly sized floral decorations. They should start a fine-dining evening once a month at Lakeside and put on something special and exclusive, like they'd done with the Gala Dinners during Advent last year. Rob the chef would definitely be up for it.

'Don't worry,' John whispered in her ear. 'This is the dead posh bit, and it's our treat. You won't mind tomorrow's do being in the merely moderately posh bit, will you?'

Stacy giggled, and passed the message on to Rico, who all but rolled his eyes. Stacy was glad when little Tom caused a diversion by catching sight of a basket of bread on the table and shrieking. His mother handed him a slice, and Tom munched his way solemnly through it, kindly handing over the odd morsel to Rico beside him. Stacy glowed inside. This was great – for the first time since she'd known him, Rico was interacting with a baby, and that could only be a good thing.

The waiter arrived with the starter – artichokes with parmesan butter – and Stacy sat back. Whatever else, tonight's dinner was definitely going to be memorable.

***

Flavia handed over a new key card to the apologetic guest who had somehow managed to fold his for the second time that week, rendering it useless. Fifteen minutes left of her shift, and she had tomorrow off, thank goodness. This time yesterday she'd been anticipating her date-that-wasn't-a-date with Alex; tonight she was heading home for a solitary supper and an early night, and boy, she could use the extra sleep. The hotel was full, and Ralph and Carol's departure at lunchtime had left an oddly rudderless feel about the place. Alex had been moody all day, too; there was little of their newly found friends-only relationship evident now. Had he spoken to his mother about his plan to move to Zurich? Maybe Denise hadn't coped with the idea after all.

Flavia gave the desk a quick tidy for Maria, due any moment. She was about to put the book someone had left on the terrace in the office for safekeeping, when the phone rang.

'Lakeside Hotel, Flavia Schneider here.'

'It's Baumann Boats in Rorschach. Can I speak to Alex, please?'

Flavia smiled to herself. This would be about the top-secret pedalos, but Alex had gone to a meeting with Rob the chef to organise what they were doing about a Welcome Home aperitif for Stacy and Rico next week.

'He's in a meeting at the moment. Can I take a message?'

'Can you tell him to call as soon as possible? Today would be good.'

'I'll make sure he gets back to you before he leaves.' Flavia rang off. By the sound of that, there was a problem with the pedalos.

Maria arrived, and Flavia spent the next few minutes updating her about the day's events on reception, and was about to phone Alex when he stomped across the hallway.

'Oh, Alex – Baumann Boats called. You have to phone back today.'

Alex stopped dead and glared at her. 'For heaven's sake! You should have let me know immediately!'

Flavia bristled. She wasn't going to put up with that. 'If he'd needed to speak to you right that moment he'd have said so. He said, and I quote, "as soon as possible, today would be good". That didn't sound to me as if I had to drag you out of a meeting there and then.'

Alex gave her a withering look and went into the office, banging the door behind him.

Flavia gaped at Maria. 'Good luck when he comes out of there. I'm off.' She marched through the front door, fuming. No matter what was going on in Alex's life, there was no excuse for rudeness. A brisk walk home was time enough for her anger to turn to concern, and she flopped down on the sofa to call Denise.

'Is Alex okay? Only he's up one moment, and down the next.'

'Oh, I don't know what's going on with him, Flavia. I told him at lunchtime about my plans to look for a place in Grimsbach, and he was pretty non-committal. I thought he'd be delighted.'

'Did he say anything... more?'

'No. Like what?'

'Oh, I don't know. D'you fancy going for lunch tomorrow? I can pick you up.' Flavia made the arrangements, then put her phone down. Interesting. Alex hadn't told his mother about possibly moving to Zurich. Why not?

26

Friday, 21st June

A knock on the bedroom door roused Stacy from a lovely sleepy doze, and she jerked upright while Rico groaned and pulled the duvet over his head.

'Are you awake? Wedding day breakfast coming up!' The door opened and Janie came in with an enormous tray, which she laid at the bottom of the bed. 'Scrambled egg with smoked salmon, toast and heather honey or whisky marmalade, coffee, and juice,' she announced. 'And the paper – your blessing announcement's in it!'

Stacy sat back as her mother swished the curtains open and let in the day, and hallelujah, it was sunny outside. 'Wow, thanks, Mum. This smells lovely.'

Janie was all smiles. 'Have a nice leisurely breakfast, darlings, then we're going to send all the boys to Gareth's, and have us girls here to get ourselves ready for the blessing.'

She left them to it, and Stacy poked Rico. 'You can come out now. And brekkie looks amazing.' She handed a plate of scrambled egg to Rico, who emerged looking unexpectedly cheerful.

'A morning at Gareth's sounds about right. I'll try to have a private word with Dad, too, and check he really is okay. Do you reckon we'll have lunch there?'

'No idea. Just let it happen. Our mission today is to keep Mum happy – and have a good time.' She attacked her egg, remembering how they'd breakfasted in bed on their wedding day. Hopefully

Ralph would have a happy day too. He'd been fine at dinner yesterday, but come to think of it, he'd packed away a lot of booze, and he'd had problems with that in the past. Drowning your sorrows wasn't the way to get rid of them. It was still early days after his fright, though. They could tackle it all together when they were home again, and meanwhile, they had a wedding – sorry, blessing – to enjoy.

Rico was flipping through the paper. 'Here we are.' He pushed the announcements page across to Stacy, who wiped her fingers on her nightie before touching it. *Mr and Mrs John Townsend are happy to announce...*

'Très chic. We can put it in our album, later – of course we're having a wedding album!' She gave Rico a little push, but his raised eyebrows and astonished face were only there to tease her – weren't they?

'You're the boss.' Rico reached for the toast.

Stacy was in her dressing gown in the kitchen when the doorbell rang downstairs. A few minutes later, Emily and Carol appeared, and Janie ushered John out to join Alan in his car. 'Rico, dear, out you go too.'

Rico put his arms around Stacy. 'See you at the church, Mrs.'

For a moment, she clung to him – it would have been fun to get ready together, but this was her mother's show. At least Emmy was here to help if Mum went into orbit.

She watched the car drive off, then turned to Emily. 'You look great – you must have reached the radiant and blooming part of being pregnant.'

'I feel fine now, thankfully. What shall we–'

The summons came from the hallway. 'Girls! Here's Babs to do your nails!'

By midday, Stacy's nails and hair were done and she was relaxing in the living room with Emily, Jo and Carol. Mum had insisted on shutting herself into the kitchen to make lunch, so what was coming now was anyone's guess.

'It'll be something posh, bless her,' said Emily, kicking a ball across the floor to baby Tom, who was sitting at his mother's feet. 'Warm duck salad, or tiny salmon sandwiches – but not from a tin, of course!'

Stacy snorted. 'Mum's having such a good time, isn't she? We'd better make sure we don't ruin our nails or hair while we're eating, that's all. We want to keep the peace.'

It was hard not to laugh when Janie called them into the kitchen to eat Spaghetti Napoli with a green side salad.

'I read an article recently that said this is the best meal to have before exams, or anything that might make you nervous,' she said, glaring suspiciously at the beaming faces around the table. 'I made it with fresh tomatoes, and there's only a tiny pinch of chilli, just in case. What's so funny?'

'We thought you'd be making something candlelight supper-ish,' said Emily. 'But this is much better. Fab idea, Janie.'

After lunch, Stacy was ushered into her room to do her make-up and get dressed, with Janie hovering between her and Emily. Carol and Jo, lucky people, were allowed to do their own thing in Janie's bedroom.

'Mum, we're fine,' said Stacy at last, attaching her fascinator and twirling in front of the mirror. 'Why don't you get into your own outfit now – we don't want the mother of the bride to look as if her clothes have been thrown on!'

'I never throw my clothes on, dear,' said Janie, blowing a kiss at Stacy. 'But you're right – the cars will be here in half an hour.'

Stacy wandered back to the living room. Was Rico ready? Someone would have to help him with his tie; a double Windsor knot was still beyond him. She thought back to their Swiss wedding day, remembering how she'd stood behind him and tied it for him. School uniforms were good for something...

'Girls! The cars are here! Don't forget your flowers!' Janie was back in full organising mode, and Stacy allowed her mother to accompany her into the car as if she was wearing a traditional long dress. Some of the neighbours and other shop owners were on the pavement to see them off, and good wishes came from all directions – English only, this time. And oh, how lovely that they'd had sunny weather both times.

Another little crowd was waiting at the church, and Stacy waved her flowers then went with her father and Emily to wait in the vestibule. The others went on inside, where little Tom soon discovered that the church made his voice sound splendidly hollow, and babbled away at full volume.

A few random notes sounded as the organist settled down at his instrument. Stacy craned her neck, but she couldn't see him from here, and good grief, why had she never thought to ask what music Mum might have arranged? Heaven knew what was coming now. Or was it...?

'Are we having "Here Comes the Bride", Dad?'

John guffawed. 'Stacy, your mother arranged this. Of *course* we're having "Here Comes the Bride". Ready?' He cocked his arm.

Tears rushed into Stacy's eyes as the opening notes sounded, and she and her father set off down the aisle with Emily a few steps behind. Look how happy Mum was, turning to watch them. As they'd arranged, people were sitting on both sides of the aisle, to make it less obvious that few Webers were here – and the flowers were absolutely perfect. And there was Rico waiting for her, and oh, this would be the best wedding – no, blessing – ever.

***

The echoing sounds of the organ vibrated through the church, drowning out Tom's small voice, and the heady smell of roses was everywhere. Rico breathed in deeply, trying to quash his nerves. He grabbed Stacy's hand as soon as she arrived beside him, and she gave him her usual grin. Phil the vicar was beaming at them both, looking very much the part today in a long white gown with a broad black stole slung around his neck and falling down his front.

'Welcome, Stacy and Rico, welcome, the Townsend and Weber families and friends to the blessing of the happy pair in front of us. I'm delighted to...'

The words washed over Rico's head as Phil explained the meaning of the blessing ceremony, which was also known as a Service of Prayer and Dedication, carried out to acknowledge the commitment made by a couple in a civil ceremony like they'd had. Rico didn't let go of Stacy's hand, and she rubbed her thumb against his. Phil announced the first hymn, and everyone stood up for *All Things Bright and Beautiful*, which even baby Tom sang along to.

Then came the blessing of the rings, which Alan as best man had in his pocket. Rico wasn't sure if this was part of every blessing, or if it was a kind of almost-a-wedding thing organised by Janie – she had expected Alan to have the rings in Switzerland, too. Whichever it was, Phil the vicar held out his bible, and Alan placed the rings on the open page. The atmosphere in the church was electric as first Rico, then Stacy repeated their vows. Janie was sniffing in the background, and Stace had tears in her eyes too. Rico cleared his throat, amazed that he'd managed to get through his own part without stumbling over the words, then slid the newly blessed wedding ring back onto Stacy's finger, feeling rather pleased with himself. A few more words from Phil, and they'd be done. The photographer was waiting at the back of the church; these would be more formal wedding pics than the Lakeside ones, but the church grounds were lovely. Rico relaxed his shoulders, then – what the heck? A sudden ripple of disquiet was surging around the church, and Rico lifted his head, sniffing. Others were doing the same, and heck – was that smoke he could smell?

A louder murmur came from the congregation, then a piercing bell rang somewhere deep inside the building.

'...and may God be with you always, amen and that's the fire alarm, folks. We'd better evacuate. That way, please.' Phil raced through his closing words, then pointed to the front entrance before diving off in the other direction.

Rico held on tightly to Stacy's hand as they joined the stampede down the aisle to the door. Outside, the wedding party regrouped at a safe distance in the church grounds, the photographer snapping in all directions as a large red fire engine swerved up, siren wailing. A clutch of firemen leapt down and vanished into the church.

Stacy's eyes were round. 'Rico Weber, can we not get married or blessed or go on honeymoon or anything without some kind of emergency service joining in?'

Ralph was shaking with laughter. He came over and put one arm around Rico and the other around Stacy, and squeezed. 'Ach, Kinder! To be honest, I wondered if it was a good idea coming here after last weekend's near disaster, but this is marvellous!'

Rico's heart sank like a stone at the unmistakable aroma of whisky coming from his father. Had that been one quick nip to calm Dad's nerves, or glug after secret glug to deaden the pain whenever no one was watching? He looked round for Carol, but she was standing with Emily's parents a little distance away.

'Oh, my!' Janie's face was an absolute picture as horror and humour combined chased across it.

Everyone was craning their necks to see if there was any sign of fire, but there wasn't. Two firemen came out of the building again and began to set up a wide tube of some kind. They didn't seem too worried, which had to be a good sign. Didn't it?

'Do you suppose it's the boiler again?' Stacy stood on tiptoe beside him to see better.

'I guess it must be.' Rico called to the firemen, 'Are we on fire?'

One of them shouted back, 'No fire, just smoke – we'll blow it outside and you can get on with your wedding in peace and quiet.'

The wedding party and the gathering crowd of onlookers cheered.

'I think we've finished, haven't we? Let's get over to the hotel and take the rest of the photos there.' John came up behind Rico and Stacy.

'Finished? We are so not finished,' said Stacy. 'I want a pic of Rico and me beside the fire engine, and one of us with some firemen, too.' She trotted over to the photographer and they went into a huddle with one of the firemen.

Rico slapped John's shoulder. 'And you thought my stag do was entertaining... that was nothing compared to your wedding blessing.'

Fifteen minutes later, the fire service was ready for them.

'Right,' said the photographer. 'We'll have the bride, groom and all the parents in front of the fire engine, please, and you–' he beckoned to the chief fireman, '–in the middle.'

It was the start of a hilarious sequence of photos. Alan murmured in Rico's ear as Stacy and her mother were posing with two burly firemen. 'The press have arrived. Reckon we'll be in the local paper tomorrow.' He pointed to two young women busily taking photos and talking into a phone.

Emily giggled. 'Janie wanted wedding of the year in Elton Abbey – I reckon she's got it covered!'

Hugely entertained, Rico watched as the photographer finished off and loped across to where they were standing.

'I'll take the more traditional ones at the hotel, and get a selection over to you in a couple of hours,' he said. 'Thanks for the commission, Mrs Townsend – most interesting wedding I've ever done!' He hurried off to the car park.

'They're expecting us at the hotel, darlings.'

Janie's voice was plaintive, and Rico grinned. She wanted to get the celebration back on more traditional lines, that was clear. He slung an arm around her. 'Janie, thank you – we'll never forget today.'

After a series of photos in the hotel garden, the photographer left to do his magic and the wedding party adjourned for dinner. Rico took his seat beside Stacy at the top table, then noticed a large white envelope between their place settings, addressed to them both in silver lettering and with a shiny white bow around two roses embossed on the front. Wow – this was very posh.

Stacy lifted it and slid a knife along the top. 'It's a card,' she said unnecessarily, pulling it out.

Rico leaned over and read the message on the inside. *Happy Wedding Blessing Day! I'll see you at Lakeside next week, and don't worry – once I get there, I'll never be leaving again... MJ xxx*

27

Friday, 21st June

Flavia emerged from the spa ten minutes before her shift was due to end on Friday afternoon. Behind the desk, Alex was having what sounded like an extremely complicated discussion about golf courses with one of the guests, but his usual smile was absent today, and Flavia deposited the spa shop basket in the office without interrupting. All she could do was hope he and Zoe, as well as he and Denise, managed to sort themselves out over the weekend; but Alex was working both days, so he wasn't going to have too much time to do his sorting. Flavia grimaced. Lucky guy. Time to herself sounded like the worst idea in the world right this minute. The busier, the better, then she wouldn't dwell on the lonely mess her life was. She had spa duty plus reception all day on Sunday, and tomorrow she was going shopping with Vreni from housekeeping, and hopefully Vreni wouldn't want all the lurid details about her accident last weekend. Flavia pushed down the memory of clinging to that tree as the hillside slid towards the valley. It was over. Finished. Finito.

Determinedly cheerful, she went to the cloakroom for her things. Tomorrow she'd have to sort out her own programme, but Sunday was going to be fun. For one thing, the surprise Ralph had planned for Stacy and Rico was due to arrive. Not that anyone had said so officially, but they were having a swanky aperitif on the terrace for Stacy and Rico coming home, and presumably the surprise was part of that. The hotel was staying open, but the spa, the restaurant and the terrace were being closed to non-residents after lunch on Sunday, so whatever was coming must be pretty special. Lucky Stacy and Rico.

Flavia bit her lip. Pity her social life wasn't as exciting as her working, life, wasn't it? Here she was, Friday night, nothing to do and no one to do it with. She wandered out to the terrace to see if anyone was sitting at the staff table, but no one was. Oh, well. Time to go home.

'Flavia, there's someone at the desk for you!' Robin, one of the waiters, swept past with two banana splits.

Flavia trudged back into the hotel. Had Denise come to suggest a coffee or something? But Robin knew Denise; she wasn't 'someone'. She marched into reception, then did a proper double-take at the slight figure gazing up at the map of the area they had pinned on the wall above the sofa. Ooh – this was the young waiter who'd brought her and Ralph coffee on Sunday. She could say thank you properly. Pity she hadn't been anywhere near a mirror for the past several hours... On the other hand, even after a full day in the spa, she could be pretty sure she'd look better now than she had last Sunday.

She ignored Alex's inquisitive face and went over to – help, she didn't even know his name. He turned and gave her a smile as she crossed the hallway – and wow. He was what you might call drop dead gorgeous, wasn't he? She hadn't noticed that on Sunday. Black hair falling attractively across his forehead, a lovely smile and shining brown eyes that were looking straight at her... Flavia swallowed. A bloke like this would have a queue of girlfriends waiting for him every day of the week, and here he was asking to see her. He'd probably asked for Ralph too, of course, but he was out of luck there.

'Hello!' she said brightly. 'I'm glad you're here – I can say a proper thank you for Sunday. That was the best coffee I've had in my life!'

He laughed. 'When I saw the state of you I was sorry I hadn't brought chicken soup, or something more nourishing! Or brandy.'

Flavia wrinkled her nose. 'I wouldn't have thanked you for brandy. Can I tempt you to a Lakeside Hotel coffee? We have a fabulous terrace. Or you could have chicken soup, if you like. Or brandy.'

He laughed again, and Flavia glowed. She led him to the corner of the terrace furthest from the staff table, showed him the menu, and ordered two iced coffees when he'd chosen. She didn't want to read too much into it, but this was going rather well. He was the easiest person in the world to talk to. His name was Ivo Schwarz, and he had a summer job at Die Trauben until he started a new job as waiter in a trendy new hotel opening in September in St Gallen. He wanted to know all about her, too, asking about her family, and her job in the hotel and what it was like, living in the area. He'd done his training in Zurich and worked there and in Winterthur, and best of all, while he told her all about his parents and sister in Rafz, there was no mention of a girlfriend. She wouldn't ask, decided Flavia. If this was meant to be, it would be.

Talk flew back and forth across the table for a good hour, before Ivo drained his iced coffee glass and touched her hand quickly on the tabletop. 'Best iced coffee I've had for a long time. Flavia, I should go, I promised my mum I'd call her tonight and she blethers on for hours, bless her. It's been great, meeting you – could we do this again? Maybe in St Gallen?'

Wow, oh wow – he was asking her out. Flavia's fingers shook as she pulled out her phone. 'I'd like that. Here's my number. You can text me sometime.'

He put her number into his phone, then tapped connect to make sure it was right. Flavia's phone buzzed, but not half as hard as her head was buzzing. This could be the start of something... of something. Take it slowly, Flavia. Play it cool.

She walked to the car park with him, and it felt like the most natural thing in the world when he kissed her cheek and drove off, giving her a wave as he turned into the road. Flavia touched her cheek, then almost danced home. Her fifteen-year-old self wouldn't have washed for a week after that kiss. Hopefully he'd text her soon. She opened the door of her flat and was immediately hit by a wall of silence, a stark contrast to her fun, sociable evening, and the old, crippling self-doubt rose. Oh heck – but he'd be in touch. Wouldn't he?

Her phone pinged at nine o'clock, and Flavia's heart raced until she saw it was a message from Carol with, oh, my goodness, a photo of Stacy and Rico in their wedding gear, with a fire engine and two firemen beside them... What was going on? Flavia sent back a long row of question marks, and was still gaping at the photo when her phone rang.

'Carol? Was there a fire at the wedding blessing?'

'Almost!'

Carol explained, and Flavia laughed. 'If that didn't take your mind off last Sunday, I don't know what would. Is Ralph okay again?'

Silence for a second, then: 'I don't know. He–' A door banged in the background, then a murmur of voices came down the phone before Carol spoke quickly. 'I'm sure he will be. I need to go, they're getting ready for the dance. See you soon!'

The call ended, and Flavia flopped back in her chair. If Ralph wasn't okay, Carol wasn't either. She got up to make tea, mentally crossing all her fingers and toes that everything was going to work out for the couple. Carol had sounded odd, and those two belonged together. Like... like Alex and Zoe belonged together. A lump rose in Flavia's throat.

Her phone pinged again as she was opening a packet of chocolate fingers, and fizzling, painful hope rose in Flavia's chest when she saw it was from Ivo. *Great to meet you properly. Am working weekend but will text on Sun. Drink on Tues?*

Flavia punched the air, then tapped. *Tues sounds good. Great to meet you too. Speak soon!* She tapped send and sashayed back to her chair with the biscuits. There. They had a proper date. Almost.

***

The musicians were poised, and Stacy put her hand in Rico's as they took the floor for the bridal waltz. Mum hadn't realised until they were eating their dessert that Ralph wasn't familiar with the custom, and spent the rest of the meal telling him ALL about it.

The dinner had been exquisite and the service faultless, and Stacy could practically see Rico making mental notes for Lakeside. The main course was what Gareth described as posh chicken salad, but it was the posh bits that made it special, and compliments flew from all directions. The only speech afterwards was her father's, as Rico had refused point blank to make one, but as Stacy pointed out, it wasn't a wedding, and Janie fortunately accepted this. She'd got her way about the bridal waltz, though.

'Ready?' Stacy held out a hand to Rico, and he rolled his eyes.

'Sooner we start...'

The band struck up, and they moved off, hopefully looking as if they did this all the time. One round of the dance floor, then they were joined by Mum and Ralph and Dad and Carol, with Gareth, Jo, Emily and Alan joining in, then masses of other couples. People were still arriving, too. She recognised most of them, old neighbours, business contacts from Pen 'n' Paper, a few she'd known at school. A dance was a good idea after all; this was fun.

The next hour or so was spent chatting and catching up with people and being kissed and wished well, and Stacy dropped down on her chair at the top table at ten o'clock and fanned her face with a menu.

'How's Mrs Weber?' Her father sat down beside her.

'Happy. Big thanks to you and Mum for organising all this. It's amazing.'

John went off to fetch drinks, and Stacy looked round to see Carol hurrying over wearing a distinctly un-party-ish expression.

'Stacy, love, you're going to have to forgive Ralph and me for being party poopers. It's all a bit much after – you know. Ralph's gone upstairs already.'

That didn't sound like Ralph; he was a pro at parties. 'Is he all right? Are *you* all right?'

'We're fine. He's – merry, I guess you'd call it, and a bit embarrassed about it. We'll call you in the morning. Say goodnight to your parents from us, will you?' She kissed Stacy quickly, then wheeled round and fled the room.

Stacy stared after her. Well. Rico wasn't going to be happy about that. Ralph's relationship with alcohol was a complicated one; he had no problems when things were going well, but when they weren't... Oh, dear.

She was still considering this when Rico joined her, a large glass of cola in one hand. He plumped down beside her. 'Busy, isn't it?'

Stacy stole his glass for a sip. Dad must be caught up in the queue at the bar; he'd been gone for ages. She leaned back to see across the room. The top table was on a little dais, so they had a good view of the guests still trickling in, young people, mostly, and – did she actually recognise any of them? Uneasiness flared inside her. This was more like the influx after the pubs had closed, wasn't it? A rowdy influx, too.

Gareth strode up with a sleeping Tom in his arms. 'Where's Dad? We're being gatecrashed.'

Stacy's hands flew to her cheeks. 'Oh no! He went for drinks – what should we do?'

Gareth handed Tom to Rico. 'Sorry, he's pretty sticky. I'll fix this.'

If it hadn't been such an awful situation, Stacy would have laughed at the sight of Rico, completely taken aback with a sticky baby in his arms. Where were Mum and Jo? Gareth had vanished into the rabble on the floor, and Stacy craned her neck.

'What's going on?' Janie rushed up, her face white. 'Who are all these people? I need to–' She moved away, but Rico spoke in a voice Stacy hadn't often heard.

'No – sit down, Janie. Gareth's gone to fix things. You stay here.'

Janie sat down abruptly. The band had stopped playing, and the buzz of talking and, yes, shouting was ever louder. To Stacy's dismay, two large police officers, accompanied by the hotel manager, Gareth, and John, stepped onto the dais with a microphone.

The older officer spoke. 'Ladies and gents, there seems to be a misunderstanding here. This is a wedding party and it's a closed event. People who don't have a personal invitation from the family are kindly asked to leave.'

The manager took the microphone. 'Yes – wedding guests only in here. We have a public bar on the other side of the building which you are welcome to visit. Please leave this room quietly – thank you.'

The commotion increased before it decreased again and Stacy held her breath, but people *were* leaving. Thank goodness. She watched as the rabble trickled back out again, then the band started playing something quiet, and the atmosphere in the room relaxed. Well. That had been close.

John arrived back, and shook his head at his wife. 'A lot of these people were under the impression that extra guests were needed to make up the numbers here.'

Janie blanched. 'I did say to a few people that lots of dance guests would be nice…'

'Word gets around.' John spoke briefly, but Stacy could see he was annoyed. She reached out and patted her mother's hand.

'Never mind, Mum. After having the fire service to help, it seems right we have the police involved too.'

Janie gave her a look, and Stacy smiled back before turning to Rico, her heart melting at the sight of him. He was holding a sleeping Tom against his chest, and his expression could best be described as soppy as he gazed down into the rosy little face. Stacy leaned across to kiss the baby's head. Thanks, Tom. Being gatecrashed was worth it for this alone…

28

SATURDAY, 22ND JUNE

It was the first day of her life as a respectably blessed wife. They'd all slept late after last night's celebrations, and Stacy was clearing the breakfast dishes into the dishwasher when Rico, who'd seized the opportunity to go to the supermarket with John, arrived back in the kitchen with the older man.

He put a hand on Stacy's shoulder. 'Dad called. He and Carol are busy packing. Do you know anything about that?'

Stacy's eyebrows rose. 'I thought they were on the same flight as us tomorrow?'

'You and me both, but they're going at half two this afternoon. I said we'd go round to the hotel now and bring them here to say goodbye.'

'Oh – I'll get something ready for lunch, then.' Janie was still subdued after the dance last night.

'Coffee and a piece of wedding cake will be fine, Mum. I'm sure we're all still stuffed after our lovely dinner last night.'

Stacy went for her jacket. It was a normal Saturday morning in Elton Abbey as she and Rico crossed the park and continued up to the sumptuous entrance of the Abbey Hotel. Ralph and Carol were on the top floor, and Rico stepped across from the lift and tapped on the door.

Carol answered, sounding pretty cheerful. 'Come in!'

Stacy joined Rico in the doorway. 'Hi there – but why the earlier flight?'

Ralph was folding his suit trousers. 'Our flights were rescheduled, remember?'

Stacy was silent, her heart sinking. He wasn't meeting anyone's eyes, which wasn't like Ralph, and although Carol had sounded cheerful, there was an unusually drawn look about her face. Maybe all the activity after her ordeal last weekend had been too much. And it had been as much Ralph's ordeal too, in a different way. Rico seemed to be struck dumb, so Stacy carried on.

'That's a pity. I wanted to show you more of the village.'

Now Ralph did look at her properly, and Stacy's heart thudded to her boots. A hangover would explain the pallor, but the dejected posture was completely unlike him. He looked as if he'd won the lottery then lost it again.

Carol spoke gently. 'Another time, Stacy, and this is the best way. We're – I'm still tired, after last weekend, but it was such a lovely blessing and a wonderful party. I'll never forget it.'

Apprehension rose in Stacy. There was something Carol wasn't telling her. 'Will – will you be at Lakeside when we get back tomorrow? Or Lugano? Or...'

'Oh, Lakeside, of course.' Ralph gave her a strained smile. 'Don't forget MJ's imminent arrival!'

Only half-convinced, Stacy helped Carol fold her clothes, then they bundled the cases and bags down to reception to check out. She took charge of the two inflight bags while Rico and Ralph wheeled the cases through the park, walking in front of the women.

Stacy squinted across at Carol. 'Will you two be okay?

Carol's mouth drooped. 'I hope so. You know what Ralph's like when it comes to talking about the touchy-feely stuff, but don't worry. And not a word to your parents, Stacy Weber, or I'll tell them how the wedding party pitch invasion was the talk of the breakfast room in the Abbey Hotel this morning.'

Stacy stifled a laugh; it wasn't really funny... 'You heard about that, then.' Carol's mouth was twitching now too, and they both giggled. And Carol wouldn't be making jokes if anything was seriously wrong, would she? Every couple was allowed a blip in their relationship, and these two had a lot to cope with at the moment.

Back home, what Rico was calling the dance disaster was the last thing on Janie's mind.

'Stacy, the photographer's sent a link for the proof photos! I'll put them on the iPad and we'll have a good look. You can choose which ones you want hard copies of.'

Stacy went to help her father clear off the kitchen table so that they could all look at the proofs together. She couldn't help smiling – golly, married life wasn't half varied. One day you were swanning around in your best gear being photographed with the fire brigade and dancing with the love of your life at the most elegant dinner-dance ever, apart from an invasion when the pubs closed, and the next you were dashing about with a damp cloth in your hand and hardly any make-up on. But it would be fab to see the pics.

Scrolling through the photos on the iPad at the kitchen table turned into the best family bonding experience they'd had here. It was as if they were all glad to have something neutral and fun to talk about. Janie, who'd been shocked by the revelation that this was Ralph and Carol's last day, soon settled down to choose the photos she wanted in her end selection, with Stacy adding several too and Ralph chuckling over the fire brigade ones.

'You should get a selection of the fire engine ones and make a collage for the front hall at Lakeside,' he said to Rico, who was grinning too.

Jamie was appalled. 'The proper ones are so much nicer!'

Ralph went back to the iPad. 'Of course they are – but so much less of a talking point. Stacy, what do you think?'

He was back to his usual self, and Stacy searched around for an answer that would please everyone. 'We'll do a collage, but we'll have some proper ones there too, Mum, don't worry!'

Janie abandoned the topic. 'It's a pity you're leaving so soon, Ralph. I feel like Carol and I have barely seen each other.'

Again, it was Ralph who answered. 'There'll be other times, I'm sure. And someone should get back to see what's been happening at the hotel, and get things properly organised for the return of the bridal pair!'

Stacy's mind whirred. Ralph and Carol were smiling, but Ralph's answer had been a bit too pat there. Although – this early return could also be because of MJ, and whatever Ralph needed to organise for that. Perhaps he needed an extra day to rearrange Lakeside around a large-sized painting of a purple mountain. Or was he dying to leave to be able to talk properly to Carol? Or – heaven forbid – were both of them dying to leave because their relationship was in serious trouble?

'Rico and I will take you to the airport.' Stacy wiped her palms down her jeans. Carol and Ralph were nodding and smiling in unison. Surely there was nothing wrong... but she'd be a lot happier when she saw them back home at Lakeside and properly recovered from last weekend.

'Thank you, Stacy.' Ralph sat back in his chair.

It was hard, no, impossible to know how either of them really were. Carol remained silent – in fact she'd been silent for most of the time. Rico's voice was even, but Stacy could tell he was feeling emotional.

He leaned towards his father. 'I wish they hadn't changed both flights, Dad – couldn't they have stuck to your original departure day at least? It would have been fun to go home together.'

Ralph's expression was nothing but innocent. 'I didn't want to make a thing of it. Anyway – you're the one who always insists Lakeside comes first!' His smile appeared entirely genuine as he winked at Stacy.

'Ahem!' She rose to the challenge, and Ralph laughed.

'After your wife, of course!'

John was tapping around on his phone. 'Pull up the local paper on the iPad, Stace – there's a whole article about the wedding blessing on the front page!'

And it was back to family bonding as they pored over the iPad again, and in the laughter about the report with no less than three photos – Stacy and Rico and the head fireman, the complete wedding party in front of the fire engine, and baby Tom in the driver's seat – nothing more was said about rearranged flights. Still… Stacy flipped her phone open. There wasn't much time left, but she was going to do her utmost to have a quick chat with Carol before that flight left Manchester.

Her chance came a few minutes later, when Carol announced she was popping down to the newsagent's along the road for some British sweeties to take back for her grandchildren.

'I'll come too,' said Stacy immediately. 'I want some for Kim's kids, and the hotel employees too.'

She grabbed her cardie and joined Carol to go downstairs. For a few moments they walked without speaking, surrounded by the bustle of Saturday shoppers on the main street.

Carol broke the silence. 'I know you're worried, Stacy, but you and Rico have to leave this to Ralph and me to sort out. It's been a tumultuous couple of weeks. What we need is some quiet time to catch up with ourselves.'

Stacy nodded. That was all true. 'Promise me if you need help of any kind, you'll tell me.'

Carol took her arm. 'That's too big a promise, my love. But I promise you'll be the first to know if I need *your* help. Come on, here's the newsagent.'

Stacy had to be content with that, and it was the last private conversation she had with Carol, as they met Emily on the way out of the newsagent's and it was all baby talk after that. Stacy's heart was heavy as she helped Janie serve coffee and wedding cake afterwards. It felt as if there was a lot being left unsaid, but as Carol said, it was down to her and Ralph to sort it, and she shouldn't be worrying about her in-laws' relationship while she was still technically on her own honeymoon, anyway. Except – Carol wasn't her in-law, was she?

Rico hugged her to him as they stood at Manchester Airport, waving frantically as Carol and Ralph vanished into the crowd of travellers heading into the departure area.

'They'll soon be home, Stace, and you know, some of Dad's oddness might well be down to Martina Johanna. And if the surprise is a ghastly picture, we should accept it in the spirit it was given in. After all, lots of people seem to love Martina's artwork. It needn't put guests off being at Lakeside. Let's enjoy ourselves now the, um, official part of the trip's over.'

Stacy shrugged. 'I guess. We can only wait and see what happens with Ralph and Carol. Come on. Mum wants to visit the church again before we leave, so that'll have to be today. Your wedding blessing duties aren't over yet, Rico Weber.'

Wait and see, and hope for the best. It sounded easy when you said it quickly.

29

SATURDAY, 22ND JUNE

This time, Rico was pleased to realise he was managing the drive from the airport back to Elton Abbey more easily – at least he wasn't so uptight about it, and pulled up outside Pen 'n' Paper almost as if he'd done it every day for the past year. Almost.

Stacy lifted her bag from the back seat. 'Nicely done, Mr Weber. Okay, today is "keep Mum happy" day, right? I want her to have happy memories of all this, and what with Carol's accident and last night's invasion, we've had enough iffy stuff. She's taken a lot of trouble to do all this, and she loves us.'

Rico saluted, and slung an arm around her as they went back inside. He'd do anything for Stacy, and keeping Janie happy was easy enough; you only had to smile and agree to all her proposals, and after all, this time tomorrow they'd be flying over France. The bigger problem would come when he had to work out how they were going to pay for all this. Their share of the bill would arrive at the beginning of next month.

Janie was waiting with coffee and tiny sandwiches. 'A nice light snack, then we'll stroll down to the church and take a few more photos. Gareth and Jo are meeting us there.' Her gaze rested on Rico's jeans, and he flinched before he could stop himself.

Stacy saved him. 'Mum, we are *not* changing into our wedding gear.'

Fortunately, John was quick to agree, and Janie, who was wearing something rather similar to yesterday's dress and jacket, subsided.

The church was bathed in sunshine, exactly as it was at the start of the blessing, minus the onlookers. Janie grouped them all in front of a tub of summer flowers by the door, and they posed for selfies as well as the more distant photos. Rico was about to suggest a wander round the graveyard, which had some ancient and interesting gravestones, when a bang and a yell came from inside the church.

'That was Phil. Oh dear – I hope he isn't hurt! We'd better go and see.' Janie opened the main door, and they all trooped in behind her.

One glance at Phil striding down the aisle was enough to reassure Rico that no ambulance would be needed this time. The vicar was clutching the black cat they'd seen before, his scowl matching the cat's colour.

'Is anything wrong?' asked Janie unnecessarily, and Phil stopped short.

'It's the last straw. I don't mind stray cats making their home here, and he does catch the odd mouse, but he attacks the furnishings too. You should see what he's just done to the new vestry cushions. It's no good. I'm taking him to the vet, and she can decide if he goes to the cat home or – whatever.'

Janie scooped the cat from his arms as if he'd been about to throw it to the lions there and then. 'A stray! There, there, darling, we can't have that, can we? Look, John, doesn't he remind you of Snowy?'

Rico grabbed Stacy, and they both collapsed on the nearest pew, shaking with laughter.

Phil met Rico's eyes, a perplexed expression crossing his face. 'Snowy?'

Rico explained. 'We rescued a stray at home last summer, and Janie took a fancy to it. It was, ah, white, though. Hence the name. And female.'

'Apart from that, Mum, they're exactly the same!' Stacy joined in, and Janie looked sheepish.

'Well, they're both stray cats. What do you think, John?' She blinked at him, eyes pleading.

'Definitely both stray cats,' he agreed, then took pity on her. 'And of course we have room for him. As long as he doesn't vandalise our cushions.'

'Tell you what,' said Phil. 'I'll put a box together for you, with a couple of things for him, and I'll bring him over whenever suits you. I guess you have plans for this afternoon?'

'Bring him tomorrow afternoon,' said John. 'We're taking Stacy and Rico to the airport tomorrow, but we'll be home by three and we'll have all the time in the world for him.'

Rico wasn't surprised when Stacy went to hug her father. John was a master at keeping the peace as well as keeping Janie happy, but then, he'd had all his married life to practise.

***

Flavia joined a crowd of other Saturday shoppers on the platform at St Gallen main station, and shifted her bags to her other hand. She and Vreni had spent all day in town, and she'd bought a gorgeous summer dress in a kind of reddish chintzy pattern for her potential date with Ivo on Tuesday, and black strappy sandals, too, so hopefully it would stay dry. She peeked into the bag, smiling. He was texting tomorrow – or maybe he'd call.

The train arrived, and she found an empty group of four seats in the rearmost carriage, always the emptiest because it left you with further to walk at most stations. Flavia arranged her bags on the seat beside her and gazed out as the train set off.

Her phone rang while they were still in St Gallen. Alex – was there a problem at the hotel? Carol and Ralph were due back today. Quite soon, actually.

'Flavia, are you busy?'

That sounded ominous. 'I'm in a train heading for Rorschach. Why?'

'Oh. It's just that they've managed to crash-land a box of fizz glasses in the restaurant and every last one broke, so we'll need more for the aperitif tomorrow. I've ordered them at that place in Romanshorn, but I can't leave reception because there's no one here to cover it and we still have six guests to check in, and Ralph's due back anytime and–'

Flavia gripped her phone. 'Tell them I'll pick them up before five. Do I need to pay for them?'

'No. You're a star. See you soon.'

Flavia gathered her bags to be ready for a speedy exit from the train. Brilliant. Now she had to rush home, grab her car key and speed to Romanshorn, then lug boxes back to Lakeside. Oh, well – it wasn't as if she had a hot date to go to, was it?

Something under an hour later she was hefting a box of twenty-five glasses through the front door of the hotel. Alex leapt over to help her.

'For heaven's sake, Flavia, haven't you heard of putting things on trolleys?'

Flavia glared. 'What happened to "thank you, Flavia, for doing this on your afternoon off"?'

'Thank you, Flavia. Sorry.' He dived into the storeroom and returned with a trolley.

Flavia relented. His hair was sticking up in all directions and his tie was wonky; it must have been a hectic afternoon. 'Are we ready for tomorrow?'

'More or less. Everyone's replied to the invitations, the, um, surprise will arrive before lunch, and the aperitif guests will come for four. Stacy and Rico's ETA is four-thirty, and let's hope their flight's on time.'

'Are you bringing Denise?'

'She'll come in a taxi. She's very happy about it, bless her.'

Flavia smiled. 'What does she think of your plan to move to Zurich?'

He wasn't looking at her, and Flavia frowned. 'Oh, Alex! Haven't you told her?'

'I'm waiting for the right time. I'd hate her to be upset, and with her thinking about moving to Grimsbach... I don't want her to do something she doesn't want to, because she thinks it would make things easier for me.'

Heavens, how convoluted could you get? Families weren't half complicated. Flavia opened her mouth to say something, but a pair of new guests arrived at this point, and Alex retreated behind the desk.

Flavia pushed the trolley out to the kitchen, where the glasses were welcomed with open arms. Alex was still busy with the couple when she returned, so she gave him a wave and left him to it. It *was* her day off. And now she had to work out something to give him a bit of a shove in the direction of Zurich and Zoe. What was he *thinking* about, not telling Denise? You could be too complicated about things...

***

'It looks great, Mum. I'm sure you'll love it here.'

Stacy walked along the edge of the corner plot that was to house her parents' new bungalow. There wasn't a lot to see, but according to the plans, this was going to be a nice wide street with trees planted along one side. Dad would enjoy the garden, too. It was small, but more than large enough for a little patio, a patch of grass and a few flower or veggie beds.

Janie beamed. 'It'll be ideal for the cat, too.'

Stacy didn't dare catch Rico's eye. He and John were strolling along beside her and Janie, with Gareth and Jo behind. Tom had held out his arms to Rico as soon as the family joined them at the church, and Stacy rejoiced. Not that she'd say anything today, but she'd start a more definite family planning chat on the journey home tomorrow.

She tucked her hand under her mother's arm. 'Any idea about a name yet? Blackie would suit him.'

'I thought Sooty. He looks like a Sooty, and it goes well with Snowy, too.'

Stacy choked. You'd think the two cats lived in the same household and were bosom buddies. No way would Denise let anyone remove her precious Snowy, anyway. Still, it was good to know she and Rico would be leaving England with her parents in a good place. Mum was happy about the blessing, apart from the dance invasion, but that would teach her not to issue such vague invitations in future. Dad was happy about the bungalow, and maybe he'd get his own way about a dog once they'd moved. So 'all' she and Rico had to do was sort out their own future in the hotel, decide what they would build on the boathouse site and when, and make sure Ralph and Carol were back on track again. Stacy pictured the pair vanishing into the crowd at the airport, each pulling a small suitcase. They must be almost back at Lakeside by now, so the usual 'home safe' message would arrive soon, and it might even include a hint about whatever the MJ surprise was. Ralph enjoyed teasing them. But oh, please let it not be a large and hideous picture.

30

SUNDAY, 23RD JUNE

Next morning, they were still none the wiser about MJ. Apart from a text from Ralph to announce their safe arrival at Lakeside, they hadn't heard a word from the older couple, far less a hint about the surprise. Stacy was disappointed.

'Leave him,' said Rico eventually. 'He knows we're almost dead with curiosity. If we stop asking, he might tell us.'

'Hm.' Stacy wasn't convinced. They'd said that before, and Ralph usually did as he wanted.

Emily came by on Sunday morning to say goodbye, and Stacy felt quite tearful. In no time at all Emmy's baby would be here too, and nothing would ever be the same again. They were hurtling towards the end of a chapter of their lives. And the beginning of a new one for Emily, of course, and oh, hopefully one day soon they would sit and watch their children play together.

En route for the airport an hour or two later, nostalgia was still uppermost. Stacy gazed out from the back of her father's car as the streets she'd once known so well passed by. New shops were springing up all over the place where familiar ones had vanished, and some older buildings had been demolished to make way for a new park. Manchester was changing and she wasn't there to be part of it. A lump rose in Stacy's throat. Her old home wasn't her home any more. But then, home now was Rico and Lakeside. The twin loves of her life.

'We'll be out to see you in October,' said Janie, turning round from the front, a brave smile on her lips and tears in her eyes.

'Lovely. Can't wait to show you our new sauna and fitness room. And you can help me choose the table stuff for the restaurant at Christmas.' Stacy tried to smile too, but oh, they would soon be gone and it would all be over, and somehow, the thought was piercingly sad. Mum could be infuriating, but she was a love too.

As usual, Stacy kept the goodbye scene short. Janie stood waving, lips trembling, clinging to John as Stacy and Rico went through the barrier into the security area and turned for a final wave. Poor Mum. Would she and Rico be in this situation, sometime far in the future? Waving a much-loved child off into their own life, knowing it was best but aching for one more hug? Oh dear... Stacy mopped her eyes.

'Come on,' said Rico, slinging an arm around her. 'We've had a great time, and it'll be October before we know it.'

Stacy set her shoulders. 'I know. Let's treat ourselves to a glass of expensive duty-free fizz to celebrate our first flight as a married couple.'

The plane wasn't nearly full, and they had a row of three seats to themselves. Stacy sat listening to the people in front speaking Spanish, then peeked into the row behind them. It only contained one person, a solitary elderly man with a hearing aid, and he was fast asleep. Good. This was her chance.

'Rico, love. About our plans for the next couple of years. I'm fine about what we do with Lakeside, but I so want to start our family soon.'

He gripped her hand, heaving a long sigh, and Stacy slumped. This was going to be a 'not now, darling' answer, wasn't it?

'Stace, you know I like kids and I do want our own some day, but we have to think about the finances, too.'

'That makes it sound so sordid. I could see you enjoyed being with Tom, and so did I. It would be brilliant having our own child.'

'I know. But we want to be able to afford it. You know what it would cost to replace one of us to do the childcare, and we've had so much expense recently, and there's more to come. The money has to come from somewhere. I wish it didn't.'

'People would help with childcare. You can't put a price on love, and babies need love more than anything, and I–' To her horror, her voice broke. 'I so want a baby for us both to love as much as we love each other.'

Rico put a hand on the side of her head, touching his forehead to hers. 'Oh, Stace. Tell you what. We'll compromise. Next year, huh? Next year at some point, we'll start trying for a family.'

Stacy blotted her eyes. It was as good as she was going to get, but it still sounded as if their baby was being put at the same level as a holiday or a piece of furniture they were saving for. But next year was definite. She could work with that. They sealed the deal with a kiss, but it still felt bittersweet to Stacy.

The second half of the flight was surprisingly bumpy, and Stacy kept a tight hold of Rico's arm as yet more turbulence rumbled across the plane. That airport fizz hadn't been such a good idea after all, and thank heavens they were going to Switzerland and not Singapore. The plane landed five minutes before schedule, and they joined the scrum in the airport.

'Right. Now to get out to the car,' said Rico, as they pulled their cases through customs and into the arrivals area. 'But – hey, there's Dad!'

Stacy stopped dead. They hadn't expected to be met; it was a long way from Lakeside to Basle Airport – had Ralph forgotten they had the car here?

'Welcome home, you honeymooners!' Ralph kissed Stacy and gave Rico their usual man-hug before leading the way to the exit. 'Everyone had a job to do today except me, so I got myself out from under their feet, and caught the train here. I'll be chauffeur, so you don't even need to drive home.'

Stacy didn't believe a word of it. Ralph's eyes were dancing; this was part of whatever he'd been planning for the past several weeks. What was waiting for them at Lakeside? The mysterious MJ, aka Martina Johanna? Or – something entirely different?

***

'Where's Carol? Is she doing okay?' Rico squashed into the back of the car beside the bear Stacy'd bought in Berne.

'She's fine. Organising a little aperitif for the staff to welcome you home – those that are working today. And the hotel's full for the next three weeks, so we'll be turning cycling tourists away.'

Rico nodded. The one-night cycling tourists were a leftover from the old Lakeside, but they were still a good source of income when the hotel had empty rooms.

Stacy was frowning. Hopefully someone was helping Carol with that aperitif.

Ralph steered the car out of the Parkhaus and east along the motorway. Rico relaxed as towns and villages, woodland and fields all swooped past, and then came Zurich. Past the city, they were driving eastwards again. After almost a week in England, it was nice to have the driver on the proper side of the car and see traffic approach from the direction you were expecting. And it wouldn't be long before they'd get the first glimpse of the Alpstein mountains. Rico leaned forward in anticipation. Yes, there they were, with just the odd patch of summer snow left on the Säntis while the green hills of the Appenzellerland rolled up to the grey stone of the higher peaks. He breathed in deeply. He was home. Almost. And what was waiting for them at Lakeside? The speedometer came into focus; his father had slowed down to a sedate – for the motorway – seventy-five kilometres an hour, and come to think of it, he'd been driving slowly all the way. Rico grinned. Whatever was going on at the hotel must need time to prepare. Ralph confirmed his suspicions a few minutes later when a service station came into sight up ahead.

'I'll stop here and get some petrol for you. My treat.'

He filled the tank, then strolled off to the filling station shop to pay, tapping his phone as he went.

Stacy twisted round in the front passenger seat. 'Taking his time, isn't he?'

Rico could still see his father, hovering around in the filling station shop, phone clutched to his ear. 'Yup. Shall we gang up on him and demand to know what's going on, or keep our cool and pretend we're oblivious?

'Oh, keeping our cool is much... cooler. Do you reckon Martina Johanna's arriving from somewhere this afternoon too? We'd better get our delighted expressions polished, if we have to thank her for a purple mountain in person. Heavens, look, he's bringing coffee. They must be running seriously late at Lakeside.'

Rico hid a smile at his father's cheerful, 'Coffee time!' when he opened the car door. Ralph's eyes were wary, and Rico swallowed a laugh. Dad was worried they were going to protest, or ask leading questions, wasn't he?

Stacy accepted her beaker and spoke brightly. 'Did we tell you about the coaster set the fire brigade sent us? Six different fire engines of the last century.' She sipped her coffee demurely, and Rico almost choked.

'Ah, lovely,' said Ralph faintly. 'Would anyone like a biscuit? I bought some chocolate wafers.'

Twenty minutes later they were on the road again, and soon Rico could see Lake Constance glinting in the distance. It would be good to get home, and good to be back in the higher summer temperatures of Switzerland. He would go for a swim this evening.

They left the motorway, and rather to Rico's surprise, Ralph took the short way to Grimsbach. He was about to say something mildly sarcastic like, 'Hey, I was looking forward to seeing the long road home again', when the car pulled into a bus stop a mile or two from the hotel.

Ralph leaned into the back for his jacket. 'Children. This is where you have to trust me and do as I say. If you don't, the entire staff will have my guts for garters.' He reached into an inside pocket and produced two blue eye masks, the kind you got on long haul flights. 'Blindfolds on, please, and no peeking.'

Rico pulled a face at Stacy, then took the mask his father was holding out. So this was why they'd come the short way; the longer road involved seeing the hotel in the distance for several minutes before you arrived, and obviously, there was something at Lakeside they weren't supposed to notice – yet. A marquee in the garden?

It was an odd sensation, not being able to see where you were going. Rico would have said he knew every inch of the road, but the various bumps and bends still took him by surprise. His ears kicked in strongly, registering sounds of other cars on the road and dull clicks and crunches as Ralph indicated and changed gear. And funny how you were more conscious of your own breathing when you couldn't see anything.

'Hold tight, kids,' said Ralph. 'We're turning into Lakeside now.'

The car made a sharp right turn and Rico steadied himself with one hand on the seat. They jerked to a halt, and he heard Ralph open his door.

'Keep those blindfolds on. Stacy, Carol's here to guide you, and Rico – out you come.'

Rico felt his father's hand on his arm, then Carol's voice came from nearby.

'Welcome home, you two! We're going round the back.'

'What on earth have you got planned for us?' Rico walked where Ralph led him, his feet crunching on the gravel and the sun's heat warming his shoulders. They rounded the corner and a breeze from the lake cooled his cheeks. He could hear Stacy and Carol on the path behind him, and murmurs, muffled giggles, people moving around nearby. A lot of people, this was unmistakably a party, but what on earth was the surprise? Could this be where they were going to meet Martina Johanna Jahn and her painting?

***

Stacy allowed Carol to lead her along the path. They were heading for the lake; she could smell the water. Was this a party in the new fitness room? That was quite likely – it would be finished by now. An opening party with Martina Johanna as guest of honour? And hey, there was an idea – they could put the painting in the fitness room.

Carol manoeuvred her a few steps to the side. 'Here we are. Stand beside Rico, Stacy.'

Stacy felt her elbow brush against Rico's arm, and reached for his hand. A duck quacked nearby; they must be right at the lake bank here – yes, water was slapping against the stone wall of the landing place.

Ralph spoke in Swiss German beside them. 'Stacy and Rico, ladies and gentlemen, friends of Lakeside – welcome to our little celebration!'

Cheers and clapping came from behind, and Stacy's anticipation rose. Ralph was good at speeches, and how nice it was to hear the melodic Swiss accent again after a week in England. She moved closer to Rico and listened as Ralph went on.

'As, er, some of you know, Rico and Stacy have been waiting to meet MJ.'

Laughter came from the crowd, and Stacy held on to Rico's hand for dear life, wishing they'd let her take off this blindfold – she was getting hot underneath it, and heaven knows what it was doing to her eye make-up. She didn't want to meet Martina Johanna looking like a giant panda.

'Rico and Stacy – before we unveil you, let's make sure we all have a glass of something in our hand to toast the new arrival.'

The new arrival. That could be a person. Or a painting. Or both. Beside her, Rico was breathing hard. Murmuring and clinking came from the crowd, and someone pressed a cold glass into Stacy's free hand.

'Ready? Here we go – but say hello to your guests first.'

Hands grasped Stacy's shoulders and spun her round before the eye mask was lifted away, and she blinked at a huge crowd stretching from the lake bank right back into the hotel garden. Golly, there were hundreds of people here, and everyone was laughing and waving at them. Where was Martina Johanna? She waved back, scanning the crowd for a mysterious stranger, then Rico went rigid beside her.

'*Dad!* What have you done?'

He was gaping at the lake, mouth open. Stacy whirled round to see what he was looking at, and she gasped.

It was the last thing she was expecting. A boat, a cruiser, but much, much larger than *Lakeside Lady*, and it was moored at the new extended landing place. Wow. Unlike little white *Lakeside Lady*, this boat – ship? – was made of shiny, warm dark brown wood, with a little cabin near the front and a canvas roof on poles to protect the passengers from the sun. The deck was metres long with wooden benches up the sides. It was the kind of boat you could use for parties or short cruises; you could even have a few tables on the deck. The red and white Swiss flag was fluttering in the breeze at the top of a pole on the cabin roof, and large gold lettering on the bow proclaimed her name: *Matilda Jane*.

Stacy gasped. What–? Who–? *Matilda Jane...* Not a painting?

Ralph winked at her. 'Rico, Stacy, meet my newest acquisition and the latest addition to the Lakeside, um, staff. To *Matilda Jane*!' He raised his glass high.

'*Matilda Jane*!' chorused the crowd, and Stacy found herself clinking glasses with Ralph, Carol, most of the Lakeside staff and everyone within reach, which included several strangers who must be hotel guests this week. She sipped cold bubbles and opened her mouth to ask what on earth was going on, but Rico beat her to it.

'Dad. Explain.'

Ralph's beam stretched from one ear to the other. 'I found her up for sale on Lake Lugano last January, and went into a huddle with Guido.' He put an arm around Carol beside him. 'We've been doing her up in Guido's boatyard ever since, and–'

'You *bought* her? How did you–' Rico was gobsmacked, and Stacy could see why. This boat must be worth tens of thousands; she was practically a valuable antique. An old-timer.

Ralph was blasé. 'Rico, stop worrying. It's the best plan ever. Those investments that matured were real and I used the money to finance it.' He tapped his chest. 'You're looking at the captain of *Matilda Jane*. I've given up my flat in Lugano, and the idea is I'll live at Lakeside in the tourist season and we can do cruises, birthday parties, you name it, with her. We have bookings already. She'll have paid for herself before we know it. Then in winter, I'll spend some time with Guido in Lugano too. It's going to be good.'

Stacy couldn't take her eyes off *Matilda Jane*. Adieu Martina Johanna Jahn, and thank goodness... She turned to Ralph. 'Wow! You've got everything sorted. I can't wait to try her out!'

Rico breathed out beside her, obviously dying to laugh. 'And here we were expecting – something completely different! You've surpassed yourself, Dad.'

Ralph slapped Rico's shoulder and winked at Stacy. 'I know. We'll have a jaunt up the lake in her soon, but for now, let's party with our guests.'

A general milling around started, and Stacy stared at Ralph's back, uneasiness spreading over her like an ice-cold wave. It all sounded wonderful, everything they could ever have wished for and so much better than they'd imagined – but something wasn't right. Carol's face was a pleasant mask, Ralph was your original hotelier-putting-on-an-act, and the dark rings under Alex's eyes were telling their own story. Yet the wedding was over, the honeymoon in the past, and theoretically they could all get back to normal.

Stacy glanced up at the hotel, where the warm brown wood was bathed in sunshine, but... A shiver ran down her spine. Something was wrong at Lakeside, fermenting under the surface, waiting to erupt. And how she was going to stop it was anyone's guess.

31

Monday, 24th June

It was almost eleven before Rico trailed into the kitchen for breakfast the next morning, leaving Stacy still asleep in bed. Yesterday's welcome home aperitif by the lake had evolved from the late-afternoon party straight into dinner on the terrace with a gathering of friends and family. When the party broke up, Carol went to bed but Rico, Stacy and Ralph sat on the living room balcony in the flat making plans for *Matilda Jane* until well after two in the morning. Ralph was full of ideas and he'd swept them along with all his plans.

Rico took Stacy a mug of milky cappuccino before heading downstairs to see what was happening in his hotel this morning. There was no sign of Ralph or Carol, but Alex on reception shot him a tired grin and went on explaining something to a couple of guests. A quick check of the spa showed a full house in spite of perfect summer weather outside, and the terrace was serving early lunches as more and more people arrived. And there was Matilda Jane, hulled in her blue tarpaulin, waiting for the first trip. Ralph had promised to take them and anyone else who wanted to go on the first voyage this afternoon, a quick trip to give them the experience of her before later in the week, when they would go on a proper outing with some paying guests. Dad was right, this boat was a real investment.

He continued down to the lake bank to examine the newly extended jetty. *Lakehouse Lady* was moored in front of *Matilda Jane*, and there was still a good couple of metres of spare jetty. Rico squared his shoulders. Right. Time to think about those pedalos. He pictured a string of brightly coloured little boats bobbing up and down in the water, a queue of guests waiting to pay their however much a pedalo cost to hire for an hour – half an hour? There was a lot to learn here; he'd better get started.

He was deep in pedalo research in the office behind reception when Ralph came in and pulled up a chair. 'Suggestion – why don't you and I and Stacy do a little mini-circuit in *Matilda Jane* now, just by ourselves? That way, you could ask any questions without having guests on board overhearing, and we can still take her out again this afternoon.'

Rico snorted. 'Guests overhearing how clueless I am about her, you mean. But you're on. I'll call Stace. Where's Carol?'

A faint shadow crossed Ralph's face. 'She's having a quiet afternoon. I thought we could all have dinner together? I'll cook. Okay, meet you at the jetty in quarter of an hour.' He went off whistling, leaving Rico staring after him. It might be an idea to get Stacy to look in on Carol later. The older woman wasn't usually one for quiet afternoons, but then she'd had a hectic week or so; she would still be catching up with unpacking after her time in England, and the plaster on her arm wouldn't help things.

Stacy was all for a mini trip on *Matilda Jane*. 'I'll check in on Carol first,' she said. 'When's the first cruise with hotel guests, did Ralph say?'

'Unofficially, this afternoon, but he has a longer one planned for Thursday. He's going to put a notice in reception, but four people have said they'll come today already. He'll do hotel guests only for the first couple of times, then when he's more used to it we can advertise for outsiders too. But go and see Carol when we're back, Stace, then you won't have to rush away.'

Stacy took his hand as they walked down to the jetty, then Rico handed her into their new possession and took his place beside her on the long bench. Ralph sat in the captain's seat up front and started the engine, and wow – Rico laid a hand on *Matilda Jane*'s side, feeling the thrum of the engine run through the ship, making tiny ripples on the water below. This boat was a lot more powerful than *Lakeside Lady*, yet you were almost as close to the water. It was a real feeling of being at one with the lake as they pulled away from the jetty and swung to the east.

'This is fab.' Stacy sat back happily, shading her eyes and gazing up at the Alpstein mountains, grey against the blue of the sky. 'The possibilities are endless. I'm so glad you bought her, Ralph. We'll need to get Guido and Julia here for a trip soon.'

'Michael and Salome are still with them in Lugano,' said Ralph. 'Maybe they can all come before the young ones go back to Berlin.'

Rico thought about big, bustling Berlin. The contrast to Grimsbach couldn't be greater, and how lucky he was to live here.

An hour later, they were pulling up at the jetty again, with Ralph oozing enthusiasm for his new career as ship's captain. 'This is just what I need, Rico. A new challenge, something positive.'

Rico helped him replace the tarpaulin, and they all trooped back inside. A glow of satisfaction settled over Rico as he surveyed reception. Alex was dealing with some people at the desk, a crowd of guests was grouped around the spa shop, and a buzz of happy chatter was coming from the tub room. Outside, barmen and waiters were rushing about with drinks and ice cream. Lakeside was living her best life, wasn't she? Beside him, Stacy's expression was serene, and love surged in Rico's heart. There was no reason not to start a family, but – was he ready? The memory of Tom's warm heaviness in his arms and that beaming happy-baby smile popped into Rico's head. *Was* he ready? Was Lakeside ready?

***

Flavia sat back in her chair at the staff table on the terrace, watching as Ralph, Rico and Stacy left the new boat and headed back into the hotel. It would be fabulous to go for a trip on Matilda Jane, and maybe they'd have a staff party on board at some point. That would be cool. She lifted her phone from the table – she should get back to the spa, and thank goodness Stacy was starting work again tomorrow.

Deep in thought, she swerved to avoid bumping into Carol on the way inside.

'Oops!' Flavia grasped Carol's arm. Exhaustion was written all over her poor friend's face. 'Didn't you want to go for a trip on the boat?'

'I'll go next time. I've come for some iced tea to take back upstairs. An afternoon of peace and quiet sounded more attractive, to tell you the truth. I'm still catching up with myself after – England.'

Not to mention being caught up in a landslide, thought Flavia. She rubbed Carol's arm. 'Let's have a proper catch-up soon.'

'That sounds good.'

Carol went on to the terrace, and Flavia went back to the spa, where Denise was peering into the shop cabinet.

'Hi, Flavia – any new gift packs needed?'

Flavia went for the stocklist, and they spent a few moments working out what needed replacing.

'Any word from your new young man?' Denise added the new list to her folder.

'Yes! We're going for dinner tomorrow, in that Italian place near the cathedral in St Gallen.'

'Oh, I'm so pleased for you, love. I have a good feeling about this, you know.'

Flavia crossed her fingers hard. It would be amazing if Denise was right, and – she had a good feeling about it too.

Denise tucked the folder under her arm. 'I wish that lad of mine was settled, you know. Sometimes I think he'll never find happiness. By the way, I saw on my way in there's a nice ground-floor flat for sale near the library here in Grimsbach. I'm going to call about it later and go for a viewing, if it's still available. It looks ideal for me and Snowy.'

'Sounds good,' said Flavia, but her mind was racing. Alex couldn't have said anything to Denise about his plan to move to Zurich. It was a bit of a catch-22 situation, Alex and his mother both trying to protect each other, with the result that nothing was moving for poor Alex. A little hint would break the deadlock...

'Alex mentioned there's an admin job going at Zoe's orchestra,' she said casually.

Denise gave her a long look. 'Right... should I be having a word with him?'

'Might be an idea. You heard nothing from me, though.'

''Course not. I'll fix things, don't worry. Thanks, love.'

Denise collected the items to make up spa gift packs and left, waving gaily to Alex at reception as she went.

He waved back, then turned to Flavia. 'Nice to see Mum in a good mood. Can you watch the desk for ten minutes, please? I haven't had my break yet.'

Flavia slid behind the desk as Rico and Ralph came round from the restaurant and went into the office behind her, both looking pretty pleased with themselves. Flavia helped a guest with a query, then looked round for Alex. He'd taken a long ten minutes. Behind her, Rico and Ralph were talking.

'I'll just ask Carol if she's planning on making her tiramisu for dessert tonight before I go upstairs,' said Ralph. 'She might want me to bring a few things for her.'

A short silence followed, then: 'She's not answering. I'll text her, there's time enough. By the way, those pedalos...'

Several minutes of pedalo chat followed, then a ping came. 'Ah – that'll be Carol.'

Another silence, then: 'She's not here. She said she needs some alone time.'

Rico sounded cautious. 'Has she left the hotel? I mean, for longer than an hour or two?'

'Shouldn't think so. I guess she needs some space for a bit, that's all. She'll be back.'

'Okay. I'll go up and see what Stacy's doing, if you get onto the pedalo people?' Rico came out of the office, smiled vaguely at Flavia, and strode across to the lift.

...some space for a bit, that's all. She'll be back... Flavia stood still as hot rage swept through her. How dare Ralph be so – so inconsiderate about poor Carol? So blasé? Talk about having blinkers on. Flavia banged her palms down on the desk, swung round and charged into the office. Ralph's eyes widened at the sight of her. Good.

Fists balled, she stood in the office doorway. 'Did you ever think Carol might need more than space and alone time after what happened to her? You didn't, did you – you were too busy worrying about your own reaction and your holiday in England. Let me tell you, Ralph, that hour I spent on the hillside waiting to be rescued was the worst hour of my life, and then think that Carol was up there for hours and hours longer. She'd have spent every minute of that time terrified the hill would slide away beneath her and bury her under a ton of rubble. What she needed afterwards was support and comfort. What she got was a guy so worried about his own fears that he didn't have time to help with her much bigger ones. Then instead of having someone to hold her up, she had to travel for hours and do heaven knows what in England, then come back to a place where she has no family and organise a bloody party. You should be ashamed of–'

'Stop.' Ralph's voice was low and shaking. 'Stop right there. How dare you speak to me like that? Go, Flavia. Now. Get out, and don't come back. You're not needed in this hotel.'

Flavia wheeled round and fled. Had she just lost her job? She had, hadn't she?

***

Stacy put another cup of tea down beside Rico. It was after seven and they were sitting in the kitchen in the flat, but neither of them were thinking about dinner. Ralph's garbled message to Rico an hour ago had come as a shock.

Think Carol's gone back to Friedrichshafen. I'm on my way there too – will be in touch.

Stacy felt sick even thinking about it. Those tensions she'd felt below the surface... they were erupting now, but could they be stopped?

Rico checked his phone for the hundredth time. 'They must have had an argument, Stace. I wish he'd switch his phone back on. I'm not sure what to do.'

Stacy heaved a sigh. 'Me neither. Oh Rico, they're both adults, and they love each other. We have to let them sort this out for themselves. I wish I'd gone to check on Carol before she left. She hasn't been herself for a while.'

'I guess. Something must have happened, though, for her to up and leave like that, and especially for Dad to go tearing after her. And hell, Stace, he doesn't even know for sure she went there! She could be holing up somewhere else. D'you think I should I call her?'

Stacy shivered. The thought that something had happened while they were on honeymoon wasn't a happy one. 'I think we should leave them both alone. They could be having a big reconciliation.'

Rico sniffed. 'Or another argument.'

'We can be here for them if they need us, but that's all. Come on. Let's make some spaghetti and look at our wedding pics again. Ralph will call when he has something to say.'

Rico agreed – grudgingly – and they spent the evening on the balcony, a warm wind from the south ruffling Stacy's hair as she swiped through the photos. What a long time ago the wedding seemed now. Even the blessing had retreated in the past, the way that holidays did when they were over.

At twenty to ten Rico gave her the most vulnerable look in the world as he went to lean on the edge of the balcony.

'Oh Stace. The last ferry's in now, and he's had time to get back here, if he was on it. He must be staying overnight.'

Stacy put an arm across his back, massaging the tension in his shoulders. 'So she must be in Friedrichshafen. It's good that he's prioritising Carol at last. Love's the most important thing, but you need to make time for it. Leave them be.'

Rico turned and put his arms around her. 'What did I do to deserve you?'

Stacy hugged back, but it was hard not to be worried. What was happening was out of character for both Ralph and Carol, and that was rarely a good sign. She and Rico had reached their Happy Ever After – but the story of Ralph and Carol was still incomplete.

32

Tuesday, 25th June

Stacy reached for her phone as soon as she was awake on Tuesday morning, but no message from either Carol or Ralph had come in overnight. Had Rico heard anything?

He was standing on the balcony in his PJs, staring moodily over the lake. 'No, nothing,' he said, and Stacy's heart ached for him.

She slipped an arm around his waist. 'I was wondering – when your mum was so ill, did he have problems coping with her then?'

Rico banged a hand on the edge of the balcony. 'None. He was love and support personified.'

Tears rushed into Stacy's eyes. Love and support personified... yet still Edie had died, leaving Ralph powerless to help her. No one would be the same after that.

She put a hand on his back and rubbed. 'We'll hear when they want us to hear. Meanwhile, my love, we have a hotel to run, and may I remind you we're working as per normal today?'

His sigh almost blew her away. 'I suppose we are.'

Rico went off to find clothes suitable for a hotel manager on duty, and Stacy started a mental list of what she needed to do today. A quick check round first, then spa duty until lunchtime, then – well she'd see what happened this morning before planning too much for the afternoon. Hopefully Ralph would have given them a small sign of life by then.

Alex was on reception when she went down, still with those shadows under his eyes. Stacy added him to her list of things to check on later, then headed into the spa to find Sabine preparing the tubs for the expected spa guests, humming as she worked. Thank goodness, at least someone was having a good day. Spa work kept her busy until coffee time, when Rico joined her at the staff table on the terrace, his face tripping him.

'I tried them both again. Still no answer.' He banged down his glass of iced tea so hard it slopped onto the wooden tabletop.

Stacy mopped it up with a tissue. It would be best if he didn't think too hard about Ralph. 'I'm sure they'll be in touch today. Ralph will know you'll be worried. How did Lakeside business cope while we were away?'

It was the right thing to ask, because Rico brightened immediately. 'Okay. Pretty well, actually. I've been looking at pedalos online. The boatyard will order them for us, and they're giving us a good discount. What do you think, red and blue or yellow and blue?'

Stacy smiley wryly. No one could call this job boring, anyway. If you weren't helping someone with their aching shoulder in a hot tub, you were considering the colour scheme of your future pedalos.

'I would get yellow. It might be easier to spot out on the lake.'

Rico finished his iced tea in a few gulps. 'Yellow they shall be. I'm off to a meeting with Peter in the restaurant – I'll put your summer Gala Dinners idea to him.'

It was almost midday when Alex put his head into the spa and beckoned Stacy over.

'Can you talk to a woman in reception, please? She isn't sure if all the meds she's on would allow her to sit in a hot tub for an hour or so.'

Stacy signalled to Sabine that she was leaving the spa, then followed Alex to the desk, where a fifty-something woman was waiting.

'Hello, I'm the spa nurse, can I–'

The hotel door crashed open and Zoe thundered in, black hair flying. She came to an abrupt halt in the middle of the front hall and stood waving her arms.

'Alex Berger, what the heck is going on? I had the most extraordinary phone call from your mother at ten o'clock last night. It didn't sound like the kind of thing we could clear up over the phone, so here I am – and don't you dare bleat "nothing's wrong" because your mother got hold of her crazy idea from somewhere, and it wasn't from me.'

As usual when Zoe was around, everyone in the room stopped what they were doing and stared at her. She strode over to the desk, still glaring at Alex, who looked completely taken aback.

'My mother called you?'

'Yes. She sounded pretty worried, but I couldn't make head nor tail of what she thinks is going on. Care to enlighten me?'

A small crowd had gathered, with Stacy and her prospective patient, a group of elderly guests in walking shoes who'd been peering at the map on the wall, and three people emerging from the restaurant, all waiting to see what was going to happen.

Stacy stepped forward. 'Um...'

Alex got in first, and she subsided.

'I don't know why my mother would call you, or why you think it's my fault, but if you tell me what you think she said, we might get somewhere.'

Now he was glaring. Zoe put her hands on her hips. 'She seemed to think that you were dying to take up the admin job in the orchestra and were using her condition, you know, the one that she's completely on top of now, as an excuse not to, and she thinks I must have said something to put you off and now you were scared I'd reject you, but that's complete nonsense. What's really going on – and why the heck did I have to find out about it from your mother?'

It was like watching tennis. Every head in reception swivelled back to Alex. Stacy opened her mouth, but again, he got in first.

'I have no idea what I said that could possibly have made her think any of that. And how did she even know about the admin job? I haven't said a thing about it to her. And I still don't see why any of this is all my fault!' His glare was as dark as could possibly be.

Oh good grief, these two were their own worst enemies. Stacy stepped forward again and this time she managed to get a word in. 'Zoe, if I were you I would just kidnap him and elope...'

Zoe looked at her, then back to Alex. 'At last someone's talking sense. Alex Berger, will you marry me? Please?'

A loud gasp came from the watching crowd of guests, and now Alex was brick-red and Zoe was in his arms and there wasn't a dry eye in reception.

Stacy seized the opportunity to take control. 'Okay folks, show's over, and it looks like we have a happy ending.' The crowd dispersed, laughing, and Stacy's attention returned to the wannabe hot tub user.

'Sorry about that!'

'Don't be,' said the woman. 'I'd have come long ago if I'd known it would be such fun!' She handed over a list of medication. Stacy read it through, then okayed a hot tub visit after their usual first-visit blood pressure check. She sent the woman in to Sabine for this, because Alex and Zoe had vanished and there was a queue at reception. Oh, well, she could cope with the desk for the moment; Flavia would here in five minutes.

Five minutes passed, then ten, and now reception was deserted and there was still no sign of Flavia. Stacy frowned. Had someone got the shift plan wrong? Flavia was usually so reliable. She pulled out her phone and tapped to connect.

'Flavia, shouldn't you be in today, or have we got crossed wires somewhere?'

There was a short silence, then Flavia's voice, and shades of Alex... were all the Lakeside receptionists taken by surprise today?

'Oh, ah... Didn't Ralph tell you? He sacked me yesterday. Effective immediately.'

'*What?*' Stacy had to lean on the desk, she was so shocked. 'What on earth happened?'

'I – I may have been a little, ah, direct about how he's been with Carol since the landslide. I'm sorry, Stacy. Letting you down was the last thing I wanted.'

Stacy stood still as the words sank in. *'...how he's been with Carol...'* She'd been right, there was a whole lot more going on here than she was aware of. What in heaven's name had happened between Ralph and Carol after that landslide that neither of them were talking about? But a sacked employee wasn't the person to ask about that. Frantic thoughts whizzed through Stacy's head. She couldn't reinstate the girl over Ralph's head, so it would be best if she and Rico sat down with Ralph to sort things out, then they'd be able to judge if Flavia had overstepped the mark so violently that it warranted sacking her.

'Right. Okay – I'll need to find out more, but I think... I mean I don't know... I mean, I'll need to get back to you about this, Flavia. I'll be as quick as I can, huh?'

She ended the call and stood taking deep breaths. Boring? This job was enough to turn anyone into an adrenaline junkie.

***

Flavia dropped her phone onto the coffee table and leaned back on the sofa, eyes closed. What a mess she was in. If she'd taken three seconds to think before she'd barged in like that yesterday, all guns blazing, she'd have gone about it differently, but too late now. That was the last time she'd interfere so hard in other people's business. And oh, no, she'd done it twice yesterday, hadn't she? Heaven only knew what Denise had said to Alex. He would hate her for the rest of her life too. So here she was, no job and a shedload of friends fewer in a place where she didn't have many friends in the first place. She couldn't even call Denise for moral support.

She trailed into her tiny kitchen to make a lunchtime sandwich. All today had going for it was her date with Ivo tonight. Flavia flung cheese and lettuce onto a piece of bread and added a generous swirl of calorific mayo before slapping another slice on and chopping it in two. Okay. Plan of action. She would go for a walk this afternoon, get some fresh air and exercise, then she'd have a lovely long bath and get ready for her dinner with Ivo. Her dress was waiting. She wasn't going to let a minor detail like losing her job stand in the way of a potentially life-changing date.

Flavia chewed morosely and swallowed. Two life-changing events in two days was a bit OTT; real life wasn't like that. She and Ivo might find they had nothing to say to each other tonight and go home as soon as possible.

She carried out her programme with no word arriving from Stacy, and arrived at the restaurant just two minutes late. They'd agreed to meet outside, but there was no sign of Ivo among the last of the shopping crowds and people heading for this or that restaurant or bar. Better and better. He had stood her up. Tears brimmed in her eyes, and she brushed them away. Another two minutes passed, then–

'Flavia, I'm so sorry! You won't believe it but there was a cow on the track and the train had to make an unscheduled stop and – what's up? I'm sorry if you thought I wasn't coming.'

Ivo took her arm and gave it a gentle shake.

Flavia breathed out. He was genuinely worried, look at those eyes. 'It's not that. I lost my job yesterday.' She nearly added 'that's all', but there was no 'that's all' about it. Losing your job was a disaster of the first magnitude.

'Oh no. Come on. You need a glass of something in front of you, then I want to hear all about it.'

He ushered her in, and a few minutes later she was sipping Merlot and telling him the whole story. He listened, his eyes never leaving her face, then he grimaced.

'For what it's worth, I think you did the right thing. Sounds like he needed a kick up the proverbial. We'll have to hope your other bosses are more understanding.'

Relief swamped through Flavia – he thought she was right. And he'd said '*We'll* have to hope...' He cared what happened to her. So she would forget Lakeside tonight and concentrate on Ivo. 'Fingers crossed. Have you ever lost a job like that?'

He laughed, sitting back to let the waiter deposit their starters. 'This isn't a good time to tell you about the summer I worked on a chicken farm... but there was the time I was kicked out of the footie team at school for punching the boy who was refereeing!'

Flavia giggled, then lifted her fork. He looked positively soppy now, and probably she did too. This was going well, and what was happening here was more important than a mere job, wasn't it?

Ivo seemed to feel the same. They were still in the middle of their pizzas when he reached across the table and took her hand. 'Hey. This is pretty special, isn't it?'

Flavia nodded, happiness flooding through her. It was, and neither of them were talking about the pizza. She was out on the best date ever, the one that was the start of her new life. She was her own woman now.

33

WEDNESDAY, 26TH JUNE

It was the morning after the night before. Flavia stirred her third coffee of the morning. With all this caffeine, she'd be bouncing off the ceiling soon, and it wasn't even lunchtime yet. To say her life had turned bittersweet was the biggest understatement ever. On the one side, there was Lakeside and her lost job. On the other, Ivo. They'd sat in the restaurant until nearly eleven last night, then he'd put her on the bus back down to Grimsbach and she could tell he hadn't wanted to let her go at all. They were going out again on Friday – two more days to go until Friday was 'today'.

Flavia sighed. Stuck in the middle of the bitter and the sweet was Alex – what was happening there? She dipped a chocolate finger into her coffee, then bit off the melted part. Days off like this one sucked, no two ways about it.

Her phone beeped as a message came in, and Flavia swiped to open it. Oh. Oh, my.... This was from Ralph. *Please come to Lakeside at 15.00 today.* What did that mean? Apart from the obvious fact that he wanted her to go to the hotel... Flavia swallowed. Pull yourself together, Mrs Own Woman Now. You can put on some glad rags and show them you're in charge of your own life, whatever they do to your job.

Half past two saw her locking her front door behind her and marching along the main road. She wasn't nervous... ha! Who was she kidding? She'd left twenty minutes early to get to the hotel, that was how much she was bricking it. Okay. She would drop into the library and see who was there. Or no, she wouldn't, because she'd have to explain about her job, and Denise might be there too, and that would open up a whole different set of complications. Instead, she turned down to the lake path, and found an empty bench facing the water about two hundred metres from Lakeside.

It was peaceful, looking out over the lake, watching a family of swans slide along towards Rorschach. The sky was its usual summer blue, reflected in the deeper blue of the water, and oh, she didn't want to lose her job at Lakeside. If only she could turn the clock back, she could try to give Ralph a piece of friendly advice. That's what Stacy would have done. Friendly, with a bit of humour... not that what he'd done was the least bit humorous, but it would have got them all further with less aggro and a lot less stress. Stress for her.

And now it was five to three; she should go. Ten to one Ralph would greet her with a box of stuff she'd left in her locker and a rubbish reference. Flavia tramped up to the hotel feeling as if she was on the way to a particularly painful dental appointment. She was going to look incredibly stupid, walking into the hotel. Did everyone know? She was behind the building here, but in the circumstances, it might be better not to charge inside through the terrace bar. She took first left and walked across the car park, her steps slowing down. Half a minute more and she'd be crawling through the front door and they would all stare at her...

A nearby car door opened. 'Flavia! Wait a moment.'

Oh – it was Ralph. Flavia stood still. He locked his car and came right up to her, hand outstretched.

'I owe you an apology. Everything you said was true, and I was too blind to see it. I'm sorry, Flavia, and please come back. Lakeside needs you.'

In a dream and semi-automatically, Flavia shook hands. 'Oh... thank you. I will. Ah – where's Carol?'

He took her elbow and steered her to the front door. 'She's here too. We came in separate cars, as she's leaving again tomorrow to convalesce for a few days with her son and his family in Munich. I'll join them at the weekend. Come on.'

They walked into the front hall, and Alex behind the desk gaped at them. He didn't come and punch her, which was probably a good sign, but Ralph gave them no opportunity to talk.

'Alex, would you ask Rico and Stacy to come to the office, please. And when they're here, call Carol too; she's waiting in her car. Then come in yourself as well.'

He swept Flavia into the office, and lifted the phone. 'Six coffees in the office, please, Rob.'

'We don't have six chairs in here,' Flavia pointed out, then her lips twitched. She was back at work already, by the look of things. And why on earth was Carol waiting in her car?

Rico arrived first. 'Dad! You should have told us you were coming!'

He slapped his father's back, then Stacy arrived, and Carol, and there were more hugs. Ralph pulled Flavia forward. 'Flavia's back. What happened was all my fault, and she was kind enough to agree to return. Ah, here comes the coffee.'

It was the weirdest tea party ever. Ralph and Carol sat side by side, and the way they kept looking at each other and grinning made Flavia think there was more going on here than anyone was saying.

She was right. Ralph stood up and raised his cup. 'Friends, it's been an eventful few days for us here at Lakeside. First of all, Flavia's back and–'

'That wasn't the first eventful thing today.' Stacy winked at Alex. 'You don't know yet, Ralph, but the first thing that happened was Zoe proposed to Alex in the middle of reception and he said yes! We'll have a second Lakeside wedding to celebrate pretty soon!'

Alex went red, and Flavia gasped. Well – her interference had worked out after all. She'd need to call Denise asap and find out more, and thank goodness she hadn't done any damage, telling Denise about the couple. Maybe this *was* all going to end well...

***

Rico held onto his coffee cup as his father resumed his speech, smirking.

'So you two are the second Lakeside wedding this year? Excellent. Now, when I went to Carol's at Friedri–'

Rico raised his eyes heavenwards. If they were having a second, they might as well have a third, and no matter what had happened before, it was plain as the nose on your face what was happening here. 'For pity's sake, Dad, cut to the chase. Just buy her a ring and be done with it. Weddings always happen in threes, don't they?'

Ralph beamed. 'Already taken care of, but we'll do it more officially for you now. Carol, will you be my wife?'

'Yup.' Carol put down her cup, and Ralph produced a ring box, slid a diamond flanked by sapphires onto her finger and kissed her thoroughly.

Tears shot into Rico's eyes. Look at them. Dad was happy, Carol was happy, Stacy was beaming from ear to ear and Flavia and Alex looked as if they didn't know what had hit them. And no wonder.

The bell on reception pinged, and Rico clapped for attention. 'We'll have a double congratulations do ASAP. Meanwhile, Alex, the desk is waiting. Dad and Carol, you'd better go and give the rest of the staff your good news. Stacy and I will get back to running this hotel, and Flavia, you can have the rest of the day off – we owe you big time.'

'You don't,' said Flavia. 'But if you don't need me to work today, I think I'll go and see Denise.'

Stacy went to the door with Flavia. 'Going to see Denise is a good idea. I have a feeling that you and she might have conspired for Alex and Zoe – am I right?'

Flavia blushed, and Rico put a hand on her shoulder. This kid was doing her utmost not only for the hotel, but for half the staff as well. They'd need to think up a suitable reward.

'We'll walk you to the gate,' he said. 'Whatever you did, it seems to have worked. Well done.'

They strolled down the driveway, then Flavia stopped. 'I'll take the lake path home. I need to get my car.'

Stacy hugged her. 'Thank you, Flavia. And oh, dear, we'll miss Alex, but him leaving means a bit of promotion for you, doesn't it? You'll be our new head receptionist.'

Rico almost punched the air. There was Flavia's reward. Sorted.

'Thank you,' said Flavia in her soft voice. 'That'll be a new beginning for me, too. Another one.'

Stacy pounced. 'Another? Spill.'

Flavia blushed. 'I might have met someone,' she murmured. 'Early days, though.'

Stacy whooped, and Rico began to feel as if there was no end to today's good news. 'Excellent. Let us know when we can get the champagne out for you, too.'

He waved as Flavia went on to the lake path, then took Stacy's hand as they turned back to the hotel. It was a fresh start for Flavia – a fresh start for more than Flavia, actually. They'd better make it a good one.

Stacy heaved a sigh. 'I hope things work out for her.'

'They will.' Rico was suddenly sure. 'Come on. Let's find Dad before he's opened every bottle of champagne we possess.'

***

It was after dinner before Stacy managed to get Carol to herself. The four of them had eaten in the flat, with Ralph grilling chicken pieces and Stacy making salads to go with them. Afterwards, Ralph pushed Rico over to the dishwasher.

'We'll clear up. You ladies can relax.'

'Let's go down to the lake, Stacy.' Carol picked up her cardigan. 'I feel like some fresh air.'

Stacy didn't wait to be asked twice. She'd been aching to have a private word with Carol and check that things were all right. The older woman was less strained than she'd been in England, but there were still dark shadows under her eyes, and she'd definitely lost a couple of kilos since her ordeal. You could tell by the way her jeans were hanging around her waist. And while it was great that she and Ralph were solid again, it had all happened so quickly, and a quick fix wasn't always the best way.

They sauntered through the garden, then sat on the little wall by the jetty. Stacy patted it fondly. 'Rico and I were sitting right here when I first tried to convince him to save the hotel. At the same time, he was trying to make me see that a nasty cheating scumbag like my ex wasn't someone I wanted to have in my life. By the next day, both of us were convinced. Talk to me, Carol. What happened to make you leave like that? And what on earth did Flavia say to Ralph?'

Carol smiled. 'She told him to stop being so self-centred, that I was the one who'd suffered most by that landslide and he should be ashamed that he wasn't supporting me. But he was shaken too, Stacy, I got that. Problem was, I needed more support than I thought I did.'

'Oh, Carol.' Guilt ripped through Stacy. Men could be so needy about emotional stuff, and no one had been there who was whole-heartedly supporting Carol. 'I wish it had happened at a different time, and I'd been here for you!'

Carol snorted. 'Be careful what you wish for! I wish it hadn't happened at all. But if it hadn't, I wouldn't be wearing this. Yet.' She waggled her ring finger. 'We can't change the past, my love, and Ralph and I are dealing with the present now. Let's leave it there.'

'As long as you're okay. And tell me the next time you're not, and I'll do the same. We're going to be stepmum- and daughter-in-law.'

Carol took her arm. 'And I couldn't be happier about that. Look, there's going to be a fab sunset.'

Stacy turned to her left. The sun was inching down over the lake, the sky orange and yellow. She pulled out her phone. 'Rico? Fab sunset approaching. Why don't we all go out in *Lakeside Lady* to watch it?'

'Okay, we'll be down in a mo – you could start taking the tarp off. Need anything?'

Stacy raised her eyebrows at Carol, who shook her head. 'Nope.'

They were waiting on board when the men appeared, Rico with a cool box and Ralph with wind jackets for Stacy and Carol. Good. Ralph was looking after Carol at last. Two minutes later, Rico was steering down the lake into the sunset while Ralph argued with Carol about putting her jacket on.

Warm happiness swept through Stacy as she sat at the back of the cabin cruiser. This was her family too, every bit as much as Mum and Dad and Gareth. She was rich. Rico swung around in a wide circle and switched off the engine.

''We'll anchor and admire the view. Let's have that fizz, Dad.' He gestured to the cool box.

'Rico Weber – you're at the wheel!' Stacy wagged a finger at him.

'One small glass won't hurt.'

Stacy pulled her jacket round her as the sun dropped ever lower then dipped into the lake and hovered there, sending glorious shades of orange sunset across the water. For long moments they sipped slowly and gazed at the spectacle, not speaking – and then it was over, and the lake went back to being a normal stretch of grey-blue water as dusk fell. Lights were going on all along the lake bank, while the first stars twinkled above and the mountains faded into a pink and blue sky. Stacy felt quite choked up. This had to be the loveliest place on earth. Home.

Rico started the engine and they chugged back up the lake. The hotel came into sight on the right-hand bank, and Stacy went to stand at the front beside Rico. Their hotel. The distant sound of guests enjoying the balmy summer evening in the terrace bar floated across the water. The old wooden chalet looked splendid, white geraniums in the window boxes gleaming in the moonlight and the lights from the bar. And they didn't have to find a place for a purple mountain picture after all...

'It's been a – a memorable day,' she said, turning to Ralph and Carol.

Ralph laughed. 'It's been an important day, the kind you remember. Like the day you get married, or the day your exam results come, or– Jeez, I completely forgot!'

He thrust a hand into his jacket pocket and pulled out a blue envelope. 'Maria on reception gave me this – it arrived this afternoon, but with all the drama, it was forgotten.'

He handed the envelope to Stacy, and she stared. Wow. Her first letter addressed to Frau Stacy Weber, and it felt like a card. A late wedding card? Or... She squinted at Ralph, but his face was completely innocent. So possibly not another MJ communication. She ripped it open, then laughed.

'Oh my goodness! I'd forgotten all about this! Rico, remember that couple we met at Ballenberg, Eva and Markus? Eva had a little boy last week!' Stacy read the message inside. Wow, this was amazing too. She waved the card at the others. 'They've called him Jan. How lovely.'

Rico took his place behind the wheel again, and Stacy stood beside him as they slid up to the landing place. Next year, they'd start a family of their own, please God.

Lakeside Lady came to a stop at the jetty, and they disembarked. Rico hugged her to him and murmured in her ear as they crossed the terrace back to the hotel.

'Come on, Mrs. Let's go and make our own babies.'

Stacy stood still. 'Now? Already?'

He kissed her head. 'Why not? You're ready, and yes – I'm ready too.'

Stacy's heart was full as she turned for a last look at the lake. Her lake, and wasn't this the perfect end to the best wedding ever? What a crazy two weeks they'd had, a real mixture of slapstick, near tragedy, heartache and happiness. Just like life was, when you thought about it. Now a whole new family adventure was looming, too. Bring it on.

Acknowledgements

Melinda Huber is the pen name I use for my feel-good fiction. In a different life, I write dark psychological suspense novels as Linda Huber. These are all set in the UK, whereas Melinda's books are set in Switzerland, in my home area on the banks of lovely Lake Constance. Most of the towns, villages and tourist attractions in the Escape to Switzerland series exist and are well worth a visit. The village of Grimsbach, however, and the Lakeside Hotel itself are entirely fictional – I wish they weren't! In real life, there's no space for Grimsbach "between Horn and Steinach", but the views enjoyed by Stacy and friends are the same views I see every day from my home a little further down Lake Constance.

For the moment, this is the final Lakeside Hotel book, but who knows, one day I might pick it up again and see what happens to Stacy, Rico and the others after the happy end.

I'm grateful to so many people for their help getting these books on the road. As always, love and thanks to my sons, Matthias and Pascal, for help and support in all kinds of ways, especially for their technical and IT know-how.

Thanks also to everyone who gave me help and advice about rewriting my original novellas, with special mentions for Helen Pryke and Mandy James for their editing and proofreading skills and generally for being great people with eagle eyes for mistakes!

More thanks to my writing buddies here in Switzerland, Louise Mangos and Alison Baillie, for help, encouragement and all those glasses of fizz.

Another special mention for James at GoOnWrite for the beautiful cover images.

And to all the writers, book bloggers, friends and others who are so supportive on social media – a huge and heartfelt 'THANK YOU. So often it's the online friends, people I may never have met in real life, who are first port of call when advice and encouragement are needed. I hope I can give back as much help as I get from you.

Biggest thanks of all, though, go to the readers – knowing that people are reading my books is adream come true. If you've enjoyed this book, please do consider leaving arating or short review on Amazon or Goodreads. One sentence is enough, and every rating and review counts towards making a book more visible in today's crowded marketplace. Thank you!

For all the latest information about my books, the characters, the writing life and life in general here in lovely Switzerland, see my website: www.lindahuber.net

(And to anyone whofancies a visit to Switzerland after reading this book – do it! You won't regret it.)

Linda x

ALSO BY MELINDA HUBER

Books in the Escape to Switzerland series:
Saving the Lakeside Hotel
Return to the Lakeside Hotel
Problems at the Lakeside Hotel
Christmas at the Lakeside Hotel

***

Standalone psychological suspense novels by Linda Huber:
The Paradise Trees
The Cold Cold Sea
The Attic Room
Chosen Child
Ward Zero
Baby Dear
Death Wish
Stolen Sister
Daria's Daughter
Pact of Silence
The Un-Family

Printed in Great Britain
by Amazon